PRAISE
NOVELS OF TH

HEXBOUND

"Neill continues building her urban fantasy geared toward tweens and teens featuring a slightly different take on magic . . . will appeal to fans of series like the Blood Coven [Vampires]."

—Monsters and Critics

"The Dark Elite series is absolutely gripping and definitely a page-turner. I could not resist this book and read it quickly. If you haven't picked up this series, you need to. This is one book that will rock your reading world."

—Books with Bite

FIRESPELL

"Chloe Neill has written an incredible cast of characters and her heroine, Lily, has a wonderful, engaging voice. . . . Fans of urban fantasy, paranormal, and young adult will definitely want to pick this one up and lose themselves in the magical underground that is Chicago."

—Fresh Fiction

"If you crave a story full of intrigue, mystery, magic, and a bit of romance, then this is your book."

—Bookstack

"Exciting teen urban fantasy."

—Genre Go Round Reviews

continued . . .

"In a genre laden with boarding school dramas, how can one possibly stand out? Ask Chloe Neill. She did an excellent job of making *Firespell* stand out above all the others. *How?* you may ask. By writing exceptionally interesting, fun characters."

—Pure Imagination

"*Firespell* separates itself from the pack by virtue of its strong characters, compelling universe, and excellent plotting. . . . [Its] pages fly by and will leave readers eagerly counting down the days until the next book in the series."   —*Sacramento Book Review*

PRAISE FOR CHLOE NEILL'S CHICAGOLAND VAMPIRES NOVELS

"With her wonderfully compelling reluctant vampire heroine and her careful world building, I was drawn into *Some Girls Bite* from page one, and kept reading far into the night."

—Julie Kenner, *USA Today* bestselling author of *Good Ghouls Do*

"If you loved Nancy Drew but always wished she was an undead sword-wielding badass, Merit is your kind of girl."—*Geek Monthly*

"A refreshing take on urban fantasy."   —*Publishers Weekly*

"The pages turn fast enough to satisfy vampire and romance fans alike."   —*Booklist*

"Neill creates a strong-minded, sharp-witted heroine who will appeal to fans of Charlaine Harris's Sookie Stackhouse series and Laurell K. Hamilton's Anita Blake."   —*Library Journal*

CHARMFALL

A NOVEL
of
THE DARK ELITE

CHLOE NEILL

 NEW AMERICAN LIBRARY

New American Library
Published by New American Library,
a division of Penguin Group (USA) Inc.,
375 Hudson Street, New York, New York 10014, USA
Penguin Group (Canada), 90 Eglinton Avenue East, Suite 700, Toronto,
Ontario M4P 2Y3, Canada (a division of Pearson Penguin Canada Inc.)
Penguin Books Ltd., 80 Strand, London WC2R 0RL, England
Penguin Ireland, 25 St. Stephen's Green, Dublin 2,
Ireland (a division of Penguin Books Ltd.)
Penguin Group (Australia), 250 Camberwell Road,
Camberwell, Victoria 3124, Australia (a division of Pearson Australia Group Pty. Ltd.)
Penguin Books India Pvt. Ltd., 11 Community Centre,
Panchsheel Park, New Delhi - 110 017, India
Penguin Group (NZ), 67 Apollo Drive, Rosedale, Auckland 0632,
New Zealand (a division of Pearson New Zealand Ltd.)
Penguin Books (South Africa) (Pty.) Ltd., 24 Sturdee Avenue,
Rosebank, Johannesburg 2196, South Africa

Penguin Books Ltd., Registered Offices:
80 Strand, London WC2R 0RL, England

First published by New American Library,
a division of Penguin Group (USA) Inc.

First Printing, January 2012
1 3 5 7 9 10 8 6 4 2

NAL
REGISTERED TRADEMARK—MARCA REGISTRADA

Library of Congress Cataloging-in-Publication Data

Neill, Chloe.
Charmfall: a novel of the Dark elite/Chloe Neill.
p. cm.
1. Paranormal—Fiction. 2. Magic—Fiction. 3. High schools—Fiction. 4. Schools—Fiction.
5. Demonology—Fiction. 6. Vampires—Fiction. 7. Chicago (Ill.)—Fiction. I. Title.
PZ7.N42862Ch 2012
[Fic]—dc23   2011043641

Set in Granjon
Designed by Elke Sigal

Printed in the United States of America

To Jeremy, with love and Schnauzers

ACKNOWLEDGMENTS

Thanks to the usual suspects who helped get Lily and Scout ready for the shelf, including Jessica, for her fantabulous edits, and Rosanne, Liz, and Jia, for their marketing support and assistance. Thanks to Lucienne, my lovely agent. Double thanks to Krista and Lisa for manning the Meritverse Forums (http://forums.chloeneill.com), editing, and marketing, and to my colleagues, friends, and family (Hi, Mom!) for their constant support. My apologies to Scout and Baxter for all the balls I haven't had time to throw, and to Jeremy, who has to put up with me while I fret about the writing—and married me anyway.

"Magic is overrated.
Courage is what matters."

—SCOUT GREEN

CHARMFALL

1

H is fur was silvery gray. His eyes shifted color between sky blue and spring green, and his ears were flat against his head.

I'd tripped and fallen, which put me at eye level with the giant werewolf in front of me. He growled deep and low, and my heart stuttered a little . . . until he padded forward and nuzzled my arm.

"I'm fine," I assured him, hopping to my feet. I may have been okay, but my jeans probably weren't going to recover anytime soon. The tunnels beneath Chicago were damp and dirty, and they left brown marks on my knees.

"Frick," I muttered, dusting them off the best I could and blowing choppy dark hair from my eyes. "I really liked these jeans." Maybe for once it was a good thing I'd be back in a plaid school uniform tomorrow morning.

A flash of light filled the tunnel, and a sixteen-year-old boy in jeans and a long-sleeved shirt appeared in the hallway where the wolf had been.

"The jeans are the last thing you need to worry about right now, Lily," he said, ruffling a hand through his dark blond hair. "I beat you in that last lap by a full ten seconds."

"I fell," I pointed out, blushing a little as I looked into his blue eyes. "Besides, you have four legs. I only have two."

He made a sarcastic sound, but winked at me. That didn't exactly stop the blushing. Actually, Jason and I had been dating for a few weeks now, and I still blushed *a lot*. He was just, you know, *cute*. The kind of cute that gave you goose bumps and made your heart flutter.

The sound of splashing echoed through the tunnels, followed by the sound of heavy panting. This time, it was just two teenagers. Scout Green, my slightly weird BFF, and Michael Garcia, her totally adorable would-be boyfriend, stood in the threshold to the next tunnel. (Would-be, if she let him. He was still working on it.)

She was one of my suitemates at the über-snotty St. Sophia's School for Girls. Michael and Jason were juniors like us, but they attended a private school a few blocks away from ours.

"You guys okay?" I asked.

"We're good," Scout said, but she didn't sound thrilled about it.

"I won," Michael said, jumping around the tunnel like he'd just crossed a goal line and spiked a ball. "I am the champion. The champion! *Ahhhhh! Ahhh!* The crowd goes wild!"

Scout rolled her eyes, and Jason gave him a fist bump.

"Well-done."

"Yeah, it really was," Michael said, dark curls bouncing as he pranced around Scout like it would actually impress her. Normally it wouldn't, but there was a tiny smile at one corner of her mouth this time. Maybe she was a little impressed.

"So we've done our sprints," she said, putting her hands on her hips. "What's next on the list?"

Jason pulled a folded piece of paper from his pocket and opened it up. "Recommended Adept Workout Number Two," he began.

"Is it, 'commence being awesome'?" Michael asked.

"It is not," Jason said. "It's dodge ball."

We all smiled. Dodge ball was one of our favorites, 'cause our version had nothing to do with lining up in a row like in gym.

See, we were Adepts—teenagers with magic. And I'm not talking about magic tricks or smoke and mirrors. I'm talking real magic—vampires and werewolves and spellcasting—and that was just the stuff I knew about.

As it turns out, the world was *full* of magic. (That fell into the category of "things that totally shocked me," which also includes turducken and gladiator sandals. Who do those things look good on?) A lucky few teenagers with some special skill or quality got a taste of magic while they were young. Scout, for example, could bind and cast spells. I wielded firespell, which meant I could control lights and send out blasts of power that could knock out bad guys. Michael could read architecture—he could put his hands on a building and figure out what had happened there recently.

And Jason Shepherd, my boyfriend, was a werewolf. He said being able to transform wasn't exactly magic, but part of an ancient curse; I wasn't sure about all the details, but being a werewolf apparently meant superstrength and a unique ability to fight. And, I mean, it was awesome to watch your boyfriend turn into a wolf and attack the bad guys in the middle of a battle. I also knew he was careful to stay away from me when the moon was full. It was too dangerous to be around him, he said.

Problem was, the gift of magic was only temporary—like an upside to puberty. Adepts like me promised we'd let the magic go in a few years, when our time came. We respected the natural order of things. Reapers, on the other hand, were magic users who started stealing the souls of others as a last-ditch attempt to hang on to their power.

That's why we were standing in the dark and dirty tunnels beneath Chicago on an otherwise gorgeous November Sunday. Adepts were responsible for keeping the Reapers—or the Dark Elite, as they called themselves—in check. That meant a lot of late nights after school running around in the dark and a lot of keeping our fingers crossed that we wouldn't run into anything we couldn't handle.

We weren't always lucky.

Anyway, when we weren't chasing Reapers or taking classes, the Adept higher-ups decided we should get in workouts to keep our magic sharp.

"Dodge ball it is," Scout said, rubbing her hands together. "Who gets the short straw this time?"

"Obviously me," Michael grumbled. His magic was more about information than offense, so he always had to do the dodging. And Jason could really only nip at us, which left the magical aggression to Scout and me.

She looked at me and grinned. "Rock, paper, scissors?"

"All day long," I said. I walked over and faced her, and put out my hands. One in a fist, one palm up. "You ready?"

"All day long," she repeated, putting her hands out.

We counted down together—"One, two, three, *go*"—then picked our sides. She picked rock . . . but I picked paper.

"Booyah," I said, covering her hands with mine. "Paper beats rock. My turn to throw."

Scout grumbled a few choice words, but picked up her skull-faced messenger bag from our dump spot in a dry bit of tunnel and slid it over her shoulder. "Fine, newbie. Just try not to electrocute us," she said, then pointed between Jason and me. "And no cheating."

"Would I do such a thing?" Jason asked, sliding me a glance.

"Frankly, yes. You would. But that doesn't matter now. Adept, ho!" she said, then turned around and began walking backward, taunting me. "Bring it."

The goal of Adept dodge ball was to practice throwing magic at a target. In this case, Scout, Jason, and Michael were the targets, which meant I had to practice throwing really light firespell. *Diet* firespell. Strong enough that they wanted to jump out of the way, but not so strong that I actually hurt anyone.

It wasn't as easy as it sounded.

"We're waiting, Lils," Jason said, moving toward Scout and beckoning me forward with a crooked finger. "Come and get us."

He was cute, but this wasn't just a race down a hallway.

This was *firespell*.

Sure, the power was still new to me. Mine was an accidental gift. I'd gotten my magic after a Reaper, Sebastian Born, inadvertently hit me with a shot of his own firespell. But I was getting better at controlling it—and throwing it at others.

"You got it," I muttered, closing my eyes and opening myself to the flow of power that spilled through the tunnels beneath me. It rose through my arms and legs, looking for a way out, a way back to ground. It tickled my fingertips, eager to move.

I opened my eyes again, the cage lights that hung in the ceiling of this stretch of tunnel flickering with the effort. I imagined gathering up a lump of power like a snowball, and as Jason, Scout, and Michael stepped over the threshold into the next segment of tunnel, I lobbed it at the ceiling above them.

Scout squealed and ducked; the firespell exploded into a shower of green sparks that vibrated the walls around us. Not exactly a comforting feeling when you were a story or two underground, but it's not like we had better practice grounds. Other than Reapers and the few nonmagical folks in Chicago who knew we had magic and helped us stay safe, our powers were secret.

"The race is on!" Michael said. He took off down the tunnel, Jason and Scout behind him.

I gathered up a bit more firespell and ran down the tunnel after them. Each caged light dimmed as I passed beneath it, like they were bowing to the power I held in my hand. I tossed another ball of firespell as the trio disappeared through an arched doorway, sparks showering down behind them.

I muttered a curse. Sure, I wasn't supposed to hit them, but I was trying to get as close as possible. And that last one could have been a little bit closer.

Water splashed in the tunnels in front of me as they ran away. The tunnels had been used for a small railroad that carried coal and trash between the buildings in Chicago. Water tended to collect in the floor between the old rails, not to mention the stuff that seeped down from the walls. The tunnels were usually dark and always cold, and they were especially chilly now that winter was on its way.

I followed the sounds of their splashing like a trail of crumbs, pausing when they slipped into a segment of tunnel I hadn't seen before. There was a thin metal bar across the threshold.

"Is that actually supposed to keep anyone out?" I wondered, slipping underneath it and hustling ahead. But when silence filled the tunnel, I stopped.

It was quiet except for the slow drip of water somewhere behind me. Quiet enough that I could hear blood humming in my ears—and still no sounds of the other Adepts. Had they stopped running? Snuck into a side tunnel to ambush me when I wasn't looking?

Only one way to find out.

I let the power flow a little more—just enough to gather a bit in my hand and scare the pants off them if they tried to be sneaky. I crept forward one step at a time, trying not to worry about the little multilegged things that were probably scurrying around me in the dark.

The lights were dimmer here, but they still flickered as I walked beneath them—*stalked* beneath them, with a pent-up dose of firespell in hand.

"Hello?" I whispered, peeking into a nook in the concrete. Empty. The firespell itching to be set free, I rubbed my fingers together.

"Anybody there?" I whispered, sneaking to the end of the tunnel and peeking into the next one, but there were no lights. It was too dark to see ahead of me more than a few feet, and every few feet that didn't reveal three grinning Adepts (or two grinning Adepts and a werewolf) just made me more nervous. Anticipation built as I waited for them to make their move.

My nerves pulled tight, I stopped. "All right, you guys. I give up. Let's head upstairs. I have party committee tonight."

There was shuffling in the dark in front of me. I froze, my heart thudding beneath my shirt. "Guys?"

"Boo!"

Somewhere in the back of my mind, I knew Scout had jumped behind me, but my brain wasn't exactly working. I screamed aloud and jumped at least two feet into the air, and then let go of the firespell I'd been holding back.

It flew from my hand, warping the air as it moved. It wavered past Jason and Michael, who'd edged against the walls of the tunnel to avoid it, but hit Scout full-on. Her body shook with the impact, and then went slack. I reached out and grabbed her before she fell, and I lowered her gently to the ground, her body cradled in my lap. Tears pricked at my eyes. "Oh, crap—Scout, are you okay? Scout?! Are you all right?"

Michael rushed to her side. He put a hand to her forehead, then tapped her cheeks like he was trying to wake her up. "Scout? Are you all right?"

"Scout, I am so sorry," I said, panicked at the thought I'd knocked my best friend unconscious. It wasn't exactly a good way to repay the first girl who'd actually paid attention to me when I'd been shipped to St. Sophia's a few months ago.

Jason kneeled beside me and looked her over. "I'm sure she'll be fine. You weren't going full force, were you?"

"Of course not," I said, but she *had* scared me. What if I'd accidentally turned up the firespell volume?

"If you wake up," I said, "I'll let you wear my fuzzy boots—those ones you really like? And I won't complain when you take my chocolate muffin anymore at breakfast. You can have it every day from now on. I swear—just wake up, okay?"

A few seconds passed in silence . . . and then Scout opened one eye and grinned at me. She'd been *faking*!

"The chocolate muffin, huh?" she said. "*And* the fuzzy boots? You heard her, boys—you're my witnesses."

It didn't bother me that she landed in the middle of a puddle when I dumped her onto the floor.

Maybe I should have firespelled her a little harder.

2

How did you top off an afternoon of being faked out by your best friend in an abandoned tunnel beneath Chicago? You helped snooty heiresses make party decorations.

Sure, party preparations were a little out of character for me, but that's exactly why I was doing it. It wasn't that I was eager to hang out with the other girls on the committee—most of them were into luxury handbags and money flaunting—but there was something seriously relaxing about playing around with glue and glitter. No rats. No spiders. No Reapers. No "workouts." Just a little mindless arts-and-craftsing. *Yes, please.*

Girls in spendy clothes—my fellow members of the Sneak decorating committee—sat in groups on the shiny parquet floor of the St. Sophia's gym, sticking beady eyes onto cutout ravens and draping faux spider web around everything that sat still long enough to be draped. There were also foam gravestones everywhere, all painted black and coated with chunky black glitter.

Sneak was the fall formal of our junior class, and the St. Sophia's girls in charge—the brat pack—had decided "graveyard glam" was our decorating theme. (The Sneak committee guys at Montclare, our brother school that Jason and Michael both attended, got to do all the audiovisual and electronic stuff.) The idea wasn't exactly original, but since I was a fan of dark clothes and good eyeliner, I didn't mind so much. Besides, St. Sophia's alumnae had rented out the Field Museum, Chicago's natural history museum, for the party, which was this Friday. I hadn't been there yet, so I wasn't really sure what to expect, but with all that money and all these decorations, there was no way it wasn't going to look sweet when we were done.

I was pretty excited about the dance. The brat pack, on the other hand, I could do without. Veronica—an every-hair-in-place type of blonde—was their leader. She was currently using a pencil to point other members of the junior class toward their glittery assignments.

I didn't like her, but I had been paying more attention to her lately. A few weeks ago, Veronica had walked right into the middle of a civil war between two vampire covens that lived in the Pedway—a bunch of passageways that connected buildings in downtown Chicago. Marlena was the reigning coven queen, and she hadn't been happy that Nicu, a vamp she'd made, had started his own clan. Nicu helped us save Veronica, and something seemed to pass between them. She'd been spelled to lock down her memories of the fight and the meeting, but I couldn't shake the feeling she was a magical time bomb waiting to go off.

Number two in the brat pack was Amie. She had a bright pink room in my suite but a quiet attitude, and she was currently painting the ravens I'd been assigned to glitter.

Mary Katherine, the third brat packer, whose dark hair was now streaked with yellow spiral curls and tiny rows of rhinestones, was painting her nails a deep shade of blue. At least, I assumed they were rhinestones. Who really knew?

Lesley Barnaby, another suitemate, walked toward me, a bundle of flat, black birds in her hand. She'd been given the task of carting the birds between the brat pack and me. Since their primary goals were being top of the St. Sophia's food chain and driving me crazy, I was more than happy to let Lesley play middleman.

"More ravens," she said, setting them down on the floor.

She sat cross-legged beside the stack, a pair of bright rainbow socks reaching up to her knees. She also wore a T-shirt with a rainbow on it and a small pair of fuzzy black cat ears tucked into her blond hair. Lesley had a very unique sense of style.

I liked clothes, and I definitely had an artistic streak. I hated the matchy-match plaid of our school uniforms. But that stuff just made me a teenager. Lesley was an altogether different type of girl. She acted less like a teenager than like a high-fashion model transplanted from some future world, complete with strange clothes and fuzzy expression. The stuff she wore might be really cool in twenty years, but right now it just seemed odd.

"Thanks," I said, and glanced over at the girls. The brat pack was possibly increasing from three to four. A new recruit, Lisbeth Cannon, had been hanging out with the crew.

"How's the brat pack?" I asked.

Lesley shrugged. "See for yourself. Veronica's handing out orders. Amie's following them. M.K.'s working on her nails."

"What about Lisbeth?"

"She's learning how to be like the rest of them."

I glanced back. As much as I found them repellant, I could admit that I was also kind of intrigued. There was a lot of fighting. They were always pairing off together, leaving one girl out until the other two got mad at each other and decided it was time to switch partners again. Some days I'd find Veronica on the couch in our suite, complaining to Amie about Mary Katherine's dramatics. M.K. usually complained to Amie that Veronica always had to have her way. Both complaints seemed right to me.

I was glad to have a steady BFF in Scout, but in an odd way I was a little jealous about the dramatics. What if deciding between BFFs were the only problem I had to face? No magic. No Reapers. No slimy nasties in the tunnels? Just deciding which friend I wanted to wear on any given day.

"You ever wonder what it's like to be them?"

Lesley looked back at me. "You mean instead of having magic?"

Lesley was one of the few people without magic who was allowed to know about Adepts and Reapers. I wasn't sure if she knew the entire story, but there was an advantage to not knowing too much—having all the details about the world of underground magic apparently put a Reaper target on your back. Lesley might have been a little odd, but she'd been a friend to us when we needed it, so I certainly didn't wish that on her.

"I mean to be popular, and for how you look to be the most important thing on your mind."

Lesley painted lines of glue onto the raven's feathers. "I play the cello," she said. "Sometimes I help you and Scout. I speak four languages, I'm super good at physics, and I will probably get into whatever college I want." She looked up at me, and it was clear she wasn't bragging. She was just giving me the facts. "So why would

I want to spend my time worrying about whether everyone else thinks my shirt is cool enough?"

Like they were following a script, raised voices carried from the brat pack corner of the room.

"I'm trying to do it right," Lisbeth said. She was attempting to carve a piece of foam into the shape of . . . Well, I'm not really sure what it was supposed to be. A gargoyle, maybe?

Veronica, who'd made her way over to the group, wasn't buying it. "It certainly doesn't look like it. You've been working on that thing for, like, an hour now."

"Seriously," M.K. said. "It looks like an angry terrier, and that's really off-theme."

I doubted M.K. cared whether the decoration was right or not. She probably just liked having someone to terrorize. And Lisbeth definitely looked terrorized. She burst into tears and ran from the room, leaving the brat pack rolling their eyes behind her.

"She is so *moody*," M.K. complained. "I was just being constructive."

Lesley and I exchanged a glance.

"See what I mean?" she asked.

I definitely did.

When the drama was over, we all went back to Sneakifying. Earlier, Veronica, as head of the planning committee, had told us Sneak got its name because St. Sophia's girls of old used to sneak out every year and host an impromptu prom in an old storage building behind the dorms. (The school used to be a convent, so even the storage building was antiquey and cool.) Add twenty years, lots and lots of money, and parents who didn't want their heiresses playing dress-up in an old storage building, and you had the modern version of Sneak.

I wasn't one of those heiresses; I'd been sent to Chicago from my home in New York when my parents went to Germany for research work.

Well, that was their story, anyway. I wasn't exactly buying it. I thought they knew more about magic than they let on, and that they'd sent me to St. Sophia's specifically because our headmistress, Marceline Foley, also knew magic existed. It wasn't something we chatted about regularly, and I don't think Foley was thrilled to be in the know, but she gave us a little bit of room to take care of business.

I poured glitter over the lines of glue Lesley had made. I'm sure I didn't exactly look like your average teenager—too much eyeliner and weird vintage shoes for that. But I didn't exactly look like a teenage witch, either. The only real sign I was anything other than a junior at St. Sophia's School for Girls was the Darkening on my back, a strangely shaped pale green tattoo that had appeared after I'd been struck by a shot of firespell—and had ended up being able to wield the power, too.

Sure—having power was better than ending up the pitiful victim of a Reaper. But was it better or worse than worrying only whether I was as pretty as the girls in *Vogue* and if my clothes were hot enough?

Lesley had clearly made up her own mind about that one. Scout had, too. She came from money and could have afforded the same stuff the brat pack wore. But she was one hundred percent Scout, and not the type to worry about what anybody else thought. Keeping the world safe from Reapers was number one on her agenda.

I shook the excess glitter from the raven and put it on the floor beside the others.

"Do you have a date for the dance?" I asked Lesley.

"No. I don't really know any boys. I'm saving that kind of thing for college." She looked up at me. "Are you going with Jason?"

"That's the plan."

"Do you have a dress yet?"

"Not yet." Spending my evenings trying to save the world—or at least some of the teenagers who fell victim to Reapers—didn't leave a lot of time to check out the fashion scene. "Scout and I were going to look this week. What about you?"

She shrugged. "I have some ideas." She stretched out her legs, revealing a worn pair of Converses. "But I'll probably go with these. They're so comfortable. And if we're going to be dancing all night . . . or running from bad guys . . ."

I looked up at her. "What makes you think we'll be running from bad guys?"

She shrugged. "I've seen television. Bad guys always attack the night of the big dance."

I made a doubtful sound and grabbed another raven, then sprinkled glitter onto its wings. "Yeah, well, that's not going to happen this time. There will be all sorts of Adepts there, and there's not a Reaper in town who'd attack a party full of high-society teenagers. They don't want that much attention."

At least, that was what I hoped . . .

It was late when Lesley and I headed back toward the dorms. The rest of the girls had left an hour before we had, but I'd been having too much fun with glitter and glue. We left the decorations in the gym, but I carried back the messenger bag that I took pretty much everywhere. Lesley, bucking the trend again, carried a small round suitcase covered in stickers. It was pea green and looked like something from the 1970s that she'd nabbed from a thrift store. Strange, but a pretty good find, actually.

The walk from the gym to the dorms wasn't far. The campus was made up of a handful of buildings, and the entire thing was surrounded by a fence with a key-carded gate. Foley'd only just had the gate installed. Probably a good idea even without the Reapers. There were weirdos in every city, and most of the St. Sophia's girls didn't have firespell to protect them.

The air outside was cool. Winter was coming, something I definitely wasn't thrilled about. Winters in upstate New York were nothing to laugh at, but I'd heard the wind off Lake Michigan was pretty miserable. I planned on using the emergency credit card my parents had given me to invest in the thickest, downiest coat I could find. I might look like a lumberjack, but at least I'd be warm.

Lesley and I walked quietly past the classroom building. There was a bench outside, where a girl in St. Sophia's plaid and a dark-haired boy in street clothes—jeans and a long-sleeved jacket—sat. His arm was around her shoulders, and he was whispering in her ear. She stared blankly ahead while he twirled a lock of her hair. I realized it was Lisbeth, the brat pack's new recruit.

It wasn't exactly unusual for St. Sophia's girls to sneak out of the building to meet with a boy. There was an old root cellar door I'd used to sneak out before—although for world-saving-type reasons.

But this seemed different. There was sadness in her eyes, and while he seemed totally into her, she seemed really, really unhappy about it. She gave off a vibe of desperation. That was quite a change from her brat pack bonding of a little while ago . . . but maybe not from the moodiness they'd accused her of.

When we passed them, I pulled Lesley around the corner of the building, my heart beginning to pound.

"That's Lisbeth," I whispered. "Who's the boy?"

"I've never seen him before."

"Did she seem okay to you?"

"She looked sad. Like she didn't think she'd ever be happy again."

That rung a bell. It sounded exactly like the effect of a Reaper stealing someone's soul. In my two months at St. Sophia's and as an Adept, I hadn't actually seen any Reaping. I'd seen the effects—girls at school whose motivation was gone, who seemed depressed, who were tired and sleepy and unhappy all the time. That was the effect of having your soul—your will to live—ripped away by a Reaper intent on keeping his magic.

I glanced around the corner, where the couple still sat, almost motionless except for his fingers raking at her hair. He leaned in like he meant to kiss her . . . but their lips didn't touch. Instead, he whispered something to her, and as he did, white wisps of smoke began to slip from her mouth and nose.

No, not wisps . . . her *soul*. It was her energy, her essence, her life's blood, that was seeping away, and this Reaper was using her for it. That explained her depression. Soon, she'd be little more than a shell of a girl with no hope, no energy, and no interest in anything.

Adults thought *hormones* made teenagers tired and moody. As if.

My heart pounded with fear, and the hairs on the back of my neck stood on end. This guy—this *teenager*—was a slow killer, a drainer of energy and taker of things that didn't belong to him.

He wasn't even supposed to be doing this. He was too young. I'd been told only adults did the Reaping because they were the only ones who needed the magic. This guy still had all of his powers, so he shouldn't have needed the extra energy.

But even if it didn't match what I'd been told, I knew what I was seeing. I had to stop this, had to interrupt it. I couldn't let him drain this girl right in front of me, right in the middle of Adept turf. My hands shook with fear, but I reminded myself that the scariest times were the only times bravery mattered. I firmed up my courage, stepped around the corner, and cleared my throat.

The guy looked up, his expression irritated as I interrupted him. And then his eyes narrowed and sharpened . . . and flashed red.

I didn't know who he was, and I didn't know exactly what the flash of color meant, but if he was willing to show off his magic, he must have known who I was.

A chill ran through me. But it was too late to turn back now. "Kind of the wrong gender to be at St. Sophia's, aren't you?"

"This is none of your business," he growled. Lisbeth cast a bored glance in my direction, and then looked away again. She seem almost hypnotized, like she was in some sort of magic-induced stupor.

"Actually, it's precisely my business. You're too far from your sanctuary, and I'm not thrilled about that." Sanctuaries were Reaper headquarters. Adepts had Enclaves.

CHARMFALL

His eyes flashed again, and this time he stood up. Lisbeth, her body limp, slumped on her seat when he moved. The boy took a step toward me. He was still five or six feet away, and I wasn't sure if he was brave enough to stay right here, but I began to feel out my own power just in case.

I was either really relaxed or totally getting used to my magic, because I hardly felt the pull of power at all. But there was no mistaking his. His eyes flashed red again, and he took a menacing step toward me, one hand outstretched. Reddish light began to dance along his fingertips. "I'll give you one chance to run away and forget that you saw anything."

I glanced to the side to make sure Lesley was safely around the corner, and called my power up. I could usually feel the energy as I pulled it up through my feet . . . but this time there was nothing. Not even a tingle. Of course, I was standing in front of two non-Adepts and facing down a really angry Reaper alone. I chalked it up to nerves and kept up my bravado.

"The thing is, St. Sophia's is my school, and I don't appreciate bottom-feeders using our students like protein shakes. I'll give you one chance to run for the gate. If you make it before my firespell hits you, you win."

His eyes widened at the mention of firespell, and I could all but see the gears turning in his head. My powers had been triggered by a shot of firespell from Sebastian Born, a Reaper, so word had traveled about me and my power.

"Yeah, I'm that girl," I admitted. "So take your magic and run."

My voice was all bravery—but he wasn't afraid. He held out his hands. Little bursts of red lightning now shot among his fingers.

"That really doesn't look promising," Lesley said, stepping out from around the corner.

"No," I agreed. "It does not." I moved over and back a little, giving my firespell a clean path. Hitting Lisbeth wasn't going to help the situation.

"I think you have the order of things confused, you bratty little anarchist." He used his magic like an exclamation mark, throwing out his hands—and a red snake of energy—in our direction.

Lesley screamed; I threw her to the ground as the magic flew above our heads, a hot streak of power. I glanced up and watched as it hit a metal garden angel a few yards away . . . and turned it to solid stone.

My chest turned cold with fear. Being turned to rock was not going to help me meet my graduation requirements.

"Stay here," I whispered to Lesley, and stood up again. "That was rude."

"You deserved it, troublemaker. Maybe you should spend a little less time planning parties and a little more time practicing."

All right, I'd had enough. I focused my energy and thrust out my hand, waiting for the sheet of firespell to fly through the air.

But nothing happened.

My heart pounded, my palms suddenly sweating from fear. This wasn't possible. I *had* firespell—I'd had it for months now. I'd done the same things I'd always done, prepared the throw the same way I always had.

Maybe I was just nervous—maybe fear had made me mess it up somehow. My heart pounded, and I tried frantically again, throwing out my arm and hoping firespell would burst from my hands and fly toward him. . . .

Again, there was nothing.

My stomach spun, panic beginning to seep through and shut off my brain. I was too scared to think, and for a split second I had no idea what to do.

And then Lesley called my name. "Lily! He's gonna do it again!"

I looked up from my hands to his. The magic was beginning to bubble around his hands again.

I shook off the fear and decided I was a fighter even if I didn't have firespell. I'd made it nearly sixteen years without it, after all.

I grabbed my messenger bag—dumped when I'd hit the ground—and slung it at him. He threw up a shoulder to block it, but it was heavy and landed on his arm with a thud. He stumbled backward a few feet, giving me enough time to reach out and grab Lesley's suitcase.

I ran toward him, swung the suitcase, and nailed him in the head.

He hit the ground like a sack of potatoes.

"What in God's name is going on out here?"

I looked back.

Marceline Foley, the headmistress of St. Sophia's, stood in the open doorway of the building where classes were held. She had a perfect bob of blond hair and always wore a suit. Today the suit was crimson red, and it matched the color in her cheeks. She looked furious.

She might have been angry about the commotion I'd caused— and the assault I'd just perpetrated. But there was something that would anger her even more.

"He's a Reaper," I said, putting the suitcase on the ground.

"He was working on Lisbeth." I pointed to the bench where she still sat, hunched over the arm.

"Oh no," Foley said, running in her skirt and low heels to the bench. She sat down beside Lisbeth, gently moved her head, and looked into each of her eyes. "Weak," she said, "but she'll manage." Foley looked back at Lesley. "Go to my office. There's a number on speed dial—it's the first one on the phone. Call it. Tell the man who answers that I need him."

Without a word, Lesley nodded and ran for the door.

Foley stroked a hand over Lisbeth's face. She knew all about magic and Reapers and Adepts. Her daughter had been one, but she'd died in the line of duty.

"It was bold of him," she said, then looked over at me. "To be out in the open."

"Maybe they're working on infiltrating the school. They've tried to take Scout's *Grimoire*—her book of magic—before."

"I remember."

"I tried to get him away from her." I shivered involuntarily, thinking of what I'd seen—the Reaper actually stealing her soul, one wisp at a time. "He was already in the middle of it."

"So I see. Why did you hit him with a suitcase? Why not use your own magic?"

That was my question, too.

3

barely paid attention to the school as I passed back through it, from the dome in the main building, to the Great Hall where we studied, and then on to the dorms. I ran upstairs to the suite I shared with Lesley, Scout, and Amie and unlocked the door.

I knocked on the door to Scout's bedroom, but didn't bother to wait for an invitation.

Scout wore black pajamas and sat cross-legged on her small bed, an open book in front of her. Her hair was blond on top and dark underneath, and it was currently sticking out of her head in a million directions. She looked a little like a Goth pincushion, not that I was going to tell her that.

Eyes wide, she yanked off a pair of earphones. "What's wrong?"

"A Reaper was outside—on campus—attacking Lisbeth Cannon. He was just sitting there, drinking her. And when I tried to firespell him, my magic was gone. It doesn't work. *At all.* No firespell at all. And then Foley came, and she called someone, I don't know who, and Lisbeth was unconscious."

"Whoa, slow down." There was concern in her eyes, but also confusion. She patted the bed beside her. "Sit down, slow down, and tell me exactly what happened."

I filled her in on the Reaper's attack and what I'd tried—and failed—to do.

"He broke through the wards."

Scout had put wards, magical guards, on the giant door in the school's basement that led to the tunnels. The wards were supposed to keep Reapers at bay, but the Reapers had at least one wardbreaker whose job was to break through those protections. Daniel Sterling, the leader of our Enclave, had recently helped Scout strengthen the wards to keep the wardbreaker out, but maybe that still hadn't been enough.

"Not necessarily," I said. "Maybe she just let him in through the gate. It definitely looked like they knew each other."

"Maybe," Scout said, but she didn't sound convinced. She unfolded her legs, then hopped onto the floor. "Let me see your back."

I stood up, lifted up my T-shirt, and showed it to her.

"Your Darkening is still there," she said.

"I'm still me," I said, pulling my T-shirt down again. "I'm just me with nonfunctioning firespell. What about you? What was the last magic you worked?"

"Uh, I turned off my alarm clock this morning."

"With magic?"

She blushed a little. "It's a new kind of spell. Hardly magic at all. Like a little appetizer-type thing. I was testing it."

"And it worked?"

"If you're not still hearing talk radio played at jet-level decibels, it worked."

"Your alarm is set to talk radio? Why?"

"Because I hate it," she said simply. "And that makes me want to turn it off faster."

I couldn't argue with that, but it also was not the point. I wiggled my fingers at her. "Try something now. I want to know if it's just me."

"But I feel fine," she said.

"So did I before the Reaper popped in and my firespell was completely ineffective."

She looked at me for a minute, probably trying to figure out whether I was really hurting or just getting upset about nothing. She must have decided to trust me, because she walked over to one of her bookshelves, which—like the rest of her room—was packed with stuff. She picked a small, glossy lacquered apple from one of her collections and put it on her bed, then stood back.

"Do I need safety glasses for this?"

"Are you going to poke your eye out just standing there?"

"Probably not."

"Then, no. Watch and learn, newbie." Scout blew out a breath and tucked her chin in to her chest, giving the apple a concentrated stare. Her lips moved with some silent spell, and I watched and waited for something to happen.

But nothing did.

Frowning, she shook out her hands and shook her head. "I'm probably just tense or tired or something," she said, and then tried again, her expression fierce and focused.

Again, nothing.

"I don't understand. I did everything right, the same way I always do it. How could it not work?"

"Probably for the same reason mine doesn't work."

"This is bad," she said. "We need to call Daniel." She dug into her messenger bag and pulled out a phone, then frantically typed out a text message.

I nibbled on the edge of my thumb, the tension in the room high while Scout texted Daniel and we waited for a response.

I hated waiting in situations like this. The anticipation killed me. Trying not to dwell on it, I pulled out my own phone and checked for messages.

There was one waiting for me—from my parents. I didn't hear from them as much as I wanted, and sometimes getting their messages hurt as much as not hearing from them. It was like a reminder they were only partly connected to me anymore. They were far away, and little bytes of data weren't the same as getting a good hug—or just knowing they were *there*.

Heck, I wasn't even really sure where they were. They could have been working in a building next door for all I knew.

The text was from my dad: "HAVE FUN THIS WEEK AT THE DANCE! BUT NOT TOO MUCH FUN! WE LOVE YOU!"

Like I said, sweet and sad at the same time. I tucked the phone away again and when Scout's phone beeped, I jumped. She looked at the screen, read the message, then glanced at me.

"What?" I asked.

"The magical blackout—it's not just us."

"The Enclave?"

"Worse," Scout said. "All the Adepts in the city."

"Awesome," I sarcastically said, 'cause it totally wasn't.

Daniel instructed us to meet him at the Enclave, which wasn't as easy as it sounded. Enclave Three was located in the underground tunnels. So to get there, we had to sneak through the school from the dorms to the main building, through the basement to the door that led to the tunnels, and then through those tunnels to the Enclave.

Was it weird that the tunnels were actually starting to feel like home? I mean, I'd walked through them, laughed in them, and firespelled my best friend in them. They weren't exactly cozy, but they also weren't as uncomfortable as they had been before. Not awesome, but not horrible.

When we reached the giant wooden door that kept the Enclave safe from the things that roamed the tunnels, we knocked and walked inside.

The mood was not good.

Enclave Three was a vaulted stone room built into one of the tunnels. The walls were covered in mosaics, but the room was mostly empty except for a round table that Daniel had added so we actually had a place to sit and talk. Now we were the Adepts of the Round Table! Somehow, Scout never found that funny.

The rest of the Adepts—Paul, Jamie, Jill, Michael, and Jason— were already seated around the table, waiting for us to begin.

Paul was a magically enhanced warrior. He was tall, with dark skin and curly hair. His girlfriend, Jamie, was a witch with fire power, and her twin sister, Jill, had comparable skills with ice. The twins were slender, with long auburn hair and pale skin. They were identical, so there was something ghostly about them when they stood side by side.

Jason and Michael sat side by side, both staring at their cell phones. Along with Scout, we made up the Adepts of Chicago's Enclave Three. Well, the "Junior Varsity" squad, anyway. We got the nickname because we were all still in high school.

Daniel, our Varsity Adept, was nowhere to be seen. He was our recently appointed team leader and a sophomore at Northwestern University. He got full varsity status because he was in college.

He was also the kind of hot that needed two syllables to pronounce. *Hah-awt.* Tall, curly blond hair, blue eyes. Very easy on the eyes, and a total doll as far as I could tell. And I was doubly lucky: I loved to draw, and Daniel was my studio art teacher at St. Sophia's.

Daniel had replaced Katie and Smith—last names unknown— our former team leaders. They were the Adepts who'd been willing to throw Scout to the wolves, who'd refused to help rescue her when she'd been taken by Reapers. They'd been coming to Enclave meetings less and less lately, not that I was going to complain. I wasn't a fan.

As we took seats at the table, Michael immediately gave Scout dopey eyes, and Jason gave me the intense ones. I took the chair next to his and squeezed his hand.

"Where's Daniel?" I asked.

"Not here yet," Paul said. "He's on his way."

"You're okay?" Jason whispered.

I nodded. "I'm fine. I'd been working on decorations for

Sneak. On the way back to the dorm, one of the other decoration committee girls was being used by a Reaper for fuel. I tried to fire-spell him, but nothing happened. I managed to knock him out, and that's when Foley showed up. Foley's our headmistress," I added for the rest of the Adepts.

Jason's expression tightened at the admission I'd been in trouble, and then it went a little fierce . . . and protective. That sent a little thrill through me.

"Scout tried her magic," I continued, "and it's not working for her, either. That's when she called Daniel. What about you?" I scanned him up and down, as if that glance would be enough to tell me whether his magic had been affected. "Are you okay?"

"I can still change," he said, but he didn't seem thrilled about it. If the blackout wasn't affecting him, maybe having a "curse" wasn't all bad.

"It's not magic exactly," he added, "so I'm fine."

"Which means the blackout is only affecting magic," Michael said. "The other Enclaves are having the same problem. But given what Lily saw, it doesn't look like Reapers are having the same trouble."

"The Reaper's magic worked," I added. "And there's a new stone angel on the grounds to prove it."

"Free landscaping for all," Scout muttered.

"Maybe he just got in one last lucky shot," Michael said. "I can't read anything." He looked sad, and even his curls looked a little droopier than usual.

"No ice for me," Jill said.

"And no fire, either," Jamie added.

We looked at Paul. "I couldn't even beat up a puppy with

magic," he said, "not that I'd want to." But then he grinned cheek-ily and flexed his biceps, which weren't bad. "But I can still use my own talents."

"Show-off," Scout said with a wink. "And that brings us full circle."

"So none of us has magic," I said.

"It's like nightfall, but with charms," Michael said. "You know, the sunset of our magical careers or something. Total charmfall."

"Charm*fail*," Jason coughed.

"In addition to the charmfall or charmfail or whatever," Jill said, "a Reaper was draining a human out in the open in the mid-dle of downtown Chicago. He was outside, and it doesn't sound like he was trying to hide it."

Reapers were usually behind-the-scenes types. They snuggled up to otherwise happy teenagers and sucked their energy a little at a time, leaving behind a depressed kid and not a lot of answers for parents and friends.

"You're thinking Reapers are changing their strategy?" Jason asked.

Jill shrugged. "I'm just saying it's a fact we should pay atten-tion to."

"He was young," I said. "He wouldn't be losing his magic, so he shouldn't have needed the energy."

"Maybe they've figured out some way to save up the magic," Paul offered. "Like charging a battery?"

"That would be a new one," Jason said with a frown.

That would definitely be bad news bears. If young Reapers figured out a way to save up stolen energy and somehow transmit it to the older ones, they could build a traveling army of teenagers who could steal magic a little at a time. But if they could do that . . .

"If the Reapers can save up that power somehow," I asked, "could they do the reverse? Like, could they pull the magic out of us? Could that have caused the blackout?"

"That's not possible," Michael said, looking at Scout. "Is it?"

"Not that I'm aware of," she said, but you could tell the thought made her nervous. "Saving up energy from one girl and somehow transporting it back to a sanctuary is one thing. Frankly, that wouldn't surprise me much. But taking the power of all Adepts across Chicago? That's different by, like, magnitudes. I'm sure there's some reason for this, and whether it's magical or not, it's not something the Reapers just whipped out all of a sudden. It would take planning."

I can't say I was convinced. We didn't have the most up-to-date information about Reapers and their activities in Chicago, and we weren't out there setting the magical pace. Sometimes it felt like we were playing catch-up, trying to keep our heads above water and hoping we didn't fall too far behind.

After that, no one said a word for a few minutes. The entire room was completely silent. Everyone looked uncomfortable, like they were wearing clothes that were a little too tight. That was when I knew this was going to be an important test for Chicago's Adepts. Maybe the most important test of all.

We'd promised that in a few years, when our magic dissipated, we wouldn't fight the loss. We'd let the power return to the universe instead of stealing the souls of others in a vain attempt to keep it.

It was easy to make that promise when you still had your

power. When you were right in the middle of the magical high life and life without magic was years away. That decision would be a lot harder, or so I figured, when you were beginning to weaken. Sure, I hadn't had firespell long, so its absence felt more familiar than having it. But wasn't it going to be hard for the ones who had gotten used to it—who'd lived with the hum of energy longer, who'd been able to change the world around them with the flick of a hand or a few words of a spell? Wasn't it going to be hard to simply shut that door and walk away?

Adepts usually talked as if the decision would be easy. And sure, there were consequences to being a Reaper that would also be staring them down—stealing souls, for one. But looking at their faces today, they were beginning to realize that the consequences of giving up their lives as Adepts were going to be harder to bear than they'd thought.

The Enclave door opened. Daniel walked inside, and from the look on his face, he didn't have any good news, either. We did the roll call and filled him in on our magical deficiencies.

"I spoke with Marceline Foley," he said. Scout and I exchanged a look. Daniel and Foley were close. He'd known Foley's daughter before she'd been killed, which I guessed was why he'd been hired to teach studio art.

"Lisbeth Cannon is going to be okay. Marceline found her family, and they're going to help her get back on track." He looked down at a piece of paper in his hand. "The Reaper's name was Charlie Andrews. He's part of Jeremiah's crew. Comes from a single-parent family, and his mom works nights. She gets some kind of stipend from the sanctuary to help them out, so she's gung ho on the Reapers. Thinks her son's a superhero."

"Fat chance," I muttered. It was a long drive from liking Reapers because they helped you pay the bills to thinking it was cool that your son was stealing a teenager's life force.

"He's too young to need the magic," I said. "Did Foley talk to him? Why was he using a girl? Does he know anything about the blackout?"

"She wasn't able to interrogate him," Daniel said. "She only heard about the mom. She didn't actually see him do anything—she only saw Lily assault him with a suitcase."

All eyes turned to me, and my cheeks flushed red. "No firespell," I explained. "That was the only weapon I had."

"Awesome," Scout said. "So he's off the hook, and we're back to square one, except that we don't have any magic and there might be an army of Reapers not just recruiting teenagers for food, but actually stealing their souls."

"It's gonna be a great week," Michael said.

Daniel tucked the paper away and took a seat at the table. "Everybody, calm down. The council"—those were the really higher-ups who made decisions about Adept strategies—"are looking into the blackout. They have our best minds on it."

"We *are* their best minds," Scout grumbled.

"Be that as it may, for *now* we leave the heavy lifting to them. This situation is temporary—if there's a cause, there will be a solution. And we will find that solution," he said, giving Scout a look. "That said, for now we have no power. So I want everyone on full alert. You go anywhere, you go in pairs. Be careful underground, and just as careful above. Until we know what they're planning, we take care."

"We always take care," Scout whispered. "It's the Reapers we have to worry about."

CHLOE NEILL

"If we're all on the same page," Daniel said. "I think we're done for now. You're dismissed."

"Excellent," Michael said, and fist bumped Jason again. "Back to the crib and a little midnight gaming."

"What is it with you two and the fist bumping?" Scout asked.

"We can't help it if we're smooth," Michael said, giving Scout a big wink. She looked away in exasperation, but not before her cheeks went pink.

"Smooth?" I asked, leaning toward Jason. "He saw that in a movie, right?"

"Three days ago. Action flick filmed in Chicago, and he won't stop quoting the scenes."

As if we needed any more action in the Windy City.

4

Daniel's motivational speech and our business done, we left the Enclave again, but stopped in the tunnel outside. We said our good-byes to Jill, Jamie, Daniel, and Paul, and Scout, Jason, Michael, and I hung back.

"Did you ever think your junior year would be this exciting?" I asked Scout.

"I was hoping it would involve a discovery that I was secretly a princess with the power to rule the world and make pop stars my minions," she said. "I have not yet become aware of any such discovery."

I patted her arm. "Keep the faith, sister."

"On to more important topics," Jason said. "What are we going to do about this blackout?"

"What do you mean 'do about' it?" I asked.

"We can't just sit around and wait for the council to do something," Michael said. "They put Katie and Smith in charge of the Enclave, after all. That doesn't show good decision making to me."

"Michael's right," Jason said. "We can't just wait around and hope they'll find a fix, and that Reapers will leave us alone in the meantime."

Scout shook her head. "We also can't just march into the sanctuary, tell Reapers we're magic-free, and ask if they're the reason. We'd be sitting ducks."

"That's not a good survival strategy," I agreed. "But how are we going to find anything else out? We don't have any leads, and no clues."

"Enclave Two," Jason said. "Their specialty is information and technology. Maybe they know more than we do."

Enclave Two was one of the other groups of Adepts in Chicago. Our focus was on identifying Reaper targets and dealing with Reapers. Enclave Two was all about information—spying on Reapers, bugging sanctuaries, figuring out what they were up to.

"And that Detroit has some crazy mechanics," Michael said. "I wouldn't mind seeing what she's been working on lately." He winged up his eyebrows dramatically. Scout punched him in the arm.

"I'm right here," she said.

"According to you, we aren't dating, so there's no harm in me looking."

"Or checking out Detroit's machinery," I added (helpfully). But Scout didn't look like she thought I was being helpful.

Detroit's magic was the ability to make things—gadgets, machines, electronics. In the short time I'd been an Adept, she'd shown off a machine that helped ghosts communicate with Adepts and a locket that was actually a projector. I wasn't sure if the blackout was affecting her in the same way, but it would be a shame if she lost those skills.

Scout might not have been dating Michael, but she wasn't above bullying him. "Keep your mind and your mitts off Detroit."

"Whatever you say, *mi reina*."

Scout made a humphing noise, but she showed a little secret smile that said she didn't mind when Michael gave her nicknames in Spanish. It did sound pretty hot.

And speaking of hotness . . .

Jason looked at Michael and Scout. "Can you give us a minute?"

Scout and Michael looked at each other, then made goofy kissing noises.

"You're both five years old," Jason said. But they did walk down the tunnel, giving us some privacy. Not that anything was going to happen; it wasn't exactly romantic down here. On the other hand, we didn't have a lot of free time, and moments in the tunnels were sometimes the only "dates" we got.

"Some days," Jason whispered, his eyes on the couple, "I feel like the only adult in the room."

"But if you need someone to cheer you up, you can't do much better than Michael. He is always on."

Jason looked back at me, a glint in his eye, and my stomach went hot.

"Okay, so you can do a *little* better," I cheekily said. "I'm a pretty great girlfriend."

He didn't answer with words. Instead, he took my hand and began to kiss the edges of my fingertips. I practically melted right then and there.

Jason sighed, then wrapped his arms around me. I buried my head in his chest. I felt safe in his arms. Secure. Like even if monsters in the dark popped out at me, he could handle them. He might be furry when he did that handling, but still . . .

He suddenly tensed up, and I knew he was thinking about the curse.

"You okay?"

He just sighed. "Yeah. Things are just . . . unsettled at home, and now I'm, like, the only Adept in town who has any kind of power. That's a lot of pressure."

"What's going on at home?" He'd hinted before that because of the curse, werewolves saw the world differently and tended to live apart from humans. At some point, his parents would even choose a bride for him from some other werewolf family. And here he was, far from home, hanging out in the middle of one of the biggest cities in the country. I bet that didn't sit well with the parentals.

"Things are . . . moving along," he said. "I've got cousins who are causing trouble, being more public about their fur than they should be, and that ends up putting more pressure on me."

He'd told me his family would pull him back at some point. I just hadn't expected it to happen so soon.

"I thought you'd have more time?"

"I might have," he said darkly, "if my cousins weren't acting like hoodlums. That changes the math. I have to step up earlier than before. When it's all said and done, my cousins may not listen to me, but at least I can be a good example."

Okay, I silently thought, but a good example of what?

He brushed a lock of hair back from my face. "You're important to me. I wanted you to know that."

I appreciated the thought, but I still moved back a little bit, giving myself some space and distance. I knew there was a risk—a really good risk—that I'd end up being hurt if we kept dating. I just didn't think it would be right now. So soon.

"I know," I said. "But that doesn't mean I don't worry."

"Fair enough," he said. He chuckled lightly, and before I could tweak him for laughing at me, his lips were on mine. He pulled me closer and kissed me like he was desperate to do it, like he might never get another chance. And as much as I wanted to just sink into the kiss and forget about the world for a little while, the world continued to spin around us. He was still a werewolf with a family that believed in curses, and I was still a girl who didn't want a broken heart.

My hesitation didn't seem to scare him. He held me even tighter, his arms enclosing me like he meant to protect me from the rest of the world. If only he could. If only it were that easy.

Eventually he pulled back and kissed my forehead. "We should get back to school. Tomorrow morning awaits. And it's a Monday."

"Yeah," I quietly said. There was no pretending I was excited about that. I mean, being an Adept was hard. But being a junior in high school was a completely different animal.

Jason called out Michael's name, and after a moment he came jogging down the tunnel, water splashing at his feet, crimson on his cheeks. It wasn't hard to guess what he and Scout had been doing a couple of passages away.

"You ready?" Jason asked.

Michael nodded. "As I'll ever be."

"Then let's hit the road. It's waffle day in the cafeteria tomorrow, and I don't want to sleep through it again."

Michael rubbed his hands together. "And that, my friend, is why I love Mondays."

That was the only reason to like a Monday, if you asked me.

"I'll text you tomorrow," Jason told me. I squeezed his hand.

Michael gave me a little wave. "See you later, Lily."

"'Bye, guys." I watched as they moved down the tunnel, trying not to get panicky about my werewolf boyfriend returning to the family who wanted to pick a bride for him. Was it wrong that I totally wanted to lecture his cousins?

Fear heavy in my heart, I tucked my hands into my pockets and walked down the passageway until I found Scout.

It was good to have a best friend, even if neither one of us was in a chipper mood as we walked back to the dorms. Turns out Michael had asked Scout about her dress for Sneak. I'm sure he asked only because he was excited, but she didn't have a dress and got panicky about "being a girly-girl."

As we walked down one dark tunnel after another, I filled her in about Jason and his possible disappearance.

She looked about as excited as I felt. "You ever have those days where you wish your life was like a keyboard with an 'undo' button? You could just hit the button and rewind recent events, go back to the way stuff was before?"

"More often than you can imagine," I said.

"Can't we just skip Sneak?" she asked. "It's not like we don't have other stuff to worry about."

"If you don't go with Michael, he'll have to find someone else to go with, and I know you wouldn't like that. What if he had to take Veronica? Or Mary Katherine?"

"He wouldn't dare," she said through gritted teeth. She was *so* easy to bait.

"So we're going to Sneak," I said, linking an arm though hers. We'll get you a dress, and me a dress, and we'll be good to go."

"Will we look more awesome than Veronica and M.K.?"

"Yes. Because we have souls. And brains. And senses of humor."

"And personalities."

This time, we did a fist bump. The boys were right; it was kinda fun.

"At least we don't have to deal with parents' night, too."

Surprised, I looked over at her. "Parents' night?"

Her expression fell. "Oh, crap on toast. I totally forgot to tell you about parents' night, didn't I?"

"That would be 'yes.'"

"The night before Sneak, all the parents come in and have dinner with their kids. It's not an official event or anything—that has something to do with insurance." She shrugged uncomfortably. "My parents don't come."

"And you didn't think to tell me because my parents are God knows where?"

She just frowned. "Sorry."

I shrugged, but it hurt. Not because she hadn't told me, but because she was right. I knew where they wouldn't be—having dinner with me the night before Sneak. They wouldn't be asking me how school was going. They wouldn't be checking out my room, or asking me about Jason, or lecturing me about how late I should be staying out or whether I was spending enough time on homework.

I wouldn't be telling them about magic and Adepts and fire-spell and Reapers—assuming they didn't already know. (I was a little suspicious about that.) I wouldn't be complaining about Enclaves and sanctuaries and Darkenings and vampires and the tunnels beneath St. Sophia's.

Maybe that was for the best.

Even if it was for the best, misery loved company. "Why don't your parents come?" I asked Scout.

She shrugged. "They have their roles, and I have mine. My role is staying put at St. Sophia's and not interrupting them. Their roles are using their money, traveling, being 'the Montgomery Greens.'"

"That's your dad?"

She nodded. "My mother doesn't even hardly use her name anymore. She's just 'Mrs. Montgomery Green.'" She shrugged. "I couldn't do it. I wouldn't want to have a kid and then stick her in a private school where I didn't have to see her or know who she was. But they came from money, and both of them went to boarding school. It's how they were raised. It's normal for them."

It was clear she wanted more, that she longed to know her parents—and for them to know her. But she also seemed to accept that they were who they were, and they were unlikely to change.

I had parents who wanted to be involved but who, for some mysterious reason, couldn't. She had parents who could be involved but, for some mysterious reason, didn't want to.

Sometimes, people just didn't make any sense.

"I wonder if I should even tell them about parents' night," I finally said, glancing over at her. "Will I feel better or worse when they tell me they want to come but can't?"

"That's a question for the ages, Parker."

I made the decision quickly, stopped in the middle of the tunnel, and took a second to send my parents a text message. At least I knew they'd be here if they could.

Lost in our thoughts, we walked silently back to St. Sophia's, then froze.

The basement was shielded from the tunnels by an antique, heavy metal door. There was a giant flywheel that locked it, and a metal bar that added a little extra security. It didn't do much to keep out Reapers with magic, but it did keep out the nastier creepy-crawlies that occasionally trolled the tunnels.

But tonight, the door was cracked open, light from the basement shining through. Now there was no magical barrier at all to whoever—or whatever—tried to sneak into the school.

My heart began to thud. "Who?" was the only question I could manage.

"I don't know." She straightened her messenger bag. "But we better go look."

I nodded, and we crept to the sliver of light beside the door and peeked into the hallway. It was empty. Whatever had opened the door—or come through it—was gone.

We walked inside and closed the door behind us, but not all the way.

"Probably shouldn't lock it in case we need to chase out whatever got in," I quietly said. She nodded. We crept down the hallway, which was pretty short, and then to the next corner. That hallway was empty, as well, but another door was open. It was marked JANITOR'S CLOSET, but it was actually called the City Room. A small model of the entire city of Chicago made in gray cardboard was spread out across the floor, like a short, three-dimensional map.

The brat pack had locked me in the City Room one night, which actually led to my getting firespell. So I guess I had Veronica to thank for that. Not that I was getting her a card or anything . . .

That was an odd place for someone to sneak into; not exactly the kind of place you expected an evil monster to hide. What was going on?

Scout pointed at the door, and I nodded. Silently, we crept along the wall to the City Room and looked inside.

"Holy crap," Scout said.

There in the middle of the City Room, legs straddled over the city of Chicago, stood Nicu, head of the newest coven of Chicago vampires.

He turned back to look at us, his black, military-style coat fluttering around his knees as he moved. He looked young, but he was handsome in an old-fashioned way. Pale skin, wavy dark hair, blue eyes. And when he was vamped out, inch-long fangs. Tonight he wore knee-high boots, snug pants, and a blousy white shirt.

No one looked that good accidentally. He looked date-night good, and that made me nervous. Really nervous. Was he waiting for Veronica? Had he ignored the fact that her memory had been erased and actually contacted her? Surely he wouldn't be that stupid. Sure, she might talk to him—but the press would be the second number on her speed dial, and vampires wouldn't be a secret in Chicago anymore.

And that was the other reason I was nervous. He was a *vampire*. With the bloodsucking and the fangs and a pretty obvious dislike of humans. Most humans, anyway.

"What are you doing here?" Scout asked.

Nicu's eyes narrowed dangerously and he flashed his fangs, as if to remind us that he wasn't a child we could boss around.

"I do not answer to you." His voice carried a deep accent, and he glowered at us—and that's the only word I could use to describe it. *Glowering.*

Sure, my instincts told me to run in the other direction and hunker down, but instead I took a step forward. I was tired, and I was out of patience for supernaturals today.

"You're in our territory," I said for the second time in a night. "You most definitely answer to us. And I repeat the question— what are you doing here?"

Nicu looked away, and this time there was sadness in his expression. I figured out his game.

"We erased her memory," I reminded him, "so she'd forget about the magic and the vampires."

"Her?" Scout asked.

"Veronica," I said, keeping my eyes on him. "Nicu's here to see Veronica."

"I am aware of the state of her memory," he said, his accent thick, but somehow fitting in the old stone convent. "I thought, perhaps, I might catch a glimpse of her." He gestured to the room. "But I find your home to be . . . labyrinthine."

He was right. The convent was like a maze, and he hadn't even made it onto the first floor yet. He must have gotten stuck in the City Room, and perhaps had been gazing at the map to find a way out.

"Why come through the tunnels?" Scout asked.

"How else would we travel? We live here, beneath ground. We do not travel in the demesne of humans. We do not stand in the bourgeois glare of the sun." His voice was flat, like that was an obvious rule of vampires I should have known about.

"She's human," I pointed out. "And she's not the type to keep a secret," I said. "Seeing her again will only cause problems, and I bet you know that. Or you wouldn't have agreed to her memory being wiped."

"We have a connection."

God only knew what he saw in Veronica. Sure, she was pretty, and she seemed smart when she wasn't using her brains for evil. But she *always* used her brains for evil.

Scout took up the debate. "If you find her, you put her and yourself in danger. Her, because she learns about magic, and Reapers might see her as a threat. You, because she learns about magic and that's one more person who knows vampires exist. Are you ready for that?"

He looked from me to Scout, and then turned again, coat spinning around his legs as he moved. He may be a big scary vampire, but he was also kind of cool, you know? Like he could have been the guitarist in an English punk band.

"You think I am not aware of the consequences? You are a child, and a human child at that. I have lived more years than you can even conceive. I know the risk."

Risk or not, here he was. I wasn't going to give a thumbs-up to a vampire sneaking around my school, but I guess the romantic in me could appreciate the fact that he was here.

"She'll be asleep," I said. "She shares a suite with three other girls. You couldn't get in and get out without being seen."

"Lily!" Scout whispered fiercely. "Do *not* encourage the fanged!"

I held up a finger. "Could you excuse us just for one second?" I didn't wait for his answer, but dragged Scout into the hallway.

"We should be threatening him, not giving him tips!" she said. "He is a monster."

"Maybe," I said, "but he's a monster with an agenda. If we don't help him, he'll sneak in, possibly leave the door open again, allowing Reapers in the school, and risk being seen by some wandering dragon lady, thus proving vampires exist to people who don't need to know that."

She considered that for a second. "You've been reading a lot of fantasy lately, haven't you?"

"It helps me sleep."

"He could hurt Veronica," she said.

Not that I'd wish her (much) harm, but that seemed unlikely. "He has a crush on her," I said. "I don't get why, and I don't think we need to play chaperone every time they hang out, but maybe if we introduce him as a human we could sidestep any of the supernatural drama? Then it's just relationship drama, and we can leave that to them."

Scout was quiet for a minute.

I knew it wasn't a great idea to escort a vampire through a sardine can of tasty teenagers. But when did Adepts ever have "great" options? My idea was the better of two crappy options, if you asked me.

"If we don't help him see her, then we don't get to control when and how he sees her."

She rolled her eyes, but finally nodded. "You're right," she said. "I don't like it, but you're right. When's your next night of party planning?"

"Every night. Sneak is Friday."

"Right. We'll play it that way, then. But I don't think he's going to be crazy about playing human."

"I'm often not crazy about it, either," I muttered, and we marched back into the room.

Nicu was standing in the middle of Lake Michigan, gazing up on the lakeshore. I bet he'd never been on the lake before. Immortality would be nice, but that would kind of be a bummer.

"We'll arrange a meeting," Scout said. "Our time, our place, our rules." She elbowed me. I guessed I was supposed to break the bad news.

"And you have to pretend to be human." I fought the urge to duck under his brutal stare.

Fire flashed in his eyes. "I will *not* do so."

"Then you will not get our help in meeting Veronica," Scout said.

He flashed his fangs. "I do not need your help."

I put a hand on Scout's arm to keep her from mouthing off. "What she means, Nicu, is that in order to keep everyone's secrets, well, *secret*, you're going to need to play it cool with Veronica. No fangs—if you can turn those things off—and maybe a little less of the I'd-just-as-soon-throttle-you-as-look-at-you vibe."

He just blinked at me. I wasn't sure vampires needed to blink, and it seemed scarier because of that. Unnerving, like he was more machine—or monster—than man.

"You will contact me," he finally said.

"Yes, yes, we will contact you. How do we do that?"

He reached into his coat, and I froze, waiting for him to pull out a musket or a ninja star or a sleek vampire weapon. Instead, he pulled out a small white business card.

He handed it over between two fingers. "Call me," he said.

And just like that—like we'd only been discussing the weather—he walked past us and out of the room, leaving the faint scent of coppery metal in his wake. The sound of his boots softened as he disappeared into the tunnels. Then we heard the metallic *screech* and *clank* as the door opened and shut again, and he was gone.

"That was fun."

Scout humphed. "Can you imagine dating a vampire? All the fangs and blood and stuff?" She gave a fake shiver, and we were quiet for a moment.

"Still," I said, "Nicu's pretty hot."

"Oh, my God, I am so glad someone else said it. Totally *en fuego*, isn't he? I wouldn't kick him out of my bed for eating crackers."

I gave her a doubtful look.

"I mean, I'm not saying I'd let him *in* my bed in the first place—I am not that kind of girl—but I feel like I wouldn't kick him out again, either."

"I feel like I'd fight you for him." We closed up and secured the basement door again, then climbed the stairs to the first floor and peeked into the main building.

The building was better lit and less damp than the tunnels, which was nice, but we still had to be careful. Instead of vampires roaming around we had Foley's minions—the dragon ladies who roamed the hallways on the lookout for Adepts breaking curfew.

St. Sophia's had been a Gothic convent, so most of the school still looked like a medieval church. The main building held the administrative wing, the chapel, and a giant circular room topped by a dome. The floor and walls were all stone, and there was a maze built into the stone beneath the dome. It was a really impressive room, but also kind of creepy. It was dark even in the middle of the day, and at night it wasn't hard to imagine monsters hiding in the corners.

When we were sure the coast was clear, we hustled through the room, and then into the Great Hall. That was our study-room-slash-library. It had tall, stained glass windows and lots of tables where we were forced to spend two hours every night doing homework. (Boarding school was fun!)

It was empty this late at night, so we ran through the hall and then into the dorm building where the suites were located. We went upstairs to our suite, and I unlocked the door with the key I wore around my neck on a ribbon. Every St. Sophia's girl got one. It was part of the welcome package.

The suite's common room was dark and empty. The room was round, with the doors to the four bedrooms around one half of the curve—mine was to the right, then Amie's, Lesley's, and Scout's. Lesley's door was the only one closed. There was no light underneath it, so I assumed she was asleep. Amie's was dark and wide-open; maybe she was bunking with Veronica or Mary Katherine, whichever girl she wasn't currently mad at.

Scout looked over at me. "Bedtime?" she whispered.

"Since we have class tomorrow, yeah. I think bedtime would be a good idea. And I hope I have sweet dreams of the firespell I used to have."

"Like they say, you don't know what you've got 'til it's gone."

We stood there silently for a minute. It was one thing to make a joke, but I did miss my firespell a little, and I hadn't had my magic nearly as long as she'd had hers. She must have felt the sting even more.

"I guess," I said. "Sleep good. I'll see you in the morning."

"Yes, you will." She walked to the threshold of her room, then looked back at me. "Sometimes our lives are too weird for words, Parker."

"Like creepy little fairy tales," I agreed. I just hoped we'd have happy endings, too.

5

I woke up grouchy after dreaming that I'd been trying to run but couldn't get my feet to move. It was like I was swimming in slow motion and couldn't get up to speed. I'd needed to escape from something, but my legs had been virtually useless, which pretty much described how I felt about magic right now.

And it was a Monday! Woot.

I pushed the hair from my face and checked the clock. It was after seven, but my small room was still dark and the suite outside my door was quiet. It didn't sound like anyone else was awake. Outside, I could hear the buzz of cars downtown. The rest of my suite might have been asleep, but Chicago was awake.

My stomach growled, and I wished I had a stash of snacks in my room. By the time I was showered and dressed, I wouldn't have much time for breakfast. That was St. Sophia's—you better be an early riser or you weren't getting fed.

Thinking Scout might have a snack in hand, assuming she was even awake, I hopped out of bed and scuffed across the common room in my pajamas—a tank top, fuzzy plaid bottoms, and thick socks. The stone floors were always cold.

I knocked on her door, and as soon as she muttered, "Come in," pushed it open.

Scout was already awake, wearing her uniform skirt and a long-sleeved shirt against the early-morning chill. Today she'd pulled her short hair into tiny ponytails that stuck out on each side of her head. She sat on her bed, her *Grimoire*—her book of magic spells—on the bed in front of her. To me and everyone else, it looked like a comic book. To Scout, it held the mysteries of magic. She was a spellbinder, which meant that not only could she cast spells, she could make them. Figure out the recipe and the words that would bring the spell to life. Her *Grimoire* held them all, which was why Reapers were always eager to get their hands on it.

I made a growly noise and sat down cross-legged on the floor. "Good morning, sunshine."

I growled again. "I still don't have magic. I can feel it in my bones." I looked up at her. "What about you?"

"No, and if I spend too much time thinking about not having it, I'm going to lose it. So I'm going to pretend it's just a blip on the screen. Just a temporary hiatus."

Somehow, I didn't think that attitude was going to last long. "Why are you already up?"

She waved a hand over her book. "I'm looking for answers," she said, rolling the "r" at the end of "answers" like a bad fortune-teller.

"Any luck?"

"About the magical blackout, not even a little. But if you have smelly ankle warts, I am your woman."

I wrinkled my nose. It was way too early to talk about smelly ankle warts. Not that there was ever a good time to talk about smelly ankle warts. While I was on the subject . . . Who even got smelly ankle warts?

"I'm going to need a lot of coffee before I'm going to be ready for smelly ankle warts."

Scout leaned over the side of her bed. When she sat up again, she held a paper cup of coffee in her hands. I snatched it immediately and took a sip. I was only fifteen, but I'd grown up at the college in New York state where my parents had been professors. I was brought up around school supplies, backpacks, and coffee, which explained why I loved fancy Japanese notebooks, cool messenger bags, and lattes.

I was a girl before my time.

I took a sip and closed my eyes. It was some kind of caramely goodness with whipped cream and just enough sugar. Maybe not diet food, but a really good waker-upper. "Oh, my God, I love you. Seriously. Marry me and business."

"That is probably the best offer I'll get today, but I must decline. Since I'm looking for answers today, I already called that Detroit. Girl wakes up at five o'clock every day. It's ridiculous."

"That is ridiculous. What did she say?"

"She used a bunch of technical words, but I think the gist was that they're working on finding the cause of the blackout. They're monitoring e-mail traffic and they have 'eyes and ears' on the sanctuaries, with cameras and video feed blah blah nonsense blah blah. Do you know what an aperture is? She kept throwing that around a lot."

"I think it's part of a camera. Is she going to call you back if she finds something?"

"Technically, she's supposed to go through her Varsity Adepts, but yeah, she said she would." She frowned. "Hey, you don't think Michael has a thing for her, do you?"

"For Detroit? Are you serious? Scout, if he was any more into you, he'd quit school and start following you around like a groupie. I mean, that's really the only other move he could make at this point."

"Fine," she said. "I get it."

"I mean, he could propose, I guess, unless he already has?"

"Are you done?"

"Oh, my God, you two could totally have a winter wedding. That would be *sweet*."

She lifted her eyebrows.

I put my hand over my heart. "Now I'm done. Swearsies." And while we were on the subject of boys . . . "Hey, is it wrong that I'm feeling less motivated about going to the dance with Jason if he's skipping out this week to maybe—*possibly*—go meet the girl his family's picked for him?"

"Did he say that's what was going to happen?"

"Well, not in so many words, but it's on the list of things he has to do at some point."

"Then keep the faith, Parker. I'm not denying he's got issues about being a wolf, but he's good people. He wouldn't string you along. He's not that kind of guy."

"I just don't want my heart to get broken, you know?"

"You'd rather bail out now than risk it, you mean? That's not exactly the brave Adept I know and love."

"Maybe my courage is in the same place as my magic." I flicked my fingers into the air. "Poofed right into the ether."

"I'll poof you right into the ether. Now, go take a shower. You're kind of stinking up my room with Adept funk."

"I do not have any Adept funk." I delicately sniffed my tank top. It smelled like laundry detergent, but I wouldn't mind brushing my teeth. "Fine," I said, turning my back on her and heading for the door. "I'm going. But I'm not happy about it."

"By the time you come back," she said, "you better have a fantastic smile on your face."

I hoped I would.

After a trip down the hall to the shower, I climbed into my St. Sophia's uniform. The plaid skirt was mandatory. We had some choices for shirts—button-down, hoodie, long-sleeved T-shirt, cardigan. It was chilly in my room, so I assumed it would be even colder outside. I opted for the button-down and a cardigan on top. It wasn't exactly high fashion, but it would keep me warm in the usually freezing-cold halls of St. Sophia's.

Thankfully, the shoes were entirely up to us. I loved shoes— especially if they came from vintage stores or thrift shops. The hunt was really the best part. The floor of my small closet was full of them—the ones I'd hauled to Chicago from New York and a few I'd found with Scout in stores in the Loop.

When my messenger bag was packed with books and my key was around my neck, I met Scout in the hallway, and we joined the horde of girls in plaid headed down to the classroom building.

The caffeine had definitely helped, but I couldn't stifle a yawn. It should be mandatory, some kind of national health rule, that teenagers didn't have to go to class until noon. We needed our rest—especially after spending our nights saving lives!

Unfortunately, the junior class at St. Sophia's was small, so we had every class with the brat pack, including art history. Over the past couple of months, I'd realized that each class had a different brat pack theme:

1. Art history: Art history was brat pack wake-up time. It usually involved putting on whatever expensive makeup they hadn't had time to apply in their rooms and drinking coffee from the expensive Italian machine in M.K.'s room. Sometimes they also made snarky remarks about naked male statues.

2. Trigonometry: The brat packers were usually awake by now, so this was when the text messaging began. We weren't supposed to have phones in class, but everyone did. The brat packers usually kept theirs hidden in pencil bags they kept on their desks. Dorsey, our trig teacher, probably just thought they were really picky about their pencils.

3. Civics: The brat pack decided Mr. Forrest, our civics teacher, was a catch—probably because he was the son of a senator from Vermont. He'd come to St. Sophia's after working on an unsuccessful election campaign, and the brat packers seemed to think he was their ticket to a fancy life as a senator's wife. Even Amie was totally smitten, and she was usually the rational one. Forrest wasn't bad to look at, but he was a believer. He worked on political stuff because he had real conviction, and there was just no way he was falling for brat pack flirting, no matter how much M.K. batted her eyelashes at him. (Seriously. He was, like, forty. It was gross.)

4. British literature: Brit lit was our first class after lunch, so

the brat packers were finally wide-awake. Amie and Veronica actually seemed to like reading *Jane Eyre* and *Pride and Prejudice*. I guess the romance got to them. Mary Katherine just whined that "nobody actually *did* anything" in the books. There was really no hope for her.

5. Chemistry: This was brat pack sleepy time. I don't know if they had an official rotation, but it seemed like they took turns taking naps in class. One day M.K. got a snooze while Amie kept watch, and then it was Veronica's turn, et cetera. If they were in danger of getting caught, the lookout would cough really loudly. Our chem teacher probably thought we were the least healthy group of St. Sophia's girls he'd ever seen.

6. European history: This class was boring for everyone, but the brat pack made the best of it. This was when they started prepping for another fun-filled day at the convent. Nails were buffed. Jewelry and shoe combinations for the next day's uniform were arranged. On more exciting days, M.K. would arrange an evening meet-up with a boy who was probably too old for her.

Somehow, even though they rarely paid attention in class, they still managed to get pretty good grades. Either they were crazy smart—and hiding it really well—or they'd made some kind of deal with the teachers. Or maybe they just all copied off one another.

Probably it was that.

Today's art history was pretty typical.

M.K. sat with her chin in her hand, looking bored and half-asleep. Amie scribbled notes furiously while Mr. Hollis, our teacher, talked about the Renaissance. Every few seconds, she'd take a sip from a paper cup that I assume held really strong coffee, because with every drink her handwriting got a little bit faster.

Veronica, the girl who had entranced a vampire so much he'd broken into St. Sophia's just for the chance to get a look at her, stared off into space. To each her own, I guess.

When the convent bells sounded after class, we all grabbed our books and headed to our lockers. Since St. Sophia's was a fancy-pants private school, juniors and seniors had glossy wooden lockers in a separate bay outside the classrooms. Mine was right below Scout's, my name engraved on a small metal plate on the outside.

Veronica and M.K. stood a few lockers down. Both of them had decided on lots of jewelry today. Yellow necklaces were loaded around their necks in gleaming tangles. If that was high fashion, I wanted no part of it.

M.K. had her back to a locker while Veronica pulled books from hers.

My mind on Nicu, I eavesdropped while I exchanged my books.

"I thought you wanted to go to Sneak with Creed," M.K. was telling her. "You talked about him for, like, two weeks."

John Creed was a friend of Jason's, and the guy Veronica had crushed—at least before she ran into Nicu.

"I did," Veronica said with a shrug. She paused, hand in her locker, and looked over at Mary Katherine. "I'm just not feeling him right now."

"Um, why? He's rich, hot, and rich. And he's a fantastic kisser."

Ick. Turned out that when Veronica had been crushing on

Creed, M.K. had been hitting on him. (I know. She was totally a class act.) Veronica looked as disgusted—and betrayed—as I felt.

"He isn't my type," Veronica said dryly. I had to agree with her. Anyone who would make out with Mary Katherine wasn't my type, either.

"He was your type two weeks ago," M.K. persisted. "You were totally crazy about him."

My stomach turned nervously as I waited for her answer—and silently bet that I knew what had changed. Yes, I'd kind-of-sort-of agreed to let Nicu meet Veronica. But if she was already so smitten that she didn't care about Creed, there was going to be fireworks. And fireworks probably meant drama for me.

"I don't know," Veronica repeated, her voice testier this time. Books in hand, she slammed her locker shut. "I don't want to talk about it anymore."

She started walking my way, and I turned my gaze back to my own locker, but not fast enough. She caught me staring and gave me a look. "You totally interrupted Lisbeth and Charlie last night. I hear you're the one who called Foley, and you practically assaulted Charlie. What are you, some kind of freak?"

"And you were with that freak Barnaby," M.K. threw in, like that was a crime.

Was Lisbeth's story that we interrupted a make-out session on purpose? So much for gratitude.

"I didn't interrupt anyone," I said, "and I didn't tell Foley. Lisbeth can do whatever she wants. We were just walking back to my room."

"Liar," M.K. maliciously said.

I glanced over and gave them a dubious look. "Have you

looked in the mirror lately? You look like a jewelry store threw up on your uniform. Now, that's freaky. Go to class."

They threw out some snarky comments, but left us at our lockers. When I looked back at Scout, her eyes were wide.

"That totally just happened."

It had happened, and I felt immediately guilty. My parents had taught me better than to be obnoxious just because someone had been obnoxious to me. But I'd *saved* Lisbeth, and I'd ended up with no firespell. Was it a coincidence? Maybe. But a thank-you would have nice.

"It totally did," I grumbled. "And not that she's my favorite person right now, but I think Nicu's in luck."

Scout frowned, and glanced back to watch Veronica walk the hallway. "Why?"

"Because she doesn't like Creed anymore."

"How is that news? I don't like Creed, either."

"I think she doesn't like Creed because she hasn't totally forgotten about Nicu."

"At least he's having a good day. Let's see how else this day can go down the tubes."

As it turned out, our trig teacher rescheduled our midterm exam.

To *tomorrow.*

I loved it when teachers were understanding.

6

We were on our way to civics—only one more class before lunch—when I got the text. I'd forgotten to turn off my phone and pulled it out of my bag assuming it was my parents, maybe with an apology about having to miss parents' night.

It definitely wasn't my parents.

It was Sebastian Born—the Reaper who'd given me firespell.

"WE NEED TO TALK" was all it said.

I pulled Scout out of the flow of traffic and showed her the phone. Her expression immediately went suspicious. Sebastian had contacted me before, and she hadn't been thrilled about it.

"Have you been talking to him?" she asked.

I rolled my eyes. "If by talking to him, you mean reading this single text message and then showing it to you as soon as I got it, then yes, I have."

"Har har har. I know you two are buds."

"We aren't buds. He thinks we've bonded because we both have firespell."

"Have you texted him back yet?"

"Not yet."

She crossed her arms and frowned like she was seriously puzzling something over. "I think you should go talk to him."

I blinked back shock. That was the last thing I expected her to say. "Excuse me?"

"I know you've talked to him before. He has some kind of connection with you. I'm not saying I like it," she quickly added, "but you use what you've got, right?"

I wet my lips and thought about it for a moment. She was right—Sebastian clearly wanted to contact me. While I wasn't thrilled about setting up a meeting, at least I wasn't doing it behind anyone's back. And maybe he had information about the blackout.

"You're right. I should talk to him." I started typing a response. "But I'm going over lunch, and you're going with me."

Sebastian agreed to meet us beside the Chicago River, which cut through the city's downtown. We were allowed to walk around our neighborhood during the lunch hour, and the River was technically too far away from campus. But what was a little rule-breaking between friends?

We were supposed to meet him beside the bridge on State Street. Sure, I hadn't been here long, and I hadn't exactly come here by choice. But there was something about this city I liked. I liked the mix of buildings in downtown Chicago, the never-ending stream of tourists who all seemed to be in awe of the city, the Italian food, and the reflection of the city on the river at night, even if

I didn't make it outside damp and chilly tunnels very often to actually *see* that reflection. I liked listening to Jason and Michael argue about the Cubs and Sox and whether Wrigley was better than U.S. Cellular Field.

Maybe a long winter would change how I felt about the city, but it wasn't winter yet. For now, Chicago was pretty good.

As we approached the bridge, we could see traffic was stopped. A crowd of onlookers stood at a stone railing overlooking the water. They stared expectantly over the edge.

"Did someone fall in?" I whispered.

"Oh, sweet luck!" Scout said, dragging me across the street as soon as the light changed.

"What are you doing?"

"There are certain good luck charms in Chicago," she said. "And this is one of them."

"Staring at the river?" I asked, seriously confused.

"Not the river," she said, squeezing us into an empty spot at the railing. "The bridge."

As it turned out, the crowd wasn't checking out what was *in* the river—they were looking at what was *out* of it. The gigantic steel bridge was rising up, its two metal arms splitting in half and lifting toward the sky so taller boats could pass through it.

"Oh, that is just frickin' sweet," Scout said, pulling out her phone to snap some pictures.

The boats were ready to go: A dozen sailboats were in the stretch of river on the other side of the bridge, waiting to pass beneath it. A few kayaks were sprinkled in the water beside them. And this bridge wasn't the only one moving. As I looked down the river, I could see two more in line behind it, now slowly moving back down again—two pieces of the road coming back together so traffic could pass.

The boaters sat on the decks of their boats, bundled up against the chilly fall wind. The boats were moving away from the lake, probably into harbors for the winter.

I heard the excited chatter of people around us and glanced over.

A few yards down the railing stood a slender girl with a ponytail of sleek, dark hair, and a big black camera around her neck. She threw her head back in a laugh, and I got a full view of her companion.

It was Sebastian Born. Tall, dark, handsome, and at least moderately evil.

I quickly looked back at the river again, suddenly nervous. "He's here," I said. "Three o'clock."

"Three o'clock? I thought you said noon?"

"He's *standing* at three o'clock. Beside the girl with the ponytail and camera."

That got Scout's attention. Very carefully, she glanced to the side, like she was just watching the next bridge begin to rise, before looking back at the river again. "That is definitely Sebastian Born."

I blew out a breath to calm my nerves. "All right, I'm going over there."

"I'll stay right here. Out of Reaper range."

"Thoughtful of you," I said, and then my feet were moving and I was walking toward him. It took only a second before he looked up and met my gaze.

The deep, dark blue of his eyes was almost shocking. They offered up a punch, and I felt it in my gut as sure as any fist. But I made myself keep walking, and stopped when I reached the girl.

"Hey," he said.

"Hey." I stuffed my hands into my pockets, suddenly self-conscious. It wasn't exactly normal practice for Adepts and Reapers to meet in the middle of downtown Chicago on purpose and aboveground.

"Oh, uh, this is my cousin, Fayden. Fayden, Lily Parker."

Fayden glanced over at me and smiled a little before turning her gaze back to the river. "Hiya," she said.

"The bridge is pretty cool, huh?" he asked.

I glanced back just as a man and woman in bright orange kayaks and puffy coats paddled by. "Yeah, it's pretty cool."

"Fayden's new to town," Sebastian. "She's a two-L at Northwestern. Law school," he added, at my confused expression. "That means she's in her second year. She transferred from California."

"That's a big change," I said.

Fayden smiled. "Seventy degrees and sunny skies made me too perky. I figured a few winters in Chicago would help balance me out."

"It's Lily's first winter, too, actually," Sebastian said.

"Oh?" Fayden asked. "Where are you from?"

"New York state."

"Huh," she said. "Cool."

Sebastian gestured toward a group of trees and a bench a few feet away from the river's edge. I guessed that was where he wanted to talk.

"We'll be right back, Fayden," he said.

She nodded just a little.

"So you're sightseeing?" I asked as we walked to the trees.

"Yeah, helping her get acquainted."

The small talk done, I cut to the chase. "So what's up?" I asked.

He looked *super* uncomfortable. "What do you know about magical power loss?"

My heart began beating wildly. Was he asking because he knew about us . . . or because Reapers were having problems, too? I decided to play dumb. "What do you mean?"

"Spells not working, powers gone."

How to lie without lying? Avoid answering the question. "Why do you ask?"

Sebastian looked back at me for what felt like a long time. Maybe he was deciding how honest he could be, wondering if he could trust me. "Because our magic is gone."

I was almost too stunned to speak. It wasn't just Adepts? It was Reapers, too? "Our?"

"Reapers. Every Reaper in Chicago."

"Since when?"

"Since this morning."

We'd lost our magic last night. They lost their magic this morning, *after* we'd lost ours. That didn't sound like a natural phenomenon. It sounded like someone had flipped a magical switch. But was that even possible? Who could flip a switch and turn off the magic of all Adepts and Reapers in Chicago? Who else was left?

"Jeremiah thinks Adepts did it," Sebastian added. "Canceled out our power somehow."

"We didn't," I assured him. "I'm not even sure we could."

"I'm not sure he'll buy that."

So many questions raced in my head. What if he was telling the truth and Reapers didn't have powers? He was taking a risk, so didn't I owe him the truth, as well? But what if he was lying? What if Reapers were the reason we didn't have power, and he wanted to confirm the trick had worked? What if he was trying to ferret out our weaknesses so Reapers could attack?

And, more important: Why was he helping me? Why was he giving me information that helped Adepts, when he didn't even believe Adepts were on the right side of things? Was he trying to lure me in? Win me over?

But I held them in. I also held in the truth. I didn't tell him we didn't have powers, either. Maybe he knew; maybe he didn't. But if he proved trustworthy, I promised myself I'd repay the favor later.

"Convince him," I said. "I promise you we didn't take your magic."

"He wants proof. He wants Scout's *Grimoire*. He thinks she did it."

That wasn't even negotiable. "He's not going to get it. Not that it would help him anyway. And if he tries it, we'll throw everything we have back at you."

It was just that "everything" we had wasn't much right now, at least not magically.

Fayden called his name, pointing at something on the river. I glanced back at her. "Is she one of you?"

His eyes darkened dangerously. "She is not," he said. "And I'd appreciate it if you'd keep her out of it. There's no need for the rest of the Dark Elite to know she's even here."

I guess he didn't trust his fellow Reapers any more than we did. But that begged a question—if I'd said I had relatives visiting, would he do me the same favor? Would he keep my family out of it?

But I wasn't a Reaper, and I wasn't looking for a way to hurt Sebastian or his cousin, so I nodded. "No problem."

He looked relieved.

"Well, I need to get back to school," I said. "Thanks for the update."

"You, too."

He walked back to Fayden and I walked back to Scout like nothing at all had happened. Like we hadn't just discussed gigantic magical developments. She started grilling me immediately.

"What did he do? What did he say? Who's the girl?"

"His cousin. The good news is, Reapers have lost their power, too."

Her eyes got really wide. "He told you that?"

"He did."

"Do you think he was bluffing?"

"The only reason to bluff would be to find out if we have magic, too. And I'm not about to give that away. At least, not now. Not until we're sure whose side he's on."

"So Reapers don't have magic, huh?" She turned around and propped her elbows behind her on the railing. "So what does that mean? Who's behind it?"

"I have no clue. Unfortunately, I do also have bad news."

"You made out with him?"

"No, jeez, no. Have some respect. Seriously, though. The

Reapers, or so they say, don't know who's done this, either. But they have a theory."

"Which is?"

No sense beating around the bush. "They think it's you."

The smile that spread across her face wasn't the fear I'd expected. "They think I'm *good*."

"They think the answers are in your *Grimoire*."

That made her pale a little bit, which I thought was good. I'd rather have her a little bit afraid than a little bit too cocky—and not as careful as she should be.

She pushed off the railing. "I'm not giving up my *Grimoire*," she said. "If they think that's going to happen, they are crazy or stupid. Or both." She looked at me. "We have to figure out this blackout thing. We *have* to."

"I know," I said.

Unfortunately, I bet that was going to be the hard part.

When compared to a meeting with a Reaper beside a bridge that had vaulted itself out of the Chicago River, classes were dull. We'd also skipped lunch for the meet, which meant we were both starving. Hunger didn't make European history any more exciting.

It was early in the week at St. Sophia's School for Perpetually Rich Girls, which meant the options in the cafeteria weren't quite as nasty as they'd get. Dinner on Thursday or Friday meant you'd be served up a stew of anything that didn't get eaten earlier in the week. The cafeteria crew called it "slurry." I called it disgusting.

Tonight they were serving burgers—the meaty kind for Scout and black bean for me. I was a vegetarian, so I made up for the lack of meat with veggies and sugar.

The brat pack seemed excited about something, but it wasn't like I was going to go over and see what was up. They were at their usual table in the cafeteria beside a huge window that looked out over the yard. It was brat pack kingdom over there, and I wasn't about to trespass.

Scout and I took seats at the end of a table on the other side of the room. We replayed my conversation with Sebastian, and she kept asking questions about what he did or didn't say as she tried to fish clues from our conversation.

But one question stood out.

"Are you going to tell Jason you're friends with Sebastian?"

I stopped in the middle of a bite of a burger. "We're not friends."

"Maybe not," she said, squeezing so much mustard and ketchup onto the remaining half of her burger that it oozed out the sides. "But I still think he'd want to know."

"Would you tell him if you were me? I mean, it's completely innocent, but I don't think Jason—or any of the rest of the Adepts—would think it's a good idea."

"Do you think it's a good idea?"

"I'm not talking to Sebastian because I want us to be buds, because I want to date him, or because I think he and the rest of the Reapers are right about anything. He's more like . . . a secret source. He gives me information, and if that information is useful, I'm going to use it. I'm not going to ignore him just because the Adepts aren't comfortable with it."

"And if Sebastian's using you?"

"He could only use me if I was giving him information. Which I'm not."

"Well, be careful he doesn't try to turn your friendship—or whatever it is—into a way to get access to information . . . and the Enclave."

"I'd never do that."

"Yeah, but I also bet you never thought you'd be talking to Sebastian on the street or making nice with his cousin. Things change. People change. Just keep an eye out."

"I will. And I'll think about whether I should tell Jason."

Scout's phone beeped, so she pulled it out and glanced at the screen. "You better think pretty fast," she said, then showed me her phone.

We were meeting at the Enclave tonight.

7

The situation was dire. We had a trig test, our magic was gone, and we had a party to prep and a secret meeting with a vampire to arrange. I had no parents for parents' night, and no dress for the dance. I also had a worried werewolf and a spellbinding best friend who was now target number one for the city's bad guys.

Pretty stressful stuff.

A lot of that stuff affected Michael and Jason, which I assumed was why we found them sitting at the table in the Enclave . . . preparing their fantasy basketball lineups.

"Is this seriously the best thing you guys have to do with your time?" Scout asked, tossing her messenger bag onto the table.

"No, no," Michael said, stabbing a finger at the table and completely ignoring Scout. "You can't put Topher at point guard. He was out half of last year because of his knee. That's ridiculous."

"I can put him wherever I want," Jason said, writing something out on a piece of paper. "I drafted him. You're just complaining because you couldn't get him."

Michael pointed at his chest with a pencil. "I didn't want him. I am smarter than that, and I know he's not going to last through the season. I took Guzman because I wanted Guzman."

So he said, but he didn't exactly sound that confident.

I sat down next to Jason. "Basketball? Really?"

He grinned over at me. "We finished our draft over the weekend, so we're comparing our lineups."

"Guzman?" Scout asked. "I can't believe you picked Guzman."

This time, Michael looked upset. "You think it was a bad pick?"

Scout snorted a laugh. "Like I know. I have no idea who Guzman is. Or the"—she looked over at the paper—"Lack-ers. Pretty crappy name for a team."

"That's *Lakers*, Scout. Lakers," Jason said.

"Whatever." She yawned. "If you two gentlemen are done, can we get this show on the road?"

"Let's do," Daniel said, and the rest of the Adepts joined us at the table. "First things first—any updates from the field?"

I looked at Scout, who nodded. "The Reapers have lost their magic," I said.

The room got really quiet, and my heart pounded so hard I wondered if everyone could hear it.

"What do you mean, they lost their magic?" Daniel asked. "How did you learn that?"

"She—we saw a Reaper near the door at St. Sophia's," Scout blurted out.

I froze, then looked slowly over at her. She had totally just lied to Daniel and the Enclave, I assumed to keep me from mentioning my meeting with Sebastian. Because she thought talking to him was a bad idea that was going to get both of us in trouble—or because she wanted to keep our secret source to ourselves?

"Near the door?" Daniel asked with a frown, crossing his arms. "And he didn't get in?"

"*She* didn't get in," Scout corrected. "She was a Reaper we'd met before, so we knew what magic she could work. But she tried the magic and it didn't work. When her attempt at mano a mano went bad, she sprinted off."

"But not before squealing something about how she was like the other Reapers and didn't have magic, either," I said.

The story sounded ridiculous even to me, but in the world of the Adepts, it probably wasn't even on the top-ten list of strange things we'd seen in our careers. Reapers trying to break into our school? Already seen it. Fist-fighting girls? Been there, done that.

"Huh," Daniel said. "So you've got firsthand info that Reapers' magic is not working?"

"Firsthand info," I confirmed.

I tried not to fidget beneath the other Adepts' curious stares. Did they know I was lying? Did I look suspicious? I was definitely not made for spy games. Thankfully, before I actually started shuffling my feet and whistling nervously, there was a knock on the door.

We all braced ourselves for impact—except Daniel.

"It's open," he called out.

So much for security.

The door squeaked open, and Detroit walked in.

I mentioned Lesley's fashion sense—odd, but pretty chill. Detroit's fashion sense was much more intense—an explosion of leather, lace, feathers, and random bits of metal. Tonight she wore a long, fitted black coat with sleeves that poofed out at the hands with a shower of lace. She wore leggings and knee-high black boots beneath it, and her blond hair was carefully curled. A tiny black hat was angled on top of her head, and she wore a small black satchel diagonally across her chest. She lugged in an old leather suitcase with gold buckles across the top.

Adepts were an odd group, and Enclave Two was certainly no exception.

"What is this?" Paul asked, walking closer.

When she had the suitcase where she wanted it, she placed it down on its side, unbuckled the straps, and flipped open the top. Unlike the vintage leather and brass on the outside, the inside was all wires and buttons that looked like they'd been popped out of old typewriters. Most of Detroit's machines looked slick and modern. This one looked like bits of junk hot-glued together. I guess that was what you got when your machinist lost her magic.

Detroit pressed one of the buttons.

Nothing happened.

She laughed nervously, then mashed the button down again. The machine clicked and then whirred into action. Little black dials flipped over on each other, and a small contraption that looked like a cheap plastic Ferris wheel began to spin.

"And what is that, exactly?" Paul asked.

She stood up again and looked proudly down at . . . whatever it was. "It's a virus remover. It will look you over and if you're infected with a virus that's caused the blackout, it will get rid of it."

Well, that was a pretty creative idea. Although it did beg one question:

"We're infected by viruses?" Scout asked with a frown.

"I'm not sure. But it's worth a try, don't you think?"

I guess I couldn't argue with that.

With the toe of her shoe, she pressed another button. A flap on the other side of the machine flipped open, and a beam of light shot across the room. "I don't have magic, but, you know, I can still make stuff. Who wants to step into the beam?"

Maybe not surprisingly, nobody raised a hand.

"Is it safe?" Jill asked, kneeling down to get a look at the machine. It *buzzed* and *beeped* as she looked at it, like the machine was filled with wicked angry bees.

"Oh, God," Detroit said, holding out a hand. "Don't move."

Jill froze in her crouch, her eyes widening. "Oh, God, what? What did I do? Did I trigger something? Is it a bomb?"

The Enclave went silent.

Detroit laughed so hard she snorted. "Ah, that gets 'em every time. Seriously, it's fine. Walk into the beam."

"Because?" Jill asked, face wrinkled with worry.

"Because, in order for it to remove a magical virus, you have to, you know, *use* the machine." She nudged Jill gently toward the beam of light.

Wincing, eyes closed, Jill put a toe into the beam. When she didn't burst into flames, she opened one eye and checked out her foot.

"See? It's fine. Now step all the way in, please."

While Jill walked into the light, Detroit adjusted the dials on the suitcase. The light wavered and flickered, but that was all it did. After a moment, the light went out altogether.

Not entirely sure what to do—or what had happened—we stood there looking at each other awkwardly, then at Detroit.

"All done," she brightly said. "You wanna see if it worked?"

Jill and Jamie shared one of those kinds of deep looks that twins had—like they could read each other's minds and knew exactly what the other was thinking. And neither one of them looked like they trusted Detroit's new contraption.

"Of course she does," Daniel kindly said. "Maybe start with something small."

The girls looked at each other, then nodded. "Does anyone have a bottle of water?" Jill asked.

"I've got one," Scout said, then dug through her messenger bag and pulled out a bottle. "It's only half-full."

"No problem," Jill said. She walked over to the table and put the bottle on top, then stepped back a few feet.

We all scooted back a little, giving her room to operate. Just in case.

She stood there for a moment, hands at her sides, and squeezed her fingers rhythmically into fists. Open. Closed. Open. Closed. Her long hair fell across her shoulders, which she rolled a little as if loosening them up.

"Is it wrong that I'm really freaked-out right now?" Scout whispered.

"That she'll turn us all into ice?" I wondered.

"That it won't work at all."

That was probably the scarier option.

Jill raised her hands in front of her body, and with a whoosh of sound—like she'd exhaled really hard—she pushed her hands out and toward the bottle of water.

The room was silent—and the water wasn't even a little bit icy.

The tension in the room was awful. It wasn't exactly fun to

watch another Adept completely unable to work her magic, especially knowing we were all in the same boat.

"Try again," Daniel said softly. "Just one more time."

Jill nodded, then repeated her magic prep again. Fists open and closed, rolling shoulders, the pushing of the hands.

But the bottle didn't waver.

Jill let out a soft sob. She turned around, tears brimming in her lashes, and went to her sister. They hugged.

"This is going to last forever, isn't it?" Paul asked, panic in his voice. "That machine doesn't work, and we don't have any other ideas, and we're screwed. Our magic is gone."

"It's my fault," Detroit said, her voice softer this time and not nearly as confident. "The machine doesn't work. I'd hoped—" she began but she shook her head, then wiped a tear from the corner of her eye. "I'd hoped I could still do it. Anyone can make a machine. You don't need magic for that. But I make machines that *interact* with magic. They recognize it. Test it. Use it. That's my power. That's my talent."

She quieted and looked away, and this time didn't bother to stop the tear that slid down her cheek. "My magic is gone," she said. "Now I'm just a two-bit hobbyist. I might as well start building battle bots."

"I like battle bots," Michael said, a quirky smile on his face. Detroit looked at him and smiled, but you could see the hurt ran pretty deep.

"Our magic isn't gone," Daniel said. "This is Chicago—not some fairy tale city. Magic doesn't just disappear without a reason. Someone is behind this—someone has turned off our magic, which means we focus on figuring out who that is and making things right again."

This might have been hard for all of us, and it might have been hard for Daniel, but you couldn't see it to look at him. He was a good motivator—a "never let 'em see you sweat" kind of guy. It was just the kind of thing we needed right now.

Unfortunately, it didn't give us our magic back.

"Don't lose your heads over a temporary circumstance," he said. "And that's what this is—a temporary circumstance."

"Or it's practice," Paul said. "Like losing our magic before we even get good at it. That sucks."

"See? It's an opportunity," Daniel chuckled. "You guys are seriously making me feel like Pollyanna today." That got a laugh in the Enclave. "Look, this is hard. This situation sucks, and I know that for sure, because I'm a lot closer to giving it all up than you are. It's hard to face a lifetime without it. But it's not impossible. It's a gift, a really particular kind of gift, but life goes on. And now you know that."

Jason's phone rang, breaking the silence. He pulled it out and glanced at the screen, then frowned. Without another word, he walked to the Enclave door, pulled it open, and walked outside. It shut with a heavy thud that sent a little frizzle of panic through my chest. Was this the call? The one that pulled him home again, never to return?

Michael walked over. "What was that about?"

"I don't know," I said, eyes still on the door. "Family stuff, I guess."

"He's been quiet about that lately. I don't think he wants to go home."

I looked back at Michael, wanting to believe him. "Why do you say that?"

Michael shrugged. "He doesn't talk about it a lot. I think he has a lot of frustration about them, about their ways. He came up here to get away from it, but it seems to follow him. He wants to have his own life, you know? A separate life."

"Separate from their rules?"

"Yeah. He told you it was a curse?"

I nodded. "Yeah."

"It weighs on him. He joined up with the Enclave to help make a difference, because he wanted something good to come of it. He thinks you're something good to come from it, too."

I felt my cheeks warm, and I appreciated the admission. "Thanks, Michael. I know he's glad you're friends."

"He should be. I kick butt." He did a fake karate chop that most definitely did not kick butt.

"And speaking of kicking butt," Scout said, loud enough for the rest of the Enclave to hear, "we can't just sit around and wait for something to happen. I have to stay busy."

"You will," Daniel said. "There's one more thing on the agenda tonight."

We all looked at him.

"The Reapers kept their magic longer than we did," he said. "That suggests the blackout is part of an organized plan. Probably not by Reapers, unless something backfired and rebounded on them. But they're even keener to keep their magic than we are. So there's no doubt they're looking into it. And if they're looking into it, they're probably talking about it."

"That's just because half the Reapers are teenage girls," Paul said with a grin. Jamie punched him in the arm, which Scout and I applauded.

"Whatever the reason," Daniel said, "that means it's time to visit the sanctuary and see what we can see. That's why Detroit is here—she'll plant a camera so we have good eyes on the place. The Council was very pleased about the last time the Enclaves worked together. Well, except for the part about imploding the other sanctuary. That wasn't exactly a Council-approved action."

Scout blushed a little, but still looked pretty pleased with herself. We had helped Detroit and Naya, another Adept from Enclave Two who could call and communicate with ghosts, investigate a sanctuary where Reapers had been looking for the solution to magical immortality. Scout destroyed it by sucking everything out of it like a magical vacuum cleaner. It had been pretty sweet, but I could understand why the Council was concerned. A magic spell beneath Chicago sucking out the building's insides? Yeah, I could see how that would worry people.

"Jill, Jamie, Paul, make a patrol of the tunnels. Make sure the Reapers aren't reacting badly to losing their magic by wreaking even more havoc. Detroit, Michael, Jason, Lily, and Scout, visit the sanctuary," Daniel said. "Get eyes on the interior and find out what you can. And if you could, come back with an answer about why we have no magic . . . and a solution for getting it back."

Oh, so a simple trip, then.

8

A few weeks ago, an order like that would have freaked us out. But now it really didn't sound so bad. Sure, we didn't have magic. But if Sebastian was telling the truth, Reapers didn't, either.

And we were getting better at sneaking around the tunnels. Visiting a sanctuary was mostly about sneaking around tunnels.

I'd been to this particular sanctuary only once—and that had been to rescue Scout. I'd used my firespell for the first time, and Jamie, Jill, Paul, Jason, and Michael and I had managed to get her out again.

But that didn't mean I was thrilled about going back. Sanctuaries were the Reaper versions of Enclaves—where they met, where they made decisions, and where people without magic were introduced to it in the worst possible way—by having bits of their souls sucked away. I was not looking forward to facing down a nest of Reapers if we managed to get caught.

This sanctuary was in a former power substation, with two access doors—one in front, and one in back. Like Enclave Three, it was also underground, but was separated from our HQ by a lot of dark and twisty tunnels.

You know, if we knew the way to get to the sanctuary, the Reapers probably could figure out how to get to the Enclave and St. Sophia's. That explained how they kept popping up at our door. Maybe it was time to think about making some new arrangements.

"You ever think it would just be easier if the sanctuary and the Enclave were right next door to each other?" Scout whispered.

The light from our flashlights bobbed up and down as we walked side by side through the tunnels, Detroit in front of us. The boys decided the "strongest Adepts" needed to be at the front and back of the team, so Jason was in the lead and Michael was last.

"I was actually just thinking about that," I said. "It's too easy to get from one place to the other. I mean, if we're supposed to be a splinter group trying to bring down the Reapers, setting up camp a few tunnels over isn't exactly a smart move for security purposes."

"It was at the time," Detroit said, glancing back at us. "The Enclaves were started by Dark Elite members who wanted to change things, but they were still considered part of the Dark Elite. Other Reapers would have been suspicious if they just stopped showing up to meetings and whatnot, so they established little hideaways not far from the sanctuaries. That way, they could sneak over after meetings or whatever."

"Which is why, if you look at the map in the City Room, the sanctuaries and Enclaves are always pretty close together," I said.

"Yes," Detroit primly said, and I had the sense the Enclave

Two Adepts knew a lot of stuff that we didn't. "Except for our Enclave. We're aboveground."

Of course they were. We had a stone room in an underground tunnel. They had labs and workout rooms and so on and so on.

Enclave Three had a werewolf.

Enclave Two had a *benefactor*.

We slowed as we got closer to the sanctuary. We also got quieter and huddled a little closer together. There was no telling whether the Reapers had patrols out and about, and it wasn't like we could do much to defend ourselves.

After a moment, Jason stopped and put a hand in the air, then made a fist.

Immediately, the rest of us stopped and switched off our flashlights. I moved a little closer to Scout. This part of the tunnel was pitch-black, and it was comforting to have someone nearby. I strained my ears to figure out what he'd heard, but could hear only the thumping of my rabbit-fast heart.

That was when I heard them—two voices, a few tunnels away, which gave their voices a weird metallic echo.

"No, it's because they think he's weak," said one man.

"He is weak," agreed another. "We don't have magic."

Scout reached out and squeezed my hand. Sebastian had been telling us the truth—the Reapers didn't have magic, either.

"You heard the rumors?"

"Yeah," the other guy said after a minute. "I heard 'em."

"You think they're true?"

"I don't know. Honestly, I don't know fact from fiction any-more."

What rumors? I wondered, and had to squeeze my lips together from calling out a question: *Who took our magic away?*

"I don't have a clue," said the first guy. "That's what I'd like to know."

"The Scions won't put up with this for long. And I don't care how the other sanctuaries do it—we're the first sanctuary, the alpha and omega. We should not be lying around and waiting for our magic to start working again."

"That's why this entire organization is going to hell," said the other one.

The footsteps moved closer, as did the faint glow of a flashlight somewhere down the line. We all froze, our shoulders pressed against one another's, squeezed into a tight knot as we waited in the dark.

"I don't even know why we bother patrolling. There's nothing out here."

"Jeremiah's nervous. No magic, and you start to think every shadow is a boogeyman."

"Says something about life without magic," muttered the other guy.

"Yes, it does." His voice dropped a little deeper, like the conversation was getting more serious.

There was silence for a minute, but the lights ahead flickered, like the guys were swinging their flashlights back and forth . . . looking for us.

"Let's go back."

"Fine," the other one said. "But if he has another fit, it's your head this time."

After a moment, we heard footsteps moving away. And when silence descended again, Jason flipped on his flashlight and turned back to us.

Michael was the first to speak. "That confirms their magic isn't working."

"And they don't seem to know why," Jason added.

"I am very happy their magic isn't working," Scout said. "I also want to know what rumors they're talking about. Let's move closer."

"Is that a good idea?" I asked. "We're, what, five hundred feet from the sanctuary? It's not going to get any safer."

"We have to plant the camera," Detroit reminded us. "We have to move closer."

"We'll go lights out," Jason said, switching off his flashlight again. "We'll get as close to the sanctuary as possible, and we'll see if they have any guesses about who's turned off the magic. If all else fails, I'll change, sneak in, and check things out. No problem."

Without a better plan, we kept moving.

After a few minutes we reached the well-lit area where the tunnel opened into an access area. From there, you could get to other parts of the city's underground tunnels or head upstairs to the street. Or, if you really wanted, you could climb the set of concrete stairs that led up to a small platform and a metal door—the front door to the sanctuary.

We crowded into the threshold of the tunnel and peered out. There was no sign of the men, who'd either gone back into the building or disappeared into a secondary tunnel. But that didn't slow my heartbeat any. Inside the sanctuary was a giant banner that bore a Reaper quatrefoil—and beneath it was the table where Scout had been used by Reapers for her own energy.

I reached out and squeezed her hand. It was cold and clammy, and when I glanced over at her, she looked a little pale.

"You okay?"

"Just . . . remembering," she said, but swallowed hard. "No problem."

"Should we go in?" Michael whispered.

For a moment, no one answered.

"I've got one more thing to try."

We all looked at Detroit. Nervously, she opened her black satchel and pulled out a black plastic beetle a few inches long. She held it in the palm of her hand.

"What is it?" I asked.

"It's like an X-ray camera," she said. "It will filter out the concrete and pipes and stuff and we can get a visual on the room. Sound, too. It's a bug," she said with a nervous laugh. "Get it?"

"What's the catch?" Jason asked.

She looked up at him. "We have to get it inside. Just sticking it on the door isn't enough. It can see through only so much concrete, so it needs to be on the wall of the room you want to look into."

Jason winced, then looked up at her. "I hate to ask—"

"It will work," she interrupted. "I promise it will work."

There was another moment of silence as we debated our options. Going inside the sanctuary was a huge risk, and if Detroit's beetle thingy didn't work, it was a huge risk with no benefit. On the other hand, if the Reapers weren't responsible for the magical blackout, who was? Who else had the power to do it? We had to find that out.

"It will work," Detroit repeated, and I held out my hand. Everyone looked at me.

"It *will* work," I said. "I know it will. And I'll get it inside. You just need to tell me how to do it."

Her eyes widened. "You believe me?"

"Your word is good enough for me," I said. After all, if I could trust Sebastian, the least I could do was trust an Adept. That was a no-brainer.

Detroit nodded and handed over the beetle. It was heavier than I thought. It was nice and solid, and that was comforting somehow.

But Jason wasn't thrilled with my plan. "It's too dangerous," he said. "You could get hurt."

I shook my head. My mind was already made up. "I'm the only one who can go. Detroit's too valuable to risk—she's the only one who can actually do something useful right now. Scout's a spellbinder—she can't be risked—and Michael's a pacifist."

That was only half-true. He probably wasn't really a pacifist, but he wasn't a fighter, either.

"And me?" Jason asked.

"You need to stay out here and keep them safe. And if I get pinched, you need to come rescue me."

I thought that sounded cute, but he didn't really look swayed. Stubborn werewolf boyfriends.

But since he wasn't going to suddenly agree this was a good

idea, I looked at Detroit. "There's a main meeting room inside the sanctuary. It's just at the end of the hall. I'll pop in, stick the bug on the wall, and be right back out before you know it."

"She's right," Scout said. "She's the best one for the job."

It took a minute, but Jason finally nodded. "Fine. But if you get hurt, I'm going to be really irritated with you."

"I'll do my best."

I hoped it would be good enough.

9

I t should be a simple operation: climb the steps, open the door, walk down a hallway, and stick the beetle on the wall outside the sanctuary's main room. I had to press a button on its back to turn it on, and as soon as a light came on that confirmed it was connected to Detroit's video screen, I was done and could run out again.

It *should* be simple, but with nerves pumping, it sounded like a lot of steps to me.

We were still stuffed into the opening of the tunnel, while Detroit walked through the steps one more time. But I hardly heard her. My eyes were on Jason, who stared back at me just as hard.

"Could this be a trap?" I asked, my hands shaking with nerves and adrenaline. I squeezed my fingers around the bug to keep from dropping it.

"It's not a trap," Detroit said. "It's an Enclave Two–style mission. You can do this."

"You can do it," Scout agreed, putting an arm around my

shoulder. "Pop in, pop on, pop out. Get it done right and I'll let you borrow my messenger bag, skull and all."

I laughed nervously. "I don't even like your messenger bag. It creeps me out."

"Even better." She slapped me on the butt like I was a quarterback who had to save the game at the last minute. Which I kind of was.

"All right," Detroit said. "The coast isn't going to get any clearer. *Go.*"

I took a step outside the tunnel, bathed in light and totally obvious, and it took me a moment to get my feet moving again.

But then I *hauled*. I ran to the steps and took them two at a time, then put an ear to the metal door. It was thick, and I couldn't hear anything through it, so I couldn't be sure there wasn't a Reaper on the other side. But no sound was better than the sound of chatty Reapers, so I turned the knob.

Nothing happened. It was *locked*.

"Crap," I muttered, and jiggled the handle again.

Nothing at all.

I glanced back at the Adepts, who all shrugged, their faces blank. If the door was locked and we didn't have a key, this mission was dead on arrival.

One way or the other, I needed to make a decision.

I looked back at the door. It was metal and rusty, and pretty old looking. Maybe it wasn't locked. . . . Maybe it was just stuck.

I stuffed the beetle into my pocket, put both hands on the doorknob, blew out a breath, and then turned it with every ounce of energy I had. It finally popped open.

I peeked into the sanctuary—the hallway was empty. I stepped inside and edged toward the wall, then crept in the direction of the door to the main room.

There were doors on both sides of the hall. On our last visit, those rooms had been empty except for some rusting equipment. Expecting to see the same thing, I peeked into one. But instead, the room held lab equipment, the kind of stuff we'd seen in the sanctuary Scout had imploded. And in the middle of the room were two ladies in white lab coats. They stood together, soda cans in hand, chatting happily—as if they weren't part of a team that sucked the wispy souls out of teenagers to survive. Sometimes, I just didn't understand adults.

I'd been so busy being angry that they were just standing there chatting that I forgot where I was and what I was doing. Both of them suddenly turned toward the door. I immediately ducked down, heart pounding, and squeezed my eyes closed. Had they seen me? Were they calling security?

But after a couple of seconds, no one burst into the hallway. It was still quiet and empty, and I took that as my cue to get on with my job and get back into the tunnels.

I ran to the end of the hall and peeked into the final door to confirm it was the room where Scout had been held. It was. The banner still hung at one end of the room, and the table where Scout had been buckled sat empty in front of it, waiting for a soul to steal. The Reapers had added more decorations now, so the room looked more like a throne room. Scary thought.

I pulled the beetle from my pocket and stuck it to the wall about five feet from the ground and a foot or so from the door. Standing back, it looked just like an ordinary bug. We might not get much use out of it before a Reaper decided to do a little pest control, but hopefully it would work for a little while. I pushed the button beneath the wings, and when the light popped on, I took off again, not even worrying about the sound of my footsteps in the hallway.

I hit the metal door at a sprint, pushed through it, bounded down the stairs, and popped back into the tunnel. Everybody wrapped me in a hug.

And for a moment, until the claustrophobia kicked in, it was pretty awesome.

"Okay," Detroit said, when they finally let me go. "Let's see what you've got." She lifted her wrist to show her giant black watch. She pressed a couple of buttons on the side, and the screen blinked to life.

It showed a grainy black-and-white picture of the banner room. I closed my eyes in relief; the camera worked. Detroit adjusted the sound until it was just loud enough to hear, and we crowded around to watch.

The banner room was mostly empty, but Jeremiah's tall, white-haired form was unmistakable. He wore a black suit, and his hands were behind his back. He stood in a circle with a few other men who were yelling at him.

"No," one of them was saying, "we *don't* trust your leadership. Why should we?"

"We have no magic," said another. "And we've heard Adepts have no magic, either. We want to know who's to blame for that."

Jeremiah tipped his aristocratic nose in the air. "You believe I am to blame?"

"We believe we have questions," said the first guy, "and we aren't getting any answers. We'd like some now. Namely, how do we know you aren't the one to blame?"

Jeremiah bared his teeth, and with lightning-quick moves, grabbed the man by the collar of his suit and pushed him until his back hit the wall. And then Jeremiah lifted him up until the guy's feet dangled a foot in the air. The man scrambled to free himself, grasping at Jeremiah's fingers.

For an old guy, Jeremiah was strong.

"Should we do something?" I wondered.

"It's not our fight," Jason whispered. "Besides—what could we do?"

"Do you have issues with my leadership?" Jeremiah asked him.

"I—I—I have issues with not having mag-mag-magic."

"I have not caused this outbreak, but I will fix it, just as I have fixed every other problem we have encountered over the years. Now, Hamilton, do you have any doubts about me?"

"N-n-no, sir."

Jeremiah dropped his hands and stepped back. The man fell to the ground and put a hand to his neck, rubbing his throat.

"What if Adepts are doing this?" he choked out. "What if this is part of their rebellion against us?"

Jeremiah dusted off his hands and walked a few feet away. "The vast majority of Adepts don't have the power to pull this off. And it certainly isn't their style to take power away from everyone."

"The vast majority?" asked a trim man who stood beside Jeremiah—one who had watched him manhandle Hamilton without blinking or intervening.

Jeremiah glanced back at him. "The spellbinder has the strength to do this, although I doubt she has the will. In either event, the *Grimoire* is more important now than ever. We will obtain it. We will find the magic that reverses whatever is being done here, and we will correct it." He looked at the man to his right. "All plans are in place?"

"Of course," he said.

"In that case, we're done here. I sincerely hope we don't need to have this discussion again." He gave everyone a harsh look, and when they murmured their good-byes, walked away.

Detroit turned off the camera, and for a second, we all stood there quietly.

I looked at Scout. Sebastian had been right again. "He thinks you turned off the power, and they're coming for the *Grimoire*. They already have a plan."

"I could do it," she said confidently. "But I didn't. And they *aren't* getting my *Grimoire*."

"But why do they think you did it?" Michael asked.

"Because she's a spellbinder," Detroit said, "not just a spell-caster. She can make spells *and* cast them, and the *Grimoire* is all that magical information together in one place. They think she has the key to fixing the blackout."

"Which clearly she doesn't," I said. "Scout didn't write the spell for it, and she didn't cast the spell for it. But if the Adepts didn't cause it, and Jeremiah's crew didn't cause it, who did, and *why?*" I said. "If they've turned off the Reapers' magic and ours, what's the reason?"

"Maybe they think magic is all bad," Detroit said. "Maybe they want to eradicate it completely."

"Maybe it's worse," I said, looking at the Adepts. "Maybe who-ever did this wants to be able to pick and choose who gets to use magic and when they get to use it."

"Someone with a lot of ego," Scout quietly said. "Someone who wants a lot of control."

"You heard those guys earlier," I said. "Someone's unhappy about Jeremiah, and rumors are floating around about who that is."

Jason looked at me. "Is it wrong that I feel better knowing Jeremiah feels worse?"

"Amen to that," Scout said. "Now let's get out of here and take that little victory while we can."

We were suddenly blinded by light.

"What are you doing in here?"

My heart nearly stopped. It was the Reapers we'd overheard earlier—now pointing flashlights in our faces and standing between us and the way out.

"We got lost," Michael said. "School project."

"Oh, yeah?" asked the older of the two men. "Doing what?"

I was surprised he even bothered to ask. I'd have thought the Reapers had our faces memorized. Scout's at least. But maybe they weren't in the loop. Maybe we just looked like obnoxious kids.

"We're mapping the tunnels," Scout said. She pulled the notebook from her bag and showed it to them. "For geography class."

The guys looked at each other, obviously suspicious. The older one began slapping his giant, metal flashlight against his hand.

"Get Jeremiah," he said, and the younger one pulled out a cell phone and started dialing.

My heart. They may not have magic, but they had a sanctuary full of Reapers and medical instruments and an abnormally strong Scion.

"Oh, God," Scout said quietly. "We are so screwed."

"We aren't screwed," Jason whispered. "I'm counting down. When I get to three, make a run for it. Go back to the Enclave, and don't stop, whatever you hear."

"I'm not leaving without you." I wasn't sure what these non-magical Reapers could do to him, but I wasn't going to leave him here alone to find out.

"I trusted you," he said, eyes flashing chartreuse and turquoise. "This time, I need you to trust me. I'll be fine. One, two, *three*."

He said it loudly enough that we could all hear. We parted ways—Scout and me on one side of him, Detroit and Michael on the other. As we split, a different kind of light filled the tunnel. With a bone-chilling growl, a great silver wolf jumped between us into the air. He landed on the men, who hit the ground on their backs. We jumped around them as they cursed and began kicking and scrapping to get Jason off them.

We ran as fast as we could down the tunnel, and made it to the end of the next passageway before a wolfish yelp filled the air.

I froze in the middle of the passage. "I have to go back. He might be hurt."

But Scout grabbed my hand and yanked me back down the hallway. "He let you do your part earlier. It's his turn. He told you to run, so you run."

"Scout—" I pleaded, but she shook her head.

It was hard to admit, but she was right. I had to trust him, even though it was one of the hardest things I'd ever done.

We made it back to the Enclave without anybody following, at least as far as we knew.

I'd hoped we'd walk into the Enclave to find Jason sitting at the table, but of course he wasn't there.

We took seats at the table and told Daniel what we'd seen.

And then we waited.

After a while, when I couldn't bear to sit any longer, I stood up and paced back and forth across the room, waiting for him to show up outside the door, all sorts of horrible scenarios running through my mind. When Scout had been kidnapped, we'd found her strapped down to a table. Was he in the same predicament? Did he make it back, or . . .

When an hour passed, I stopped pacing and looked back at Daniel. "I can't stay here anymore. I have to go find him."

"He told you to stay here," Scout said. She was sitting cross-legged on the floor against the wall, Michael beside her, his head on her shoulder, staring off into space. I wondered if he worried like I did. They were best friends, after all.

"Yeah, but they also told me not to go look for you."

"True," she said. She gave that a nod, then looked at Daniel. "What do you think?"

He checked his watch. "The tunnels are deep. He could have led them on a chase to get away."

"Or he could be stuck in there right now," Detroit said. "I'll go with you if you want me to."

I smiled at her. "Thanks," I said, but unlike the last time I'd gone off on a rescue mission, I was now part of a team. I wasn't going to go without an okay from the boss.

"He's good at being a wolf, Lily," Michael said. "And if we walk into his plan, and you put yourself in danger, he's not going to like it. Give him five minutes more."

"I don't know what five minutes is going to do—" I began, but stopped when someone kicked open the door.

We all looked up. Nicu stood in the doorway, Jason at his side.

He was back in human form, but he was pretty well scratched up, and he was leaning on Nicu for support.

Daniel and Michael rushed to the door and helped Jason to the table. I ran to him, pulled off my cardigan, and pressed it to a cut on his cheek. It was long and deep—deep enough to leave a scar.

"What happened?" Daniel asked.

"He was being chased by Jeremiah's minions," Nicu said, straightening his dark coat.

"They have a wolf," Jason said, then let out a string of curses. "A *wolf*."

"Not someone you knew?" Nicu asked.

"We don't all know each other," Jason grumbled, wincing as I touched the fabric gently to his face.

"I'm sorry," I said. "I'm trying not to hurt you. Worse, I mean."

"It's okay. Thanks for taking care of me." The slightly goofy smile on his face brought tears to my eyes. He was hurt, and I did not care for that. If I'd had firespell, the Reapers would be in for a very, very bad night. And speaking of bad nights . . .

"How did you two find each other?" I asked Nicu. He looked away, and that irritated me even more.

"You were going *back* to the school?"

"I was *walking*," he said, sounding a little like an irritated teenager. "And I brought your wolf back to you. You should be grateful, child."

"You know each other?" Daniel asked.

"Daniel, Nicu. Nicu, Daniel," Scout said, sounding like a bad game show host. "One's the head of a slapdash band of magic-wielding teenagers. The other heads the city's newest vampire coven." She must have been tired; her jokes were getting worse.

Daniel rolled his eyes and looked back at Nicu. "And why are you visiting St. Sophia's?"

Nicu looked at me, a little bit of panic in his eyes. Was he . . . embarrassed about wanting to see Veronica?

As much as I would have liked to call him out—just to tone down his attitude—I was grateful for what he'd done, so I held it in.

"He was coming to see us," I told Daniel, earning me looks from all the Adepts. "We promised him a meeting. Kind of."

Nicu relaxed a little.

"Tomorrow," I promised. "We owe you one, and we'll get that meeting arranged tomorrow."

He nodded, and with a flurry of fabric, he was gone.

If only all supernatural problems disappeared so quickly.

Scout and I were exhausted when we made it back to St. Sophia's, but still too wired to sleep. That was the bad thing about late-night espionage—it was physically and emotionally tiring, but your brain was still pretty ramped up when bedtime finally came around.

After sneaking back into the suite, we went to her room. I sat down on the edge of her bed. She went to a drawer and pulled out a plastic zip bag of trail mix. She poured some in her hand, and when I extended mine, did the same for me. She dropped the bag on top of the bookshelf and stretched out on the floor.

For a few minutes, we quietly munched our snack. I picked through the pile in my palm, eating the raisins and other dried fruit first to get them out of the way before moving on to the nuts and—last but not least—chocolate chips. There may not be an order to the world, but there was definitely an order to trail mix.

"It happens, you know."

I munched a piece of pineapple in half. "What does?"

"Some Adepts can't hack it. Sometimes they decide they're going full stop with the magic, but after years with powers, they can't do it. They feel empty, or they miss the camaraderie, or they don't want to go back to feeling plain or ordinary. Usual."

I guess that explained what she'd been thinking about.

"It's easy to be brave when the decision isn't staring you down. When you're young and powerful and the world is your oyster. It's easier to judge a hard decision when you don't yet have to make it. It's a lot harder from the other side when you feel like the one thing that makes you who you are has been taken away."

"I can see that," I said. "And I can definitely see that in the Enclave. It's hard for them, this decision. And having to face down the life after magic is clearly not looking as fun as they thought it would."

"Not being responsible for the fight against Reapers is one thing. Being average, though, is something completely different. You're no longer one of the Dark Elite; you're just one of the millions of people in Chicago. You work. You raise a family. You pay your taxes. Stealing a little of someone's essence might feel like a small price to pay to feel like you matter."

"Are you regretting it?"

"Not regretting it." She looked up at me. "But definitely thinking about, I don't know, the gravity of it? When you talked to Sebastian that first time, I wasn't thrilled. Or the second time. But you said some things about the world being gray instead of black and white. That makes more sense to me now."

"So you're saying I was right?"

I thought I was being funny, but I got a peanut in the face for my trouble. I tossed it back at her, but it landed on the shelf behind her in front of one of her tiny owls. She had a collection of those, too. In our more magical days—like last week—I wouldn't have been surprised to see the owl come to life and pounce on the peanut. But now . . . it was just a bit of wood and some glue.

"There is something to be said for believing in magic," I agreed. "It's the keeping it that's the trouble."

"You said it." She finished the rest of her trail mix and dusted off her hands on her pants. "Honestly," she said, "who am I without magic?"

"You're a girl," I said. "A smart girl with a great education, rich parents, fabulous fashion sense, and a great friend. And even if not having magic means you'll be closer to 'ordinary' than 'magical,' you're still pretty extraordinary if you ask me."

"I'm glad your parents dumped you in Chicago, Parker."

"Right back at you, Green." Time to talk about even more uncomfortable subjects. "Jeremiah is gunning for you and your magic. It's probably time to think about getting the *Grimoire* somewhere safe."

"The safest place to keep the *Grimoire* is with me."

"Yeah, but what if you're the Reapers' target? What if they take you again to get to the *Grimoire*?"

"I understand the point," she said, her voice low and serious. It wasn't a tone I heard her use often. "But there's no way I'm giving up my *Grimoire*. That's exactly what they want—to separate me from it and get their hands on it. That's why they took me to the sanctuary in the first place." She shook her head. "No. The *Grimoire* stays with me. I'll find a hiding place for it."

"Okay," I said. "You're the expert." I looked around her room, imagining where she might hide it. A cutout inside another book? A secret compartment in her closet? Under her mattress?

"Where are you going to put it?" I wondered.

"I'm not sure yet."

We sat quietly for a second.

I wanted to be supportive, but I wasn't really sure how. "Do you want me to stay . . . or go?"

"You should go," she said, but she didn't sound happy about it. "If they think you're the key to the *Grimoire*, they'll use you to get it."

Maybe, but it didn't make me feel any better that I wouldn't have any information to tell them. Wasn't that when they usually stopped the torture on television—when someone gave up the goods? But this wasn't the time to bring that up.

"You're right," I said. "This is between you and your book." She nodded, and I stood up and walked to the door. "Just don't forget where it is."

"Fat chance," she said.

I walked into the common room and closed the door behind me. This was one of those things she'd have to do on her own. Putting distance between herself and her magic wasn't comfortable, I knew, but we also couldn't deny the reality.

After all, we were getting used to that distance.

10

The best way to top off an evening of Reaper spying had to be a morning of trigonometry exams. *Not.*

But we were students as well as Adepts, so we headed into trig class after cramming as much as possible in the few hours we had left, took our seats, got out our freshly sharpened St. Sophia's pencils, and waited for the show to start.

"Good luck," I whispered to Scout, who was in the seat behind me.

She gave me a serious nod. However silly Scout may be most of the time, she was apparently serious about magic . . . and trig tests.

"Make us proud, Parker," she whispered.

Our trig teacher went through the normal test-taking rules: Don't talk. Don't cheat. Stop when time is called. No calculators. Pencils only. Show your work. Then he passed out the tests and wrote the finish time on the board.

"Begin," he said, and we got busy.

It took a few minutes for me to get into the zone—but I got

there eventually. Each problem had two or three parts, so I tried to focus on finishing each part, quickly checking my work, and then moving on to the next. There were a couple I wasn't sure about, and I hoped I hadn't screwed up parts two and three because of some stupid error in part one. But we had a limited time to finish the test, so it wasn't like I could do anything about it.

We were fifteen minutes from the end when a shrill alarm ripped through the silence.

I nearly jumped out of my chair. Some of the other girls did, grabbing their books and dropping their half-finished tests on Dorsey's desk before running out of the room.

"Fire alarm," Dorsey dryly said. "If I had ten dollars every time a fire alarm went off in the middle of a test, I'd . . . well, I'd certainly drive a much better car. Turn in your tests and exit the building."

"But I'm not finished!" cried out one of the brainier girls in the class, the kind who raised her hand to answer every question and always asked about extra credit points, even though there was no way she needed them.

"I'll take that into consideration," Dorsey said, holding his hand out and staring her down with a stern expression until she walked toward him and handed it over. It took her a moment, but she finally did, then trotted out of the room with a pile of scratch paper and pencils in hand.

I glanced back at Scout, who was shoving her stuff back into her messenger bag. "Fire alarm?" I wondered.

"For now we assume it's a fire alarm. And then we see."

We turned in our tests and joined the traffic toward the exit doors. When we got outside, we clumped together with Lesley, just close enough to the classroom building that we could get a look at the action. But there wasn't any action that we could see, not even the sound of a fire truck rushing down the block toward us. And there were *always* fire trucks in downtown Chicago. There was a station pretty close to the convent, and rarely a night went by when we didn't hear at least one call.

But now . . . nothing.

"I don't smell smoke," Lesley said.

"And the building's stone," Scout added. "There's not a lot in there that could actually go up in flames."

"Suspicious," I said, watching Foley emerge from the main building followed by a gaggle of dragon ladies.

I looked back at Scout. "We need to know what's going on—if there's a fire, or if this is some kind of distraction."

"And you think Foley's gonna tell us? Doubtful."

"Maybe not," I said. "But I think we know someone who can get some intel." I looked at Lesley.

"I'm in," she simply said, then tilted her head as she looked at Foley and the dragons. "This is easy."

Without any instructions or warnings, she walked over to Foley. Hands on her hips, she began talking to her. Foley looked surprised, but it looked like she answered whatever Lesley had asked, and then Lesley walked back to us again.

We crowded around her. "What did you say?"

"I asked her if my $78,231 cello was safe in the dorm, or if the dorm was on fire."

You couldn't fault her for being direct. "What did she say to that?"

"She said there's no fire. The company is working to turn off the alarms."

Scout and I exchanged a glance. "Would someone have tripped the alarm just to get us out of a trig test?" I wondered.

"Like Dorsey said, it wouldn't be the first time."

"Maybe, but it happened now that we know Jeremiah's gunning for your *Grimoire*? When he thinks he really *needs* it? Remember what they said—that they had plans?"

She shrugged. "That's a lot of coincidence."

"They could be searching our rooms right now."

"They could be," Scout agreed. "But they won't find it. That would be impossible. And I'm not going to tell you where it is," she added before I could ask. "I don't want you tortured for it."

"In that case, thank you very much. Still, we need to get back inside."

"Yeah, but that's not exactly going to be easy, is it?" She gestured to the crowd around us, which was still growing as folks filed out of all the school's buildings. "There are people everywhere."

"We need a distraction."

"I'll take this one, too," Lesley said, her expression kind of devilish. She cleared her throat and smoothed out her plaid skirt, then began waving her arms in the air.

"My cello! My cello! My gorgeous cello from 1894 that may be burning to a crisp right now! What if it's on fire? What if it feels pain? Oh, woe, my cello!"

She sounded completely ridiculous, and she looked pretty ridiculous, too. She was running back and forth in a zigzag across the grass, arms flopping around in the air like she'd completely lost it. But she did make a really good distraction. Everyone turned around to look at the crazy teenager who was yelling about her cello. You just didn't see that kind of thing every day.

As soon as Foley's back was turned and the rest of the girls were watching Lesley, we snuck around the corner of the building and then raced back to the dorms. But I stopped her before we went inside.

"If this is part of their plan to take the *Grimoire*, they could still be in there."

She looked down at her empty hands. "Days like this make me wish I had a wand, you know." She made two finger guns and pointed them at the door. "*Pew pew!* Abracadabra."

"Not really the time for humor."

"Sorry. I'm nervous."

I nodded my head, completely understanding the emotion. I was freaking out too, and not just because we might soon be facing down Reapers again. As if last night hadn't been enough.

What if we were also facing down Sebastian? What if he was part of a team sent to destroy our rooms to find the *Grimoire*? What if I'd been totally wrong, and he was even worse than I thought he was? What if helping me had all been a plot to get closer to me and Scout . . . and her spellbook?

He was right. I'd never really be able to trust him. I'd never really be able to ignore the possibility that I was being played and he really was as bad as everyone else thought. The first question in my mind would always be "what if," and I didn't think there'd ever be a good answer. Especially not if I found him rifling through my stuff.

Oh, God—what if he was rifling through my underwear drawer?

I didn't hear my name until Scout shouted it. "Lily!"

"What?"

"Where were you just then?"

"You don't want to know." I gestured at the door. "Are you ready to go?"

"We have no magic, no weapons, and a school full of dragon ladies on high alert. 'Ready' doesn't really cut it."

"Actually, we aren't completely unprepared." I pulled my cell phone out of my pocket. "It's broad daylight, and any Reapers would be trespassing. Even if we can't nail them magically, we can nail them with the law."

"That totally deserves to be a line in an action movie. I mean, a really crappy action movie, but still." When I rolled my eyes, she held up her hands. "I know, I know, inappropriate timing. Let's do this. First sign of trouble, you dial nine-one-one. Got it?"

"Right behind you, Tex."

We slowly pushed open the door to the dorm building, then walked inside and held it until it closed slowly behind us. We stood inside for a moment, just looking and listening.

And for a moment we didn't hear anything . . . but then we heard rustling and shuffling that didn't sound like dragon ladies looking for fire or St. Sophia's girls returning to their rooms.

"They're up there, aren't they?" I asked, my stomach beginning to ball with nerves.

"It sounds like it." She looked back at me, fear in her eyes. "We have to do this, don't we?"

I squeezed her hand, faking a confident smile I didn't really feel. "We do. But we can do it. I promise."

She blew out a breath, and off we went.

We trekked up to our floor and peeked into the dim hallway. Our door was open, a beam of light shining into the hallway. We could hear rifling and throwing of objects even down the hall. That was when our moods changed.

"You know what?" she whispered. "I was scared. But now I'm really ticked. Who do these people think they are?"

"Infallible, apparently."

Scout harrumphed, and we tiptoed down the hallway to the suite door. She pointed to herself, and then she pointed up. She pointed at me, and then she pointed down. I think she was telling me to go low, and she'd go high.

I nodded, and just like two totem pole heads, we peeked into the room.

The suite was in shambles. Every bedroom door was open, and our formerly organized belongings were thrown about everywhere, including little bits of pink from Amie's room that were mixed into the rubble. It looked like her stuff had bled into the room. Either they didn't know whose room was whose, or they had a suspicion that Scout had hidden her *Grimoire* in there. As if.

And on the floor in front of my doorway was the fractured remains of the crappy—but important—ashtray that Ashley, my best friend from my hometown in New York, had made for me. One big hunk and a lot of shards and crumbs were all that was left of a treasured memento.

I probably could have cried a little, but instead I got even angrier.

We couldn't see the Reapers, but it sounded like there were two of them—one in Scout's room and one in mine. I glanced down at the floor of the suite and looked for a weapon. There was a pink golf club on the floor—expensive-looking and surely Amie's.

I crept inside and picked it up, then held it like a baseball bat. Scout did the same thing with a silver desk lamp that had probably been in Lesley's room.

"All right, buttwipes!" she yelled out. The noise stopped immediately. "We're here, and the cops are on their way. You aren't going to find what you're looking for, so I suggest you find your way out of our rooms before we move in with our crew to bust some heads!"

"Our crew?" I silently mouthed to Scout. She just shrugged, but I took her point. We probably weren't much of a threat on our own.

"One, two, three!" she mouthed, and then let out a loud whoop and charged toward her room. Sucking in a breath, I did the same thing toward mine, and stared in shock.

There was a cheerreaper in my room—a Reaper in a green and gold cheerleading uniform, complete with blond ponytail and bow perched right at the top of her head.

Lauren Fleming, a Reaper who'd tried to sneak into the school before, was standing in the middle of the room, a pair of my quilted patent leather boots under one arm, the remains of the rest of my stuff at her feet.

"What do you think you're doing?" I asked, raising the golf club.

She snarled at me like a crazy little Chihuahua. "Get out of my way, peon."

"Yeah, that's nice language. The cops are on their way, so you might want to put down the boots. If you leave now, since you clearly aren't going to find what you're looking for"—the expression on her face proved that was true—"we might manage to not beat the crap out of you for breaking in here."

"Whatever," she said, then hurled the boots at me. I half turned to dodge them, then swung out with the golf club. I missed, and took a chunk of stone out of the wall. Lauren darted around and plucked books from my bookshelf, then began hurling them at me. I batted them back with the golf club, but missed my history book and winced when it hit me in the shoulder.

Lauren saw her chance and tried to slip past me into the common room. I managed to swat her back with the club, but the shot didn't land very hard. She took off out of the suite and down the hallway. I ran out and pulled out my camera, snapping a picture of her back before she took the stairs.

Since I could still hear the sounds of fighting coming from Scout's room, she apparently didn't have any regrets about leaving her partner behind. I stuffed the phone back into my pocket and ran to Scout's room.

Despite years of being a teenager and months of being an Adept, there in the middle of Scout's room was probably the strangest thing I'd ever seen.

Lying on the floor was a girl I knew only as "French Horn"— another Reaper who'd previously tried to break into the school with Lauren. She and Lauren hadn't been friends then, and if Lauren was willing to run away without helping her partner, I was guessing they hadn't gotten any closer.

She was a larger girl, and she had a thing for black clothes and Goth looks. And she lay in the middle of Scout's room on her stomach, with a very angry-looking spellbinder sitting on her back, lamp in the air like a samurai sword.

"Everything okay?" I asked.

French Horn spewed some curse words that were pretty typical Reaper.

"Language, language," Scout said, tapping the bottom of the lamp gently against the Reaper's head.

"Did she come in through the tunnel again?" I wondered.

More cursing.

"Seriously, I don't know about your high school for angry misfits and teamsters, but we are classy at St. Sophia's. Enough with the swearing. Now answer the girl's question."

"Tunnel," she said, then turned her head away. Reaper or not, this couldn't exactly be a comfortable position for her to be in, especially since her partner had left her at the mercy of two irritated Adepts.

"Tunnel plus fire alarm equals breaking and entering," Scout said. "And I'm going to guess you're looking for something that doesn't belong to you."

When French Horn began to answer, Scout flicked her on the head. "I wasn't asking for a response. Hear this, Reaper. What's in my book won't help you. If it did, don't you think we'd have used it already?"

She didn't seem to have a good answer to that.

"Exactly. So here's the deal. You're going to advise your fellow Reapers that my *Grimoire* isn't what you're looking for, and you're all going to leave me alone. Maybe you could spend a little time working on solving the blackout. After all, it's probably some irritated Reaper anyway. How about that?"

French Horn opened her mouth—probably to start swearing again—but was interrupted by a tall blonde standing in the doorway.

Foley's mouth dropped open at the sight. "Green! Parker! What in the name of God is going on in here?"

Scout stood up. Freed from her bonds, French Horn stood up and made a run for the door, before Foley blocked it with her arms.

Go Foley, I thought.

"May I help you, young lady?"

An idea struck. I walked toward Foley and put an arm through the French horn player's. She seemed sticky.

"As it turns out," I said, "this lovely individual was walking past the school when she heard the fire alarms and rushed through the building to see if she could help."

"She did *what?*" Scout asked.

"She helped," I insisted, looking intently at French Horn. Yes, I was giving her an escape route, but Scout was right—the Reapers needed to know the *Grimoire* wasn't going to help them, and maybe helping her out of this pinch increased the odds she'd take that message back to her sanctuary.

"Scout surprised her and then, you know, fell on her. And then you came in!" I brightly added.

No one in the room seemed convinced of my story, least of all Foley. "You fell on her?" she asked, slowly lifting her gaze to Scout.

Scout looked back at me, and I nodded just a little, hoping she got my silent message: *Trust me.*

Her expression was easy to read: *You better have a good reason for this one, Parker, or I'm bringing the pain.*

When I nodded, so did she. "It was the strangest thing."

"She tripped," I said.

"I tripped . . . and then I fell on . . . this girl here . . . who was clearly trying to help us out."

French Horn looked completely flustered, but she wasn't going to let the opportunity pass. "I need to go now," she said. "I have an . . . appointment."

"She's very busy," I said.

"Very busy," Scout grumbled.

Foley looked completely shocked, but she pulled in her arms and let French Horn pass. We heard her scurry through the common room, and then the suite door opened and closed again.

Foley looked pointedly at us. "Is there anything else you'd like to share about this particular incident, ladies?"

Scout and I looked at each other. "Is there, Lily?"

"Um, well, someone clearly trashed our rooms during the fire alarm. Perhaps that's why the fire alarm went off in the first place. Like it was all a ploy or something."

"A ploy," Foley repeated. She didn't exactly sound convinced, but as she glanced around the room, she hardly could have thought we'd done this ourselves. "I don't believe your suitemates are going to take this very well."

She couldn't have timed it better. The brat pack burst into the suite in a flurry of dramatic wailing. Amie, actually, wasn't all that loud. Veronica and M.K. were doing most of the yelling, and they didn't even *live* here.

And then they caught sight of us in Scout's room.

"This is your fault," Veronica said, snapping her gaze to Foley's. "This has to be their fault. They're always involved in something, always sneaking around."

You could actually see the shutter going down over Foley's eyes. They turned cold and glinty, and she narrowed her gaze at Veronica, then Scout and me.

"I'm not entirely sure what went on in here, although I don't believe either Ms. Parker or Ms. Green were responsible for the destruction."

I sighed in relief.

"That said, I also must wonder if their behavior somehow tempted this destruction?"

I opened my mouth to argue with her, but what exactly could I say? It wasn't like we invited the Reapers to pop in and destroy our stuff, but they'd clearly been here—and in Amie's stuff—because of us.

When neither one of us answered, Foley turned her attention back to Veronica. "Rest assured, Ms. Parker and Ms. Green have already assured me they'll take full responsibility for cleaning up the mess. I assume that's an appropriate solution for all parties?"

"Fine by me," Amie said, her worried gaze on the stuff on the floor.

Foley looked back at me and Scout, her gaze daring us to disagree with her.

"Our responsibility," Scout muttered, voice defeated. "We'll clean it up."

"Sure thing," I agreed. "But maybe everyone could clear out and give us room to work?"

The brat pack didn't look thrilled at that suggestion—they probably wanted to lie around on the couch and eat grapes like Cleopatra while we worked, but they eventually nodded. Foley escorted them out.

When the door closed again, I looked over at Scout. "This blows."

"Yep. I mean, it's not like we haven't seen this before, but yeah, totally blows."

I sighed. "I really wish you had magic. You could probably spell the crap out of this and get everything back in order again. That would be sweet."

"Yes, I could, in fact, go all *Fantasia* on this mess. But for now there's only one thing I can do." She disappeared back into her room, and after a few seconds club music—the kind with the *thub thub thub* bass—filled the room.

"If we must clean," Scout yelled over the music, "let's clean with rhythm."

And then she shook her butt and got to work.

11

I took us two hours, but we managed to get the suite put back together. And surprisingly, it was pretty easy to figure out where everything came from. Amie's stuff was all pink, so anything with Barbie coloring went back into her room. Lesley's stuff was just odd, so anything with unicorns, rainbows, or anime characters went back into hers. (Including tons of Japanese comic books about schoolgirls who were also vampires, or vampires who ate schoolgirls, or something like that. You'd think she saw enough of that kind of thing just being friends with us. But to each her own.)

When we were done, we flopped onto the couch in the common room.

"So, I guess that was part of Jeremiah's plan," I said.

"I guess so. I'm really starting to not like those guys. I mean, jury's out on Sebastian, but the rest of them are *hateful*. Trying to steal a girl's *Grimoire*. That is a total breach of magical etiquette."

"It's also messy. And illegal."

"Seriously." Scout looked over at me. "Do you think they'll try again?"

"Until they solve the blackout or realize you have nothing to do with it."

"So they won't stop coming after us until they get their power back . . . and *actually* have the ability to come after us. I don't really like that strategy."

"They probably don't, either. And what sucks worse? Other than knowing Reapers have lost their power and Jeremiah's totally mad, we have no other clues." I let out a frustrated sound and rolled my shoulders a little. "I need a break."

"You've got one until study hall," she said. Because of the shenanigans, classes had been canceled for the rest of the day. "Maybe we could take a walk, get a little fresh air. *Ooooh*," she said, jumping up off the couch. "Let's go to Gaslight."

"What's Gaslight?"

"Only the best magical trade shop in the tri-state area, offering magical surplus, supplies, and books for the exceptional spellbinder!"

I was caught between two emotions. Sadness that she was excited about something she may never get to use again, and amusement about how truly geeky that sounded.

I decided to feel amused.

"Wow. That was so geeky it, like, transcends normal geeky and moves straight into hella geeky. Or maybe über geeky."

She stuck out her tongue at me. "Grab your messenger bag. It's a short walk. We'll grab a snack while we're out."

"Are we supposed to be leaving campus like this?"

"We just saved Foley a whole lot of grief by skipping the magical details. She owes us one."

Scout was leaving out the part about how the fire alarm had been faked to get to her *Grimoire*, which made the whole incident our fault. But I didn't think she'd appreciate the reminder.

"Fine," I said. "But this time you're the one who has to make up an excuse."

She got her chance pretty quickly. We'd gotten our gear and were just preparing to leave when the door opened, and Veronica and Amie walked in.

Amie smiled. "It looks much better in here. Thanks for getting it taken care of."

"You're welcome," Scout said. "Sorry for the mess."

Veronica looked us over suspiciously. "Where are you two going?"

Scout jumped in with an answer. "Lily's out of craft glue," she said, "and she still has more, you know, decorations to do. So we were going to run down to the pharmacy and grab some. Sneak errand!" She waved her hands in the air excitedly.

"Wow," I muttered under my breath, but Veronica must have bought it, or at least was bored by the conversation, because she and Amie moved back into her room.

"Let's get going," Scout said, "before she changes her mind and follows us."

Probably a good idea.

A sign above the door read GASLIGHT GOODS. The door was framed by two old-fashioned lanterns, small flames flickering in the breeze.

"A bookstore?" I asked her.

"Calling it that hardly does it justice," Scout said, pushing open the door and jingling a leather strap of bells that hung on the inside.

The store smelled faintly smoky. Not in a bad way—more like "fall campfire" than "burnt toast." It wasn't a big store, and it was divided neatly into areas by tall white bookshelves loaded with books, spices, and candles. Long ropes of beads and stones hung along one wall beside a set of tall wicker urns that held branches in various colors. The walls were painted cheerily white, and clerks in white lab coats milled around with feather dusters. Unfortunately for them, they were just about the only other people in the store except for a family of obvious tourists—complete with matching I ❤ CHICAGO baseball caps.

Scout picked up a red wire basket from a stack by the door and immediately headed for a shelf that held various kinds of salt.

"Don't people wonder about a magic store in the middle of downtown Chicago?" I asked quietly.

Scout picked up a small glass bottle of pinkish salt, held it up to the light, and squinted at it. "They don't wonder because they assume it's a joke." She put the bottle back on the shelf, and grabbed a bottle of gray salt instead.

"Why gray instead of pink?"

Scout shrugged and moved over to the next bank of shelves, which held old coins and metal knickknacks. "It's my go-to shade."

"Veronica has lip stain; you have salt."

"Not just salt. Brittany sea salt from France. It has great stick."

"Stick?" I asked, picking up a small metal dog that looked like a miniature schnauzer. It was heavy for its size, and had a crazy level of detail—little ears, little tufts of fur, and a perky little tail.

"Stick," she repeated. "It means . . . the spell has staying power. It sticks around for a long time. Doesn't just fade away like cheap perfume."

She picked up a coin, weighed it in her hand, and then put it back on the shelf again.

While she perused the coins, I put the tiny dog back and looked at the rest of the metal items. There were lots of them, and they were all just as detailed—a tiny Ferris wheel; a lantern; a potted sunflower; a laptop.

"What are these?" I asked Scout, holding up the lantern.

"They're called icons," she said. "It stands for Iterated Condensations of Normal Space."

"Using English—no magic speak—explain to me what that means."

"Just call 'em icons," Scout said. "You use them to symbolize something in a spell. Something you want. Something you want to effect. A quality you want to give something."

My gaze went back to the tiny dog, and I picked it up again. I know it sounds weird, but I liked the way it felt in my hand. It was a cute little dog with a funny little expression. But it felt kind of *right*.

"I like this one."

She looked over. "Good choice. Dogs have good energy."

I put the dog back on the shelf again. "So is this stuff just for people who do spells? Spellcasters or spellbinders or whatever?"

"Not at all. There are books, gear with the Adept and Reaper symbols on them if you want to go full out. And people who can make stuff with their magic sometimes sell the stuff they make. You can get all that here. *Oooooh*," she suddenly said, making a beeline for the wicker urns of branches. "I need to look at those.

The books are over there," she said, pointing to the other side of the room. "If you want to take a look."

I watched her pick through the branches, pulling out one after another, looking it over, and shoving it back into the basket. I'm not sure what she was looking for, but it was certainly beyond anything I could see. As far as I could tell, they were just tree limbs—the kinds of sticks an interior designer might throw into a vase on a dining room table.

I took her advice and walked to the book area, which filled the shelves on the back wall of the store. They looked like comic books and graphic novels, but then again, so did Scout's *Grimoire*.

"I wonder if these are magic books, too," I muttered.

"Can I help you?"

I glanced behind me. A guy whom I guessed was in his twenties, with short black hair, a Gaslight uniform, and a name tag that read KITE smiled at me. His teeth were a little bit crooked, which made him seem cuter, actually. Friendlier. More real.

"Are these really graphic novels? Like, comic books?"

"They really are."

I looked at him for a sec, trying to figure out if he was telling me the truth and these were just normal books . . . or if they were magic books in disguise and he wasn't sure whether he could trust me.

"If I was, um, *special*, would they still be graphic novels?"

"Yes," he slowly said, looking at me with an odd expression. "Can I help you find something?"

"Hard to believe," Scout said, joining us, "but she is totally for real. 'Special,' she says. Poor girl thinks everything in here is magical." She fluttered her hands in the air. "Woo woo!"

Kite laughed knowingly. "Noob?"

"Totally. But got firespell her first time out."

Kite's eyes widened, and there was a little more respect in his face. "No kidding. Nicely done."

Not that I'd had any choice in the matter, but I said, "Thanks," anyway.

"I just thought they might be—"

"Because we're in a magic shop," Scout hurriedly finished. "We know, we know. Silly girl. Hey, do you have any of those beeswax candles I like?"

Kite frowned. "There weren't any on the shelf?"

"Not that I saw."

"Maybe we have some in the back. Let me check."

"Thanks!" Scout said. As soon as he was out of sight, she gave me a sharp pinch on the arm.

"Hello, *ow*," I said, rubbing the spot. "What was that for?"

"Ixnay on the graphic novel bit. The form of my *Grimoire* is just between you and me. Gaslight Goods is Switzerland."

"It's Switzerland?"

"Neutral territory," she explained. "Reapers and Adepts are both allowed in here, and Kite loves gossip. That can work well for us—he gives us info when he's got it to give, but he gives it to the other side, as well. So you have to be very careful what you say, because the information's probably not going to stay here."

"What happens in Gaslight Goods does not stay in Gaslight Goods?"

"Precisely."

My stomach turned. I had almost given away the secret form of Scout's *Grimoire* to some guy I didn't even know just because he worked in a magic shop. Just because I'd assumed he seemed like a nice guy and, therefore, would have been some kind of Adept sympathizer. I was a magical disaster waiting to happen.

"I am *so* sorry," I said, but she shook her head. "I had no idea."

"No harm, no foul. Even if he figured it out, I could always change the form. We just have to be careful."

We might have to be careful, but if Kite really liked to gossip, maybe we could use that to our advantage.

Kite emerged from the back room with an open cardboard box in hand. We followed him to the candles, where he began restocking the shelves.

Scout grabbed a couple. "So, Kite, how are things around the store?"

He made a low whistle. "Very, very slow. The blackout hasn't exactly been good for business. Not many people stocking up on supplies when they aren't sure when they'll be able to use them again."

"You know about the blackout?" I asked. Scout rolled her eyes.

"It's not exactly common knowledge," Kite said, "but I like to stay in the loop."

Speaking of which: "Kite, we've heard Reapers are having some internal issues. Like, folks are really mad at Jeremiah. What's your take on that?"

Scout's eyes widened at my question, but then she smiled a little. She must have figured out where I was going.

"Only that the hierarchy's getting nervous."

"Hierarchy?" I asked.

"The Scions," Scout put in. "Jeremiah and the others. The ones who lead the rest of them into committing heinous acts."

"Switzerland," Kite reminded her, and she gave him a canny smile.

"So why are they getting nervous?" I asked. "We've heard there are lots of rumors floating around the sanctuaries. Are the rumors making folks nervous?"

Kite shook his head. "My theory? People are nervous, and the rumors are how they're coping."

"How so?" Scout asked.

"Well, there are two tiers within the Dark Elite. Just like with Adepts, there are the ones who fight the war—who hang out in the sanctuaries and are in touch with the leadership, and there are the ones who stay home and mind their business. They're called the 'old ones.' They keep their magic quietly. They take energy a little at a time. Slowly. Carefully. They don't get wrapped up in the politics, and they tend to believe in fairy tales."

"Fairy tales?" I repeated.

Kite nodded. "Think old-school fairy tales—the terrifying kind where everybody learns an important lesson about wandering around in the dark alone. Only they tend to think of them more like history than children's stories."

Okay, that was weird. But it got weirder.

Kite looked around, then leaned in. "Anyway, last week a few of these old-school types come in, and they're fretting about leadership, and one of them mentions this old Scottish fairy tale about a boy named Campbell."

"Who was he?" I asked.

"Supposedly, he led an army against the evil baron who was controlling their area of Scotland. He was helped by a band of fairies and pixies—little magical creatures—but after he won control of the country, he became as evil as the guy he'd replaced. Eventually, he banished the fairies and pixies from his country."

Scout and I exchanged a glance. It was sad, sure, but an old fairy tale didn't exactly help us figure out who was making trouble in modern-day Chicago.

"I don't get it," Scout said. "What does this have to do with Reapers?"

"They're repeating the story like it's gospel," Kite said. "Every time they talk about Jeremiah, someone brings up the tale of Campbell."

"Okay," Scout said, "but maybe they're just saying the grass is greener, or whatever. You know, don't complain about what we have, 'cause the next guy could be worse?"

"Honestly," Kite continued, "I don't know if they believe it or if they just want to. They're completely without magic right now, and they want someone to blame. Jeremiah's the obvious choice. I think the rumors are making the Scions nervous. Rumors have power, after all." He slid us a glance. "Have you heard anything else?"

"Not really," Scout said, and Kite frowned.

Maybe, I thought, it was time to get more specific. "Kite, have you seen Sebastian Born in here lately?"

He blinked, then seemed to mull it over. "Sebastian? Not for a few days. Again, that's probably because of the blackout."

"Could you give us a call if he comes in again?" I asked.

"Is there anything in it for me? I mean, to be fair, I am running a business here. And business is *slow*."

I was already committed, so I kept pushing along. "How about information?"

He perked up. "What did you have in mind?"

Scout had mentioned that trying to take her *Grimoire* was a breach of magical etiquette. Maybe if Kite knew about it, and spread the word about it, Reapers would get embarrassed enough to back off. Long shot? Sure. But I was grasping at straws.

"Members of the Dark Elite broke into St. Sophia's today," I finally said.

His eyes widened. "Oooh, that is interesting. Why did they do it?"

I glanced at Scout. She nodded. "They're trying to take magical property that doesn't belong to them. A spellbook."

Kite's mouth dropped into an "O." "You are not serious."

"Scout's honor," I said. Literally.

Kite stood up again. "That's definitely interesting. If he comes in, I'll call you." He flattened out his box and glanced down at Scout's basket. "If you're ready, I can head over to the register and check you out?"

She picked through the stash. "Yep. Got everything I need."

"Cool," he said, and we followed him back to the register. He slipped each item into a paper bag with handles after scanning them in. When he was done, he pulled off the receipt and handed it to Scout, who looked it over and pulled a wad of cash from her pocket. Kite took Scout's money and handed over her bag.

"Thanks, Kite."

"You're welcome, Scout. You girls try to have a nice day."

We always tried; we just weren't always successful.

"So now you want to follow Sebastian? Do you think he's a bad guy?" she asked when we were out the door and a few steps down the street.

"I have no idea," I said. "And that's exactly my point. Maybe he really wants to help us. Maybe he doesn't. I don't think there's any harm in listening to him . . . or in keeping an eye on him."

"I guess. I'm glad we went in there, but I'm not really sure it was helpful. I mean, a fairy tale? How could that possibly help us?"

"I have no idea, unless . . ."

She stopped and looked at me. "Unless what?"

An idea began to blossom. "What if the old ones don't think it's just a fairy tale?"

Scout frowned. "What do you mean?"

"What if they're not just repeating the story because it's like a symbol, but because they think someone named Campbell is going to overthrow Jeremiah?"

She waved a hand. "That's not the way fairy tales work. They're just repeating them because they're nervous about what might happen if someone tries to kick him out—and someone worse gets put in charge. And PS, a little warning about Kite. He's well-intentioned, but he tends to be kinda dramatic. Just because he heard people talking about it doesn't mean it's a big deal."

"Sure," I said, as we started walking again, but I wasn't convinced. Maybe it was just a hunch, and maybe it would turn out to be wrong, but I had a feeling this fairy tale was more than just people talking. I think they were talking about that specific fairy tale for a reason, and I knew someone who might be able to shed a little light on it. I didn't want to call Sebastian right here; I felt weird calling him in front of Scout. But I would later. The opportunity for more info was too good to pass up.

"Should we tell Daniel about the fairy tale?" I asked.

"For all the good it'll do, yeah, we probably should." She patted down her messenger bag. "Crap. I left my phone in my room. Do you have his number?"

I searched through my bag, but it wasn't in there. I must have put it down after the battle with the cheerreaper. "I apparently do not."

"No worries. We can tell him tonight at Enclave."

Perfect. That would give me a little time to do some investigating of my own.

We'd walked only a couple of blocks when Scout stopped short. "How about a snack?" she asked. "I am starving."

Since breakfast had been a handful of fruit candy and a bottle of orange juice, I was also starving. "Fine by me."

"I know just the place," she said, then headed down a side street. I could smell something cooking—something fried and buttery. The smell was coming from a small shop tucked between two hotels—with a line out the door ten to fifteen people deep.

We walked past the door, but the store was so small I couldn't see what they were selling.

"This is the place?" I wondered.

"This is the place," she said, then walked to the end of the line, crossed her arms, and faced the door, her expression all business.

Whatever they sold, this girl was serious about it.

"Any hints about what this is?" I whispered, as more people joined the line behind us. Folks were leaving, but the stuff they'd bought was hidden in small paper bags and coffee cups. Doughnuts, maybe? Muffins? Cupcakes?

"That would really ruin the surprise," Scout said.

Ten minutes later we reached the threshold, and I could finally see inside the shop. Two men and a woman stood behind a counter. The woman was at the cash register. One of the guys stood in front of a giant round fryer, and the other was mixing a giant kettle with a wooden spoon.

"Churros con chocolate," Scout said, in a pretty good Spanish accent. "Fried dough and this crazy thick chocolate. You'll love it."

Of course I would. I mean, it wasn't exactly a hard sell. Chicken-fried grasshoppers would have been questionable. Eyeball of eel would have been a no-go from the start. But pastries and chocolate? Yeah, I'd give that a whirl.

The place smelled like grease, sugar, and chocolate. Totally intoxicating. When we finally got to the counter, Scout ordered for us and handed over some cash. The girl took the money, then used tongs to lift long fried thingies into a paper bag. Scout took the bag; I took the two small foam cups that followed.

We took the booty and headed outside again. I felt a little guilty as we passed the other folks in line. They looked longingly at our stuff, probably wishing they were the ones with food in their hands.

I followed Scout across the street to a stone office building with a low concrete railing around it. She popped up onto it, then patted the railing beside her. "People watching 101."

I took a seat and handed over her cup while she offered up a churro. It was still hot and a little greasy. More crunchy than soft, with ridges along the edges.

"Behold," Scout said, then pulled out her own snack, opened a cup of chocolate, and dipped the churro into it. "Dip and munch," she said, then took a bite.

I followed her example . . . and had to close my eyes to take in all the flavors. Hot. Crunchy. Sweet. Bitter. Smooth.

Amazing.

"OMG, you are a *goddess*," I said, going back for another bite. At this rate, I'd have the thing finished before she even answered.

"That's not even the best part," she said. "Look up."

Still munching, I lifted my gaze. With the sidewalk in front of us, and streets all around us, we had a fantastic view . . . of people. All shapes and sizes. All genders and ethnicities. A short, prickly-looking man with a tiny dog. A couple of tired-looking tourists with a baby stroller.

"Oooh, peep this," Scout quietly said, nudging me with her elbow. Two of the tallest people I'd ever seen were walking past us. They wore the same outfits—neon-bright pants and even brighter shirts. They were blindingly bright. Where could you wear that kind of thing?

"Maybe they work in really dark rooms," Scout said, reading my mind. "Or they direct traffic."

"Or work in a highlighter factory. Or make paint chips."

"People are just odd," she said, and I really couldn't disagree with that.

We ate our churros, and when they were gone, I followed Scout's lead and took a sip from the cup. The chocolate was thick, rich, and delicious. Not that there was a chance it wouldn't be—we were basically drinking melted chocolate.

"I would take an IV of this every morning," I murmured.

"Seriously, right? I wish they had a delivery service. I need to wake up every morning with chocolate and churros outside my bedroom door."

"Oooh, and the brat pack would have to be banned from the store forever. I mean, if we're talking big dreams here."

"I like the way you think, Parker. I've always said that about you."

"Speaking of the brat pack, what are we going to do about Veronica?"

"Ignore her?"

"Nicu won't appreciate that," I pointed out. "We promised him a meeting tonight. And since he brought my boyfriend back in one piece, I'd really like to keep it."

"All we have to do is get them in the same place at the same time. I assume we need to do it at night because, you know, Nicu is a vamp, but it can't be too late, because she'll be in pajamas and we won't be able to convince her to leave her suite."

"We're going to have a hard enough time convincing her to leave at all. She'll think we're up to something."

"What about during party prep? Can we arrange a meet then?"

I shook my head. "She'll be there with Amie and M.K., and they'll follow her. We need to separate her from the herd."

Scout chuckled. "If that was so easy, I'd have saved her years ago. How do you separate someone who doesn't want to be separated?"

I thought about that for a minute. "Don't give her a choice."

"I'm not going to kidnap Veronica."

"That's not where I was going, but good to know." I shook my head. "No, we need to make her *want* to be there."

"And how do we do that?"

"I'm still working on that part."

While we thought it through, we sat on the stone rail and finished our chocolate quietly, watching the passersby. They all
looked normal, but then, so did we.

I turned to Scout. "How many of these people know about
magic, do you think?"

"None of them, if we're playing the odds. There are six Enclaves in Chicago. Figure twenty or so JV Adepts per Enclave."

"Twenty? That's a *ton*." We had only seven.

"We're wee. Most Adepts don't go to school in the Loop."

She had a point.

"So twenty JVs per Enclave, six Enclaves in the city, that's
roughly one hundred and twenty Adepts total. Maybe add in a few
who don't know they have magic or haven't been identified—"

"Or just don't want to be involved," I added, feeling sympa-
thetic.

"Or that. I don't know—maybe you end up with two hundred
active Adepts at any given time. And in a city of nearly three million, if we're talking members of the Community, probably more
than that. They don't 'age out' like we do, so their numbers grow
over time. Well, unless Reapers take them out."

We got quiet at that suggestion. I didn't want to think about
the Community members I'd met so far being harmed because
they agreed to help us. Of course, they seemed to believe in the
cause, so maybe it wasn't a hard choice for them.

"So odds are, most of these people walking past don't know
about us." I sipped at my chocolate. It was cooling, so it was getting
thicker and almost gritty—and it was already chocolaty enough
that it made my teeth ache. But it was the best kind of hurt.

"Probably not," Scout said.

Realization struck as I took the final sip. "We're thinking about this Veronica thing too hard."

"How so?" Scout asked.

"She's already thinking about another guy, right? Someone other than Creed? She said so at her locker the other day. She just doesn't know who the other guy is."

"So?"

"So we bring the guy to her."

"Parker, I am intrigued."

"I knew you would be," I said, and laid out our plan.

12

I didn't waste time when we got back to the suite. Scout headed to her room to unload and organize her stuff from the shop. I was still thinking about the stuff we'd *heard* at the shop, including that fairy tale the "old" Reapers were supposedly talking about.

And what was the most efficient way to learn more about Reaper topics of conversation? Ask one. So I headed to my room, grabbed my phone, and called Sebastian.

"Lily?" he answered.

I sat down on my bed. "Hey, I need a favor. Well, information, anyway."

"Okay," he slowly said. "What do you want to know?"

I swallowed down a moment of panic, then threw it out there. "Do you know the story of Campbell? The fairy tale, I mean?"

There was a pause. "The fairy tale of Campbell?"

There was something strange in his voice, but I kept going. "So, there's this fairy tale about a boy named Campbell who overthrew an evil baron or something. I hear Reapers are talking about that story a lot—maybe because they're unhappy with Jeremiah. Do you know anything about it? Have you heard the story?"

Another pause, which just seemed that much more suspicious.

"Sebastian?"

"I'm here."

"Okay. Any ideas?"

"I have—I have to go," he said, and the line went dead.

I blinked at the phone for a minute, then flipped it in my hand while I thought through the call.

I'd asked Sebastian only about a fairy tale, and he seemed to freak out. He definitely hung up. Did the fairy tale mean something to him? Or did he know a boy named "Campbell" the Reapers might be secretly referring to?

"Maybe there's a Campbell out there trying to make a name for himself," I said quietly.

I grabbed my laptop from the bookshelf and carried it back to the bed, then flipped it open. The hard drive whirred a bit while the computer started up. As soon as it was ready, I dug into the Internet and tried my first search: the words "Campbell" and "fairy tale."

Sure enough, I found a Web site of old Scottish fairy tales, including one called "Campbell and the Evil Lorde" that was pretty much the same as Kite had explained. Boy managed to win despite huge odds against him, but boy became as evil as the guy he'd overthrown. I think the moral of the story was basically "the grass isn't always greener."

Chin in my hand, I scrolled through the search results just in case there was anything else interesting. I didn't see anything . . . until I got to the end of the fourth page. There, on the very bottom, was another Campbell story—a news report. The title read:

CAMPBELL KIN RETURNS TO CITY FATHER CALLED HOME. And when I clicked on the article . . . a color picture of *Fayden freaking Campbell* stared back at me.

"Oh, crap," I muttered, an uncomfortable flutter in my chest, as I scanned the article.

Turns out, Fayden Campbell's father—Sebastian's uncle—was from Chicago. He'd been a big shot in a tech company in California before he died earlier in the year. And just like Sebastian had said, Fayden had moved from California to Chicago, her father's hometown, to finish law school.

So, to review:

Sebastian's cousin, Fayden, just moved to Chicago. The Reaper gossip was about some fairy tale "Campbell" who was looking to take over the Reapers. And Sebastian's cousin's last name was "Campbell."

Sebastian said she didn't have magic. But this whole "Campbell" thing was a coincidence, wasn't it?

Crap—I'd just told Sebastian that we suspected a "Campbell" might be involved. Sure, only in fairy tale terms, but I'd just given him the only clue I had, and he'd immediately hung up. What if he'd called Fayden and given her a heads-up?

Suddenly sick to my stomach, I shut the computer again. Had I done something awful? Had I trusted Sebastian too much?

Unfortunately, this wasn't the kind of thing I could stash away and refuse to think about again. I had to tell someone. I had to tell *Scout*. And eventually, probably, I'd have to tell Jason and Daniel and the rest of Enclave. There was no avoiding it.

I flopped back on the bed. How did I get into messes like this? How did I end up in this bedroom in Chicago afraid to tell my new best friend that I might have accidentally given away details about our magical investigation to a guy who may or may not be totally evil . . . or who may or may not have told his cousin, the bad girl, that we were on her case.

I put my laptop back on the shelf in case I needed to run back into my room and flop on my bed in tears—or to hide from whatever Scout might throw at me.

I blew out a breath, and headed across the room.

Scout was organizing her new Gaslight Goods stuff when I opened the door. But when she looked back at me and saw the expression on my face, hers drooped.

"What's wrong?"

"I think I screwed up."

She put her hands on her hips. "How did you do that?"

I closed her door behind me. "I called Sebastian to ask about the fairy tale. He hung up almost immediately—like the question freaked him out."

"Or like he knew something about it?"

I nodded and took a seat on her bed. "Yeah. And I looked around on the Internet and maybe figured out why."

Scout's eyes widened. "Why?"

"Because his cousin—the one we saw outside—is Fayden *Campbell.*"

Her eyes widened. "That's convenient."

"That's what I thought. I mean, he said she wasn't a Reaper, but what are the odds? And here's the thing—when he hung up, what if he went and called Fayden and warned her?"

"Warned her what? That you figured out her last name was Campbell? I mean, that's really the only thing you've proved."

I deflated a little. I mean, I didn't want to put Adepts in danger, but I also kind of thought I'd been onto something. "I only told him that we'd heard about the fairy tale."

"That's my point—you didn't tell him anything he couldn't have found out from Kite. What you did find out is that he *knows* something. If that fairy tale didn't mean something important to him, he wouldn't have hung up. We just need to find out what that is."

She patted me on the back. "You actually did good. This is nothing to freak out about. Now, the fact that you called Sebastian—that's going to raise a few eyebrows."

"Can't the Enclave just think of me as a spy or a double agent or something? Making Sebastian think I'm a friend while actually using him for information?"

"Is that really what you're doing?" Scout asked.

I didn't have a good answer for that.

"I didn't tell them about the time you met him in that Taco Terry's," she pointed out. I'd met Sebastian in the Mexican fast-food chain near St. Sophia's over one lunch hour.

"But now you're actually going to him for information. These people are putting their lives on the line just like you are, and I think it's only fair that you tell them you have a source." She shrugged. "It's possible they won't be really mad."

"They?" I wondered. "Or Jason?"

She grimaced. "Yeah. You might want to think about a bribe."

I made a face. "I got helpful information from Sebastian. I'm not going to feel bad about talking to him."

She patted me on the shoulder. "Just keep telling yourself that, kid."

When did things become so complicated?

Scout texted Daniel to arrange an Enclave meeting. I prepared myself mentally to make my confession about Sebastian, and then tried to put it out of my mind. I knew—or at least I thought I knew—I was doing the right thing by communicating with him. But I also knew there was a pretty good chance the others wouldn't see it that way—some Adepts would be upset. There was no point in worrying about something that was guaranteed to happen.

In the meantime, I needed to get Veronica and Nicu together, as unfortunate as that assignment was.

Scout used Nicu's business card to get his number, then called him to arrange a meeting. The rest was my responsibility—I had to get Veronica to Nicu. I figured the easiest way to do that was to simply invite her.

I found some off-white drawing paper among my art supplies and a really old calligraphy pen. We decided study hall was the best time to get Veronica to the meeting place without making the other brat packers completely suspicious. Amie wasn't the type of girl to leave in the middle of a cram session, and Veronica probably wouldn't even tell M.K.—not if she thought she was meeting a secret boy.

The trickier part was getting Scout and me out of study hall to follow her, but we'd cross that bridge when we came to it.

"What, exactly, should I say on this note?" I asked, nibbling on the end of my pen. "How do you entice a brat packer to go to a secret meeting?"

"Promise them free makeup and Neiman Marcus gift cards?"

"I was hoping for something more poetic."

"Ah," Scout said, then cleared her throat and broke out the worst European guy accent I'd ever heard.

"Mizz Veeee-ronica," she said. "I have dee love of you, greatly. You will meet me in dee night, and we will make dee beyoooteeful music."

I just stared at her. "Really?"

She shrugged. "I don't know. I'm not really into the whole romantic thing. Just keep it vague."

That probably was for the best. I went with something simple.

Veronica—
   I'm the one you've been waiting for. It's time we meet. 8:15 tonight. Thorn Garden.
                                             Yours Truly

Pretty romantic if you asked me, but not so romantic that it sounded, you know, stalkery.

I folded it up and wrote Veronica's name on the outside. Then Scout and I waited until dinner started and slipped the note under the door to Veronica's suite.

And then we waited.

The great hall was quiet and chilly, and most of the girls in St. Sophia's wore sweaters or sweatshirts over their uniforms. With an elbow on the table, I sat with my chin in one hand, flicking my pencil against the table with the other.

I should have been upstairs in flannel pajamas. Instead, I was in study hall, a notebook and tattered copy of *Sense and Sensibility* on the table in front of me . . . and Veronica Lively on my mind.

We were already an hour into study hall, and Veronica hadn't done *anything*. She sat with M.K. and Amie just like usual, and it looked like she was studying. If she planned to go through with the meeting, she certainly wasn't acting like it . . . and that was making me antsy.

What if she didn't show at all? What if she stood up a vampire and he blamed us? No more trips through the Pedway for us.

Seriously, these old-fashioned British romance novels were tame compared to the stuff we were living.

Since Veronica hadn't so much as moved in five minutes, I looked down at my book and forced myself to read three more pages.

I looked up at Scout, who sat at the table across from me, actually reading her own copy of the book. She may have missed her parents, but there were some reasons for which she wouldn't want to see them. Like failing out of school.

"What's a whippet?" I asked.

"Whip it," Scout said. "Whip it good." She drummed on the table. "Duh duh duh, duh duh."

"Not 'whip it,' *whippet*. It's a dog, I think."

"If you think it's a dog, why do you want to know?"

"I just wanted confirmation. Thank you for being so helpful."

"We aim to please," she whispered, turning a page.

Apparently I wasn't going to be able to get her to procrastinate with me.

Suddenly, Veronica all but jumped out of her chair. She walked over to one of the dragon ladies, said something with hand gestures, and then walked to the doors that led into the main building.

I guess she'd gotten excused from study hall.

I tapped my pencil on Scout's book. When she looked up at me, I gestured toward Veronica, who was opening the door.

She nodded. "You go," she said, then motioned at the patrolling dragon ladies. "How are you going to get past them?"

Trying to think up a plan, I gnawed the edge of my lip. And just as Veronica slipped outside the door, I spied my solution.

"There's a water fountain in the great hall," I whispered.

"And?" Scout asked.

"And," I said; then I coughed—loudly.

The dragon lady glared over at me for interrupting the silence.

Pile it on, I thought, and launched into a spasm of coughing that would have impressed an Oscar winner.

"All right," Scout barely whispered. "She's walking over. Make your move. I'll follow you if I can get outside. If I can't, keep an eye on the lovebirds."

I didn't wait. I scooted my chair back and hustled over to her. Every few steps I faked a gigantic cough that turned every head in the room.

"I need to . . . you know . . . It's an emergency." I winged up my eyebrows and put a hand on my chest for dramatic effect. I also fake coughed enough that I made my eyes water, which probably helped, too.

The dragon lady didn't look convinced, but she gestured toward the door. "*Quickly*," she warned.

I didn't waste any time. I half jogged to the door and slipped through it, fake coughing all the way like it was my theme song . . . at least until I was out of the room and the door was shut behind me.

I got out just in time to see Veronica slipping into the administrative wing. That was when I knew we had her. The only reason to visit the administrative wing this late at night was to use the secret exit—an old root cellar that led directly to the St. Sophia's grounds. No alarms. No dragon ladies. It was a miracle Reapers weren't pouring through there every night.

I walked as quietly as possible across the stone labyrinth to the hallway, then looked around the corner. It was empty, but I could see Veronica's shadow shrinking into a thin line at the end of the corridor.

When I got down the hallway, the door to the final room—which held access to the root cellar—was cracked open where Veronica had disappeared through it. Waiting for a moment to ensure I hadn't been followed, and that she didn't know I was following her, I headed down into the cellar and outside again.

The weather had turned colder, and a strong breeze had blown up. It wasn't exactly great weather for a romantic meeting, but there was only so much I could do.

Veronica crept outside the school's front gate, and then up the block around a couple of the buildings beside the school. The thorn garden was behind those buildings. It had once been part of the St. Sophia's grounds, at least until someone discovered the school didn't actually own it.

It was a pretty cool area during the day—lots of green grass punctuated by pointy concrete columns that poked through the ground like thorns.

At night, it was scarier. The columns seemed almost menacing, and it was easy to get lost in the maze of them. I stayed behind Veronica, creeping behind her as quietly as possible while trying not to lose her in the dark. Which, of course, I did. I hung back behind a column, scanning the rest of the park until I heard her footsteps in the grass, and finally caught sight of her.

She stood in the middle of a clearing, her arms crossed. She'd paired a short-sleeved shirt with her uniform skirt and had to be cold. She also looked nervous.

But before she could change her mind, Nicu emerged into the clearing. He may have been willing to pretend at being human to meet Veronica, but he hadn't done much about his clothes. His coat was a little shorter today—knee-length instead of down to his ankles—but he still looked like the hero from a Jane Austen novel. He just needed a musket. And maybe a whippet.

They faced each other across the clearing. Veronica, slim and blond, and Nicu, tall and dark, both beautiful enough to be like fairy tale characters.

"You are . . . Veronica," he said.

"I—yes. Who are you? And how did you know my name?"

"You can call me . . . Nicholas. I know your name because we've met before."

"Before?" she repeated, and I could see the confusion in her expression . . . but also a glimmer of recognition. Maybe because of the blackout, the block on her memory seemed to be losing its power. She may not remember exactly how she knew Nicu, but I could see in her face that he seemed familiar.

"Before," she repeated, this time a statement. "Do you go to school around here?"

"I do not," he said. "I . . . work."

"How did you get the note to me?"

"The note?" he asked, brow furrowed. But then he looked up and across the garden . . . and caught my eye.

He nodded at me and I nodded back, my debt cleared.

"I have friends," he told her. "You look cold. Perhaps you should return to your school."

"I think . . . I want to stay here with you."

For a long, silent moment, they looked at each other with such emotion I nearly got teary eyed. How could they have that kind of bond so quickly? How was that even possible?

Possible or not, there was no point in denying it. 'Cause here they were, in the middle of a park in the middle of the night, staring like they could save each other.

"You should go," Nicu said, then picked up Veronica's hand and lifted it to his lips. He pressed a kiss to the inside of her wrist, and then held her hand against his cheek. His lashes fell, and for a moment he just stood there.

"How will I—" Veronica began, but he opened his eyes again and shook his head.

"This is only the beginning," he said. "I will find you."

If this was only the beginning, my life was about to get a lot more complicated.

And then, like he'd been only a figment of her imagination, Nicu disappeared into the thorns again.

Veronica stood there for a moment, and, like nothing had happened, walked back into the building and rejoined the brat pack in study hall. Amie, her head in a book, seemed uninterested in the fact that Veronica had been gone. M.K., on the other hand, looked plenty curious. I wondered what Veronica would tell them later. That she'd snuck outside to meet a guy who left a secret note in her suite?

Scout leaned over the table when I took a seat. "What happened?"

"They met."

"And then what?"

"I'm not entirely sure. But it looks like love to me. And good luck to them."

With Marlena angry at Nicu, and M.K. ready to sabotage Veronica's relationship at a moment's notice, they were going to need it.

13

When study hall was over, we dumped our books, changed into jeans, and headed out to the Enclave. Tonight, there was no Detroit, but we were joined by Katie and Smith. They both looked unhappy to be there. Actually, they both also looked like they were wearing the same skinny jeans. Not a fashion statement I was fond of.

Everyone was seated around the table when we walked in. Michael smiled when Scout sat down beside him, and Jason smiled a little at me, but he looked distracted, like he had other things on his mind. Maybe his family was giving him more trouble than he'd let on.

"We're here," Daniel began, "because we need to talk about the blackout."

Scout and I exchanged a glance. Did he already know about Fayden Campbell—that we suspected she might be involved? Did he already know I'd been talking to Sebastian?

"An Adept from Enclave Four, apparently frustrated by the loss of her magic, attacked two of her fellow Adepts last night."

"She attacked them?" Michael quietly asked.

"I understand that Enclave had been on edge since the blackout began, and the lack of magic hit them harder than some of the others. This particular girl was taking the loss of magic very poorly. She was nervous. Excitable. Angry. An argument at the Enclave escalated, and . . ."

"Are they okay?" Scout asked.

"One was released from First Immanuel Hospital this morning. The other is still in serious condition. She hasn't woken up since the attack."

The Enclave went silent.

"Not having magic is difficult for all of us," he said. "But that is an explanation. It is not an excuse."

"What if that happens to us?" Jill asked. "It could happen to us. We could lose it just like she did."

"You're not going to lose it," Daniel said. "But that doesn't mean we don't stay vigilant. We are all experiencing something we thought we had years to prepare for. Instead, we went cold turkey. Not everyone handles that transition well. I didn't tell you this to scare you," he added. "I told you this because you need to understand the risks. You have a right to understand the risks."

He let that sink in for a minute, and then put his hands on the table. "All right. Let's get to business. Scout, you had news?"

"Um, well, Reapers broke into St. Sophia's today," Scout said. "Two girls tried to steal my *Grimoire*. We're assuming that's part of Jeremiah's plan to steal it because he thinks I had something to do with the blackout. Which, obvs, I did not."

"Did they get it?" Daniel asked, his voice tight.

"Of course not. They wouldn't have found it anyway, but Lily had already suggested I hide it, and I did."

Daniel blew out a breath. "Good," he said. "Good."

"And, in addition to being awesome," Scout continued, "we also have a lead on who *might* have something to do with the blackout. We went to Gaslight Goods. Kite told us some of the Reapers were talking about a fairy tale that involved a guy named 'Campbell.'"

"What's that?" Michael asked.

"Supposedly Campbell overthrew an overlord, but then went evil when he took power," Scout said. "Kite told us Reapers were talking about the fairy tale like they thought it might be real. Lily did a little research, and it turns out Sebastian Born has a cousin named Fayden Campbell. She just moved back to town."

Scout pulled out a copy of the article from her bag and handed it to Daniel.

"That's a pretty big coincidence," Daniel said, looking it over. "But it's still only a coincidence. Do we have information tying Fayden Campbell to the blackout? Or to any Reaper activities?"

Scout looked at me.

"I've actually been told she's not a Reaper," I said. "But I don't think that's true."

Daniel tilted his head in curiosity. "Where did you hear that?"

Nerves flooding me, I squeezed my hands into fists. "Sebastian Born. He's my source in the Reapers. He helped me use firespell to rescue Scout, and he gives me information sometimes. That's how I found out their magic was working even when ours was gone—at least at first. I saw him and Fayden on the street earlier this week.

He introduced us, but he didn't mention her last name. When Kite told us about the fairy tale, I did some Internet research and found her picture." I left out the part about calling Sebastian to check if he knew anything about her. I was only so brave.

Without saying a word, Daniel sat back in his chair and crossed his arms over his head. I was afraid to look at Jason, afraid of what emotion I might see in his face.

"You have a source in the Reapers," Daniel finally said.

"Yeah."

"And you talk to him often?"

"I don't talk to him at all, really. Occasionally, he gives me information."

"Out of the goodness of his heart?"

"Honestly, I think he thinks he can sway me to his side. Which is ridiculous," I added. "I know who the good guys and the bad guys are." *Or I mostly did,* I silently added. "But I'm not going to ignore him when he's trying to help me out, whatever his reasoning."

"Yeah," Scout said. "Does this really matter? The point is, Lily has a contact in the Reapers and helped us figure out what's going on. We need to focus on this Fayden Campbell person. We need to track her down and get some eyes on her—some Enclave Two cameras or something."

Daniel sat forward again, crossing his hands on the table. "I'm going to need to think about this one. A source is nice, but I find it hard to believe he'd be so helpful without some secret motive."

"That's all you're going to say?" All eyes turned to Jason. "Seriously. She's suddenly friends with a Reaper, and that's it?"

My stomach dropped. There was no doubting the fury in his

gaze. He looked like I'd committed an unforgiveable sin. What if, no matter how good my reason, he couldn't forgive me?

"Scout's right," Daniel said. "Whatever the source, we have to follow the lead. It could send us right to the source of the blackout."

"There is a way we can track her, maybe," I said, forcing myself to keep my gaze on Daniel and not think about the fury in Jason's voice. "We went to Gaslight Goods yesterday. I asked Kite to call us if Sebastian Born came in. When he does, maybe we can follow Sebastian and see what he's up to. It may not be much of a lead, but it's better than nothing."

Daniel thought about it for a second, then nodded. "Agreed. When he calls, go to Gaslight and follow him. See where he goes. Maybe the clue leads nowhere, but it's worth the trip. And keep us posted."

Without saying a word, or looking at me, Jason pushed back his chair, grabbed his backpack, and headed for the door.

"Jason, wait!" I pushed back my chair to follow him, but he closed the door in my face. I pulled it open and ran into the tunnel, but he kept going.

"Jason, please stop."

Nothing.

"Please, can we just talk about this?"

He finally turned around . . . and he looked *furious*.

"What are you doing?" I asked him.

"What am *I* doing?" He pressed a hand to his chest. "*I* am trying to keep all of us safe. And it looks like that's more than I can say for you. Talking to Sebastian? Helping out Reapers? What is that about? He's the one who got you into this mess in the first place, and you're talking to him?"

"That's not what it's like. He's helping us. Ask Scout."

"He's *helping* you? Do you even hear yourself?"

I forced myself to stay calm. "Quit yelling at me and listen to what I'm telling you. Sebastian helped me. When we were in the sanctuary, he helped me use the firespell and get Scout out alive. And he's helped me since then."

"If he's helped you, it's because he has an ulterior motive—just like Daniel said. He wouldn't just do it out of the goodness of his heart."

"Because he's evil?"

"Because he's a *Reaper*, Lily, God. Haven't you been paying attention for the last few months? Reapers are manipulative. This is how they operate. They take sane people and convince them that everything they know isn't true."

"Isn't that what you and Scout did to me? Convinced me there was more to the world than just what I saw? Convinced me magic existed?"

His eyes flashed. "Sebastian convinced you of that when he hit you with firespell."

I could see the anger in his eyes, and I knew what he thought. He thought I'd been swayed by a Reaper, convinced by Sebastian's words. But I was still able to think for myself. I just had a different view of the world—a bigger view of the world—than I'd had before.

"He hit me with firespell accidentally," I said. "He was aiming for Scout. And I'm not going to apologize for actually thinking about what's happening here, instead of just accepting what you and Daniel say."

"Great. Go think for yourself. And when I need someone level-headed to talk to, someone who isn't trying to screw up my family life, I guess you aren't the person I should call. You may not even believe a word I say."

"You know that's not true."

"No, I really don't. I don't think you're the girl I thought you were. I do know I can't handle this right now."

He put his backpack back on his shoulder and began walking down the corridor.

"Where are you going?"

"Honestly, Lily, I'm not sure. I'll let you know when I get there."

With that, he disappeared into darkness.

I bit my lip to hold back tears. I didn't want to cry in the tunnels, I didn't want to cry over a boy, and I didn't want to feel bad for thinking things through instead of just buying what everybody told me.

Yeah—it was scary to give up your assumptions and actually think, but wasn't that the entire point of being an Adept?

The door creaked open, and Scout peeked her head out and looked around. "Where's Jason?"

"He left."

Frowning, she walked into the tunnel and closed the door behind her. "He left?"

I wiped at the tears on my cheeks. "Yeah. He's really mad that I talked to Sebastian. He thinks I'm a traitor."

"Aw, Lils," she said, and held out her arms for a hug. I walked into them and sobbed my heart empty of tears.

Scout went back into the Enclave, grabbed my messenger bag, and got us excused so the other Adepts wouldn't have to see me standing in a damp, nasty tunnel with tear tracks on my face and raccoon eyeliner eyes.

"I am definitely not going to the dance now," I said, as Scout put an arm around my shoulder and we began walking back toward the school.

"You never know. He could come to his senses. And even if he doesn't, do you really have time to worry about a werewolf with a bad attitude? Or a dress? You haven't even had time to find a dress yet."

"Do you really think he has a bad attitude?" I stopped short in the hallway. "Scout, am I making a huge mistake by even talking to Sebastian? It's just information—he's not going to sway me from one side to another. I'm a smart girl; I can make up my own mind."

"I know you can. But Jason doesn't think there's any choice. In his mind, there's clearly good and clearly evil and there's no meeting in the middle. You talking to Sebastian totally crosses his wires, you know? He doesn't see how you could do that if you were really a good guy . . ."

"Which makes him wonder if I'm really a good guy," I finished.

"I think so, yeah."

We started walking again. Feeling totally rejected, I kicked at a rusted chunk of metal on the ground. It skittered away into the dark.

"Do you wonder if I'm a good guy?"

It took her a scary long time to answer. "I want to think you're a good guy. But you have to make that decision for yourself. And maybe being a good guy isn't the same for everyone. It's different for members of the Community than it is for us. So maybe it's different for some Adepts than others."

I didn't exactly like the sound of that. But I knew how I felt. "No one has the right to take something that doesn't belong to them," I said. "And that includes stealing souls or energy or whatever Reapers take. But I didn't grow up with this stuff, Scout. It's new to me, and the only things I know come from other people. You tell me Reapers are bad, and I believe you. But I also think there's more going on here than we know. Something more than Reapers-bad, Adepts-good. And I think we need to figure out what that is."

I think she had a decision to make, too. I'd disrupted her world, made her think about things she probably didn't want to— the possibility that truths she'd known weren't entirely truth. That was the risk I took by telling her how I felt about it. I could only hope that she was strong enough to take that leap with me.

"When I first figured out that I could bind spells," she said, "my parents were appalled. Fortunately, the Enclave found me pretty quickly after my powers popped through. They were nice to me, and what they said made sense, you know? But I was also told Reapers were bad. Always bad. Always self-centered. I don't want to believe that it's more complicated than that. I don't want to believe that the world is this gigantic gray hole and you never really know wrong from right."

She sighed, and looked back at me. "But that's not exactly a good way to live, and it can't be the best way to spend the few years I've got this power. If you're in this, then I am, too. I don't want to be part of a team just because it's a team I grew up in. I want to be part of a team because it's the *right* team."

"There's a risk it won't be, you know. There's a risk we'll find out things we don't want to."

She nodded, and that was when I knew she was all in. "Then let's find out."

I knew Jason needed time and space, but that didn't mean I was thrilled about the fact that he'd walked away. I checked my phone every few seconds, hoping I'd find a text message saying he'd rushed to judgment and was sorry he'd left me crying in the tunnel.

But my phone was silent.

When we made sure the tunnel door was locked up tight, we headed upstairs to bed.

"Long night," she said after I followed her into her room and locked the door against nosey brat packers.

"It really was."

"Do you think you'll hear from Jason?"

"Right now I really don't know."

And I was getting so mad at him for walking away, I wasn't sure I cared.

"You know what we should do?"

"What's that?" I asked, but she was rifling through her messenger bag. She pulled out a cheap spiral notebook and a pen, then pulled off the cap.

"Are you starting on your novel?"

"Har har har, Parker. And someday, yes, but not today. It's going to be called *The Wicked Witch of the Midwest*."

"Promise me you're joking."

The expression on her face said she was dead serious. Which

was sad, really, because that title was awful. "It's, what, like, your memoir or something?"

"It will be," she said, sitting down on the bed. "But I can't write it, of course, until people know we actually exist."

"So they don't assume it's just fiction?"

"Precisely," she said, pointing with her pen. "But that's not the point. We're going to do something fun, Parker. We're going to start a list."

"That might be the boringest idea I've ever heard. A list of what?"

"Just, you know, *stuff.*" As if to prove her point, Scout flipped open the book and wrote THE LIST in big capital letters at the top of the first page. "It will be like our scrapbook of words. You know, instead of saving ticket stubs and homecoming ribbons and crap like that, we'll have this list of all our memories, and stuff. You know?"

I didn't really, but I did kind of like the idea of having a memory book for the two of us. I wasn't sure there was a lot of my high school experience I'd want to remember—and I was hardly going to forget life as an Adept—but this would just be for Scout and me. Something to look back on in our old age . . . if we made it that long.

"Okay," I said. "Let's try out this list thing. What do you want to put on it?"

She flicked the pen against her chin. "I feel like the first thing that goes on there should be pretty significant, you know? Something we'll definitely remember later on."

"Firespell? Brat pack? Reapers?"

"All good words, but so . . . common. For us, I mean. No—we need something cooler. Something better."

"Werewolf? Sanctuary? Enclave?"

She shook her head. "Too specific."

"You know, I've already named all the stuff we do on a daily basis. Pretty soon I'm just going to be listing off nouns in alphabetical order. Aardvark. Antelope. Architecture. Avalanche. Stop me when I'm close."

She must have thought of something, because she began to furiously scribble. And when she finally showed me the page, she'd listed down all the things I mentioned. But at the top of the list, in her scrawly handwriting, were a couple of simple words that meant a lot.

Best friends.

I bit my lip to keep my eyes from welling with tears again. "Good choice, Green."

"I know," she quietly said. "But that's what this is all about, right? Now," she said, tapping the paper, "let's do the Adepts."

In twenty minutes, we filled three sheets of paper.

14

lasses were bad when you were happy, when the weather was nice, or you wanted to be outside doing anything other than studying.

But they were even worse when you were depressed. When you wanted only to sit in your room staring at your phone and waiting for a call that probably wasn't going to come. The more you wanted that phone call, the harder you waited for it, the longer it took. The slower classes became, and the more you wanted to fall down into yourself and just make the time go faster.

But, of course, it didn't. And Jason didn't call. He didn't text. He didn't contact me at all, not even to confirm that we were definitely off for Sneak.

It was total radio silence, and it drove me *crazy*.

Scout thought it was a good sign he hadn't called—that if he'd really wanted a permanent breakup, he would have already told me. I wasn't sure no news was good news, but it wasn't like there was anything I could do about it. I wasn't going to text or call him. He'd walked out on me, not vice versa. I'd stuck with him when he told me he was facing down a curse and his family was pressuring him. I could have told him it was too much drama for me, too much risk that I'd get my heart broken later on.

But I didn't. I stayed.

He'd walked away because I'd gotten information from Sebastian. It's not like I didn't get why he was irritated, but what was the difference between me texting Sebastian and Detroit planting a camera? Not much, as far as I could see.

I muscled through the day without crying even though every minute felt twice as long as usual. And by the end of the day, I was ready for a night of pajamas and movies instead of Enclave drama. But since we were in the middle of a magical crisis, there was no way that was going to happen.

I was still a member of the Sneak planning committee (however stupid that idea seemed now), so after class I walked to the gym and helped make fringed garland out of sheets of black crepe paper. Lesley was at cello practice, which left me alone in a nest of brat packers and brat pack wannabes. I could hear their sniping across the room while I cut strips of paper, but I was having enough of a pity party that I hardly cared. There was something kind of Zen about cutting one strip of paper after another. It wasn't exactly exciting work, but I got into a rhythm that helped clear my brain of everything else.

And sometimes that's what a girl needed—a clear brain for just a little while.

It didn't take long for Veronica and the rest of them to take advantage of the fact that I was vastly outnumbered. Veronica and M.K. walked over, leaving Amie and Lisbeth on the other side of the room.

"What's up, Freak?" M.K. asked.

I ignored her and made eye contact with Veronica. I wondered if she had any idea who'd left the note at her door, or arranged her meeting with Nicu. But if she suspected I was the one, she certainly didn't look it.

"I'm here to make garland," I said. "Not talk to you."

"Like we'd talk to you on purpose," M.K. said, apparently not realizing that's exactly what she was doing. "Do you even have a date for the dance?"

Honestly, I had no idea. But I wasn't about to tell her that. "Of course. And he's even my age."

M.K., who tended to date guys old enough to drink and rent cars, rolled her eyes. "Like you could even get an older guy, Parker. What kind of freak would want you?"

A werewolf, I guessed, at least before he thought I'd betrayed him.

They made another snarky comment, then picked up armfuls of the garland and gave me a dirty look before walking back to the rest of the group.

"Freak," M.K. muttered.

"Totally," Veronica said, but she glanced back at me and dropped her eyes guiltily. Maybe the girl had a conscience after all, as little good as it did. Next time I had the urge to help her out, I decided to stick a pencil in my eye instead. I'd probably get less trouble out of it.

"Thanks," I called out. "You're welcome for the garland."

They rolled their eyes and offered snorty laughs.

Ugh. I was not a fan of today.

I got a little pickup after dinner when Scout found a giant box addressed to her outside the suite door. She brought it inside, but didn't seem the least bit interested in what was in the box. I was plenty interested, so I followed her back to her room.

"Don't you want to open it?"

She sat down on her bed and rifled through the stuff in her messenger bag. "It's from my parents. I already have a pretty good idea of what it is."

"Which is?"

"Something stupid expensive."

"Electronics? Fine linens? Heavyweight diamonds? What?"

"Do you really have to know? Like, right this second?"

"I'm not very patient."

Scout rolled her eyes, but gave in. "Fine."

She pulled the box onto her lap and slid a fingernail beneath the seal to open the box. When she lifted up the lid, she revealed neatly folded pinstripe tissue paper.

"Clothes?"

"Not just," she said, unfolding one delicate sheet of paper at a time. "Clothes picked out by my mother."

She pulled out a dress in the greenest green I'd ever seen. It was sleeveless, knee-length satin with a swingy skirt. The satin was topped by a layer of black lace in huge whorls and flowers.

"That is hideous," she said, just as "That is amazing" escaped my lips.

Our answers were simultaneous, and we immediately looked at each other.

She held the dress out at arm's length, nose wrinkled in disgust. "How can you like this thing? It's so . . . *green*. And it probably cost, like, three thousand dollars. Somebody at some fancy store convinced her it was the latest thing and she picked it up. I guess the thought is nice, but the dress is awful."

"Are you kidding? How can you possibly say that? That lace is fantastic. And I like the green."

"Maybe so, but it's not me. It's not who I am." She lowered the dress and looked at me with a sneaky glint in her eye. "But it might be you."

"Me? Oh, no." I shook a finger at her. "First off, I probably don't even have a date. And even if I did, I'm not wearing a three-thousand-dollar dress. Are you crazy? What if I spilled punch on it? What if I got a rip in it?" I pointed at the ground. "What if demon zombies burst out of the ground and get their, like, putrescence on it?"

"Putrescence?"

"Doesn't that totally sound like something a demon zombie would have? You know, like, oozing from its pores and stuff?"

"That is heinous. But you have a point."

"I always do. That dress is yours. It's a gift from your parents. What if they found out I'd worn it?"

"And got zombie putrescence on it?"

"Precisely. They'd probably get me kicked out of school. Not that there wouldn't be advantages to that. But, no. *No*. As much as I appreciate it, that's a lot of responsibility."

Scout looked at me for a moment, and then placed the dress back in the box. "Look, I'm not going to wear it, so it's only going to sit here. If you decide you're willing to take on the challenge, you let me know."

"I won't."

Scout sighed and packed the box away again. "People always say that, you know. That they won't succumb to the lure of the money." Once closed, she shoved the box under her bed.

"Money isn't everything."

"No," she said, sitting up again. "It's not." She hopped off the bed and walked to her closet. She opened the door, and pulled out a handful of clothes on hangers that still had the tags on them. "But sometimes parents confuse money with attention."

"They bought you all that stuff?"

She tossed a long-sleeved silk shirt onto the bed. "They forgot my thirteenth birthday." A tweed jacket—that was totally not her style— followed it. "They didn't come to the beginning-of-year assembly."

Scout threw shirt after skirt after jacket onto the bed until there was a pile of brand-new clothes—brand-new *expensive* clothes— there. "When they forget something important—or when they can't make room in their schedule of polo watching and sun-tanning, they buy me things."

My eyes widened when I caught the price of one of the shirts. "I guess 'spare no expense' is their motto."

"Yep."

I picked up the stack of clothes and handed them back to her. "And the green dress?"

"That's probably an early apology since they'll miss parents' night."

Even I was disappointed in that. Someday I'd like to meet Scout's parents, the man and woman responsible for creating this totally brilliant, unique person . . . and then ignoring her.

"I'm sorry, Scout."

"Eh," she said, hanging up the clothes again. She may not have liked them, and she may not have worn them, and she clearly wasn't happy about what they represented. But the clothes were still hanging in her closet, taking up space. She probably preferred to have her parents here, but I guess if she couldn't have them, she kept their gifts as a substitute.

"You know," I said, fingering the nubby tweed on the jacket, "some of these things aren't bad. Maybe I'll borrow them sometime."

"Knock yourself out," she said. And then her phone began to whine out a really loud piece of classical music that sounded a lot like buzzing insects.

"This is Scout," she answered. When her eyes went wide, I assumed it was interesting news. "Okay. Thanks for letting us know, Kite. 'Bye."

She put the phone down and looked at me. "You might have gotten your wish earlier than you thought."

"Sebastian?"

"He's in the store," she confirmed. "Let's get moving."

We decided it was too risky to wait for backup, but we should let someone know where we were going. I wasn't about to call Jason.

If he wasn't ready to talk, I certainly wasn't going to call him first, so Scout called Michael and told him the plan.

We changed into dark street clothes and geared up, then snuck out the same cellar door through which I'd followed Veronica outside.

We walked quietly over to Gaslight, then crept along the edge of the building and peeked inside one of the storefront windows. At first, we didn't see anything, but we could hear muted yelling from inside the store. After a couple of minutes we spied the source. Sebastian and Fayden emerged from an aisle.

She was in the lead, rolling her eyes in irritation, a Gaslight Goods bag in hand. She looked like she was making an emergency visit. Her dark hair was pulled into a messy topknot, and she wore her dark, cat-eye glasses. She wore a thin T-shirt, yoga pants, and flip-flops. She was very trim, so the outfit didn't look bad, but it was definitely more suited to running errands in California than in Chicago.

Sebastian was behind her, dressed in clothes more appropriate for fall. But his gaze was narrowed at the back of her head, and he looked really, really unhappy.

"We may have just missed some fireworks," I murmured.

"Apparently," Scout said. "They're heading for the door. Let's get out of the line of sight."

We scooted into the doorway of the pharmacy next door to Gaslight. When the bell on the Gaslight Goods door began to ring, we snuck a peek.

Fayden walked out first. Sebastian followed her. They made it to the end of the dark and empty block before they started talking.

"You need to chill, cuz," Fayden said. "I told you this would all be fine."

His eyes narrowed. "You lied to me."

"No, the family just omitted a few things. My status in the DE isn't your concern."

"You don't think I should know that another member of my family has magic?"

Her bag on her arm, she poked an escaping tendril of hair back into her topknot. "I think unless it affects you, it's not really any of your beeswax." She patted his arm. "Maybe this blackout is getting to you. But never fear. I think you'll find, cousin, that your life is about to get a lot more interesting."

She took a deep breath of chilly Chicago air. "A whole new world is about to open up."

Sebastian grabbed her arm. Hard. "What is that supposed to mean? Do you have something to do with the blackout? Have you taken magic from us?"

Fayden had been all smiles, but in that second her expression changed to something much more nasty. "You will take your hand off me right now or you won't live to regret it."

Whatever Sebastian saw in her eyes must have convinced him, because he pulled his hand away.

"Much better," she said, smiling again. "The blackout is what the blackout is. Don't you think it's an exciting time, though? There's something new in the air. Something mysterious. A new era."

A taxi pulled up to the curb, and before Sebastian could argue the point, Fayden hopped inside. "Thanks for the chat. I'll catch you later."

The cab pulled away.

"We have got to follow her," Scout said. As soon as the cab had passed, Scout ran to the street and hailed another one. I followed her to the street, and Sebastian picked that moment to look over at us.

I gave him an apologetic look. He nodded back—an acknowledgment, maybe that something was up that bridged the gap between Reapers and Adepts.

A cab screeched to a stop, and we jumped inside. "Follow that cab," Scout said. "But not too close."

The driver looked at us in the rearview mirror. "We don't really do that—"

"Follow the cab," Scout repeated, "and there's a hundred dollar tip in it for you."

"Following the cab," the driver said, and pulled into traffic.

Wherever Fayden was going, she was going there in a hurry. We zigzagged other cars, and I think we were moving toward the lake.

"Do you think she knows we're back here?" I wondered.

Scout looked around at the traffic. It was night, so it wasn't exactly heavy, but there were taxis here and there. "Hopefully she thinks we're just coincidentally moving in the same direction." She glanced down at the driver's badge, which was stuck to the dashboard. "And John here is doing a fantastic job of keeping a few cars behind her."

"I drive NASCAR on the weekends," John dryly muttered. "This is just my day job."

Scout rolled her eyes.

"I think she's stopping," John said. Sure enough, the cab ahead of us pulled to a stop at the next corner. John sneakily pulled his cab into a parking space at the other end of the block. Scout pulled a hundred dollar bill out of her wallet and pushed it through the little box in the plastic guard between the seats.

"Run the meter," she said, "and there's another hundred in it for you."

"You're the boss."

"I guess being a Green pays off sometimes," I whispered. Scout humphed.

We got out of the cab, but hung back between the cars until Fayden got out. She walked toward a fancy-looking apartment building that was eight or ten stories tall. If she disappeared in there, we'd never find her.

"Let's get closer," Scout whispered. "Maybe we can at least figure out which apartment she's going into."

We moved up, peering at the door from behind a four-foot-tall hedge that surrounded the building. Turned out, we didn't need to know where she was going. We needed only to watch how she got in there.

The front door had a really big keypad lock. Fayden held out a finger like she was going to punch in a code.

"Maybe she lives here," I suggested softly, thinking she meant to unlock the door. But no sooner had I said that than a giant green spark shot from her finger and right into the keypad. The door unlocked with an audible *click*, and she walked right inside.

That was *magic*. And not just magic—like, electrical power– related magic with its pretty green tinge.

"Holy crap," Scout said.

"Holy crap," I agreed. "Fayden Campbell has *firespell*. And hers is still working."

I guess that answered the blackout question.

Problem was, even if we had pretty good evidence Fayden Campbell had used her still-existent magic to create the blackout, we didn't know why she'd done it, or where she'd done it. Maybe most important, we didn't know *how* she'd done it. Firespell, as far as I knew, was the ability to control energy—turning off lights and sending shock waves and stuff. So how had she managed to turn off everyone else's magic?

We let the cab wait for a few minutes while Scout called Daniel and filled him in. He promised to get eyes on the building and try to figure out what Fayden was doing there—and if she'd managed to stash some sort of ongoing spell or magic machine that we could hack or destroy or just plain turn off.

But I had another idea.

I wiggled my fingers to borrow the phone from Scout.

"Hold on, Daniel," she said. "Lily wants to talk to you." She handed it over.

"I think Fayden lied to Sebastian," I said into the phone. "And I don't think he was happy about it."

"And your point is?"

"My point is I suggest we set up a meeting with him. If he feels like he's been betrayed by his cousin, maybe he'll be willing to talk about her. Maybe he can tell us more about her powers, or who her friends are, or something like that."

Daniel was quiet for a second, giving me time to think about the consequences of what I was asking. Yes, a meeting with Sebastian was necessary to solve the mystery and try to get our magic back. But Jason wasn't going to be happy about it. He was probably going to be even madder than he already was, if that was possible.

On the other hand, what was I supposed to do? I couldn't ignore leads or information just to make him more comfortable. That was definitely not good Adept behavior.

"Do it," Daniel said. "Arrange a meeting, and make it formal. Maybe we'll get to her before then and it won't be necessary. But we have to do something."

I agreed. I just hoped this was the *right* something.

15

G etting Daniel to agree to let us meet Sebastian was easy. Getting Sebastian to agree to meet us was a little harder. He wasn't answering his phone, and he didn't call me back until the next morning. Turned out, that was fine, because the apartment building had been a dead end anyway. There'd been no sign of Fayden when Daniel—or whichever troops he'd called out—had arrived.

The hardest part? Working out the details of the meeting.

Daniel sent a message with a whole list of rules and procedures for us to follow. We had to set a time (way too early in the morning), a location (the middle of the bridge over State Street), and the rules that applied to the meeting (no magic allowed, which was easy since we didn't exactly have any). Daniel also asked Jill and Jamie to take positions near the bridge just in case Sebastian tried something. Since he'd had plenty of other chances to zap me without Adept bystanders, I felt pretty safe.

Unfortunately, once word got out, I was afraid I wouldn't be hearing from Jason anytime soon. That thought hurt, but there was nothing I could do about it now. The wheels were already in motion.

Daniel got an okay from Foley for us to skip art history, although we probably could have snuck out without much trouble, as we realized when we walked outside and watched one wickedly expensive car after another pull into the drive in front of St. Sophia's. As the blue and yellow flag above the door waved in the wind, a Mercedes convertible pulled up, followed by a Bentley, a Rolls-Royce, and a really long limo driven by a white-capped driver.

I'd forgotten—the dance was tomorrow, so this was parents' night.

"Aren't they here early?"

"There are events throughout the day," Scout explained. "They have breakfast together; then, while the girls go to class, the parents go to seminars about raising bratty little monsters or something."

"Or financial aid for college," I said.

"Like these kids need financial aid," Scout grumbled. "Let's go."

I pulled my hoodie around me and followed Scout down the street.

The city smelled like smoke and wetness and dirt, and there was a chill in the air that said winter wasn't far away. I wasn't looking forward to that any more than I was looking forward to putting Scout and Sebastian together in the same place. She'd watched him knock me out with firespell, he'd been there when the Reapers had kidnapped her, and he was at least part of the reason I was sad about Jason. So he wasn't exactly at the top of her popularity list.

We walked silently toward the river through a part of downtown Chicago I hadn't seen yet. The streets were a little quieter over here, and there weren't as many tourists. It looked more residential, like the folks who worked and shopped in the busier parts of downtown lived here. Even the bars and restaurants looked smaller—more like neighborhood joints. They all had little patio areas with stand-up heaters, I guess for Chicagoans who weren't quite ready to give up the fight to winter.

The bridge appeared at the top of a rise in the road. There was a stone tower on each side of the roadway, and symbols were carved into the walls. As we walked closer, I could tell there were two kinds of symbols—a "Y" within a circle, and a quatrefoil. These were the signs of the Adepts and Reapers. *Appropriate meeting place,* I thought.

There were cars on the bridge, and plenty of tourists and businesspeople going about their days, but no Reapers as far as I could see. We walked to the edge of the bridge where the sidewalk narrowed to cross it, then stopped. Scout put her hands on her hips and surveyed the area with a critical eye.

"He's not here yet," she said.

I frowned. I couldn't see the other side of the street because of the angle, and she wasn't much taller than I. "How do you know that?" I wondered, a little spark of hope fluttering that maybe, somehow, she'd gotten her magic back.

That wishful thinking didn't last long.

"Jill just signaled it," Scout said, then pointed over to one of the high-rise buildings that lined the river.

Jill stood beside the building's front door, arms wrapped around herself in the chill, her long auburn hair nearly horizontal in the wind. She uncurled a hand and gave me a little wave. But her head suddenly whipped to the side toward the river—she'd seen something.

When she looked back at us, she raised her index finger, then made a fist, then pointed to the bridge.

"A Reaper has arrived," Scout translated. "That must be Sebastian."

"I guess so." I pushed down a bolt of fear. Fear wasn't going to do any good right now. Besides, if Sebastian didn't have magic, what could he do? Water balloons? Slap fight? It didn't seem likely that he'd start punching two girls in the middle of downtown Chicago.

I glanced at Scout. "Are you okay with this?"

"Am I ready to have a civil conversation with a Reaper who didn't lift a hand to help me when I was lying on the table? I'm not sure. I'm certainly not ready to forgive someone who had a chance to do the right thing but cowarded out. And I'm not convinced he's the good guy you think he is."

"I don't think he's a good guy," I said, not realizing I'd decided that until I said the words aloud. "But our lives are weird, and sometimes you make friends with strange people."

"Frenemies?"

"I guess so." I nodded with confidence, trying to convince myself as much as her. "Let's do this."

We started across the bridge, and as we walked closer to the middle, Sebastian appeared over the hill. He wore jeans and a black leather jacket, his hands tucked into his pockets. With the dark hair and blue eyes, he looked like a bad boy from a movie poster—the kind that was charming and handsome, but turned out to be not so good by the end.

It probably looked like I was a helpless schoolgirl in a plaid uniform, but my guard was all the way up.

We met him a few feet from the middle, a gap between us.

Sebastian looked at Scout, then me, and it felt like his eyes were boring into my soul—like he knew I had doubts.

He raised his hands, palms facing us.

Scout did the same thing. They looked like street performers pretending to be stuck behind a glass wall. She elbowed me. "Hands up," she murmured.

"Why?" I asked, but did what she said.

"Tradition. Proves you aren't holding a wand or something."

"I could have a wand?"

"It's a personal preference. Come on." Apparently satisfied that Sebastian wasn't about to throw bad magic at us, she put down her hands and walked forward.

We walked closer and faced him down, two Adepts against a Reaper.

"I request a temporary cease-fire," Sebastian said.

"Granted," Scout said. "South side rules, no snipe hunt."

Slowly, I turned my head to look at Scout and tried to ask a question with my eyes: *What in the crap are you talking about?*

But it was Sebastian who understood the look and answered me. "Cease-fire means no magic will be used during this meeting. South side rules mean we're fair game after we leave the bridge, but we can't snipe hunt—so only the people on the bridge can work the magic, not the folks we brought with us."

I guess it was a tradition, but it seemed silly to have rules like that when there was no magic to use.

"We didn't bring anyone with us," Scout said. She didn't make a very good liar.

Sebastian didn't take the bait. "We did," he said, then pointed behind him. Two teenagers stood at the edge of the bridge. One was Alex, a blonde who'd been with Sebastian when he hit me with firespell. She'd also attacked us when we went in to rescue Scout. She was not one of my favorite people.

The other was a really tall girl with dark skin and really short hair. She wore a T-shirt with what looked like a techie joke, skinny jeans, and a really big pair of mean-looking boots. She smiled. She was a pretty girl, but that didn't mean I wanted to run into the business end of those boots anytime soon.

"None of them have magic," I said, looking back at Sebastian.

His gaze shifted to me. "Not at the moment. And that's why we're here. What did you want to know?"

Scout got to the point. "We think your cousin is behind this, and we don't think that comes as a surprise to you."

Sebastian looked at me. "She didn't tell me she was a member of the Dark Elite."

"I know," I said. "We saw you fighting outside the store."

"Spying on me?" he asked.

"Honestly, yes," I said. He'd seen us outside the store, so there was really no point in lying. "You hung up on me really fast when I asked about the fairy tale. I thought that was worth a little consideration. But that's not the point—we actually saw Fayden do magic. She has firespell."

"I know."

"Tell us what you've seen," I said.

He didn't look at me, but his face was tense. He *definitely* knew something. "I can't."

"You can, and you have to," I said. "The blackout is taking your magic, too. The only way we solve this problem is if we work together."

"You want us to work together?" he asked, but there was a little bit of a smile in one corner of his mouth. I think he was actually enjoying this.

"It's a limited-time offer," I said. "We want things to get back to normal." If chasing Reapers through tunnels beneath Chicago could ever be considered normal. "Start at the beginning. How did you find out she was involved?"

"When I realized she was the only one in the city who could actually do magic."

"You might have mentioned that to us," Scout grumbled.

"I didn't know. Not until I saw her turn off a light. I think she forgot she was standing in front of me. And I wasn't exactly thrilled. She played it off like it wasn't any big thing. Like being the only person in town with magic wasn't any big thing."

"Why would she be doing this?"

He turned to face the river, putting his hands on the railing.

"I don't know. I mean, she was a bully when we were growing up. Bossy. Manipulative. Always telling the younger kids what to do."

"She mentioned something last night about a 'new era,'" Scout said. "We know people are unhappy with Jeremiah right now, and we know the old Reapers are talking about a fairy tale involving someone named Campbell, like, overthrowing the government or something. Is it possible she's working the blackout because she wants that kind of control? Because she wants to determine who gets to use magic and under what circumstances?"

"If that was true, why hasn't she announced it?" I wondered. "I mean, it's all well and good that she wants to be in charge. But at some point, she'd actually have to, like, *be* in charge."

"Maybe she can't," Scout said. "Look, first the Adepts' magic turned off, right? And then the Reapers' magic turned off. As far as we know, she's the only one in the city who has it. But if she's going to control who gets to use it, she has to be able to give magic *back* to someone."

"And maybe the spell isn't working that way," I finished. "She got the magic turned off, but she can't figure out how to turn it back on again?"

"She ordered some things from Gaslight," Sebastian said. "Maybe she was looking for a solution to that problem."

"What did she order?" Scout asked.

"I don't know. It was already bagged when we got there."

"Had she been to Gaslight before?"

"Not with me," Sebastian said. "But the girl at the counter knew her name."

Scout looked at me, and I could already see the wheels turning. She wanted to find out what Fayden had bought, and that was how she was going to find out what kind of magic she was working—and how to stop it.

I looked at Sebastian. "She has firespell, right? Is turning off other people's magic something you can do?"

"Not as far as I know. You?"

"Nope. So either she's got some new version of firespell we don't even know about, or she's got friends helping her—donating their magic, maybe." That kind of thing wasn't impossible; I'd used my firespell to help Scout take out the imploded sanctuary.

"Do you know who she hangs out with?" Scout asked him.

"No. Like I said, as far as I knew, she was new to town. I didn't lie to you," Sebastian said, looking earnestly at me. "I wouldn't do that."

Before I could answer, Scout cut in. "You're a Reaper," she said. "Lying is just par for the course."

"Not for me, it isn't," Sebastian said, his eyes going wide with anger.

"Oh, please. Reapers kill without a second thought."

"Taking energy for food is one thing. No one has to die because of that. Killing someone out of revenge is something else completely."

Scout made a sarcastic sound.

"I get it," Sebastian said. "You don't like me, and you don't trust me."

"Not even as far as I could throw you."

"You don't even know me."

"And you don't know me, but that didn't stop you from kidnapping me."

"I didn't kidnap you."

"Your friends did," she countered, "and that's close enough for me. And it's not like you stopped them, did you?"

"No," he admitted. "But I helped Lily get you out."

That wasn't enough to sway her. "You're a malicious little jerk who takes things that don't belong to him."

"You don't know what you're talking about."

"Don't I?" She put on her best know-it-all expression. "Sucked any souls lately?"

His expression went flat. "We have a gift. And if we can't use it? Then what happens?"

"The rest of us live happily ever after?"

"Our magic helps people. If we don't have the magic, we don't get to help."

Her eyebrows shot up. "Help? Name *one* thing Reapers have done to help *anyone*."

"What we do is confidential."

"What you do is *nothing*. I've heard the 'confidential' story before, Sebastian. You think they don't try to sway us with the nonsense?"

Okay, I wasn't thrilled my BFF and a Reaper were arguing in the middle of a bridge, magic or not. But this was stuff I hadn't heard about before.

"Who is 'they'?" I asked. "And what's confidential?"

" 'They' are the Scions," Scout said, narrowed gaze on Sebastian. "The ones who make decisions for the Dark Elite. And the confidential crap is just that—a load of crap."

Sebastian looked at me. "It's a long story, and there are details I can't reveal. But we do help people. I promise you, Lily."

Scout was standing there, but I still felt like he was saying that just to me. I definitely believed they were doing secret things; I just wasn't convinced they were for anyone's good but their own. Willing to believe? Maybe. But I was going to need hard evidence, and we didn't have time for that kind of proof today. So I changed the subject.

"Let's save the argument for another time," I said. "Right now we have a more immediate problem."

"She's your cousin," Scout said. "You can just call her up and tell her to give you your magic back."

"If she's done something, invented something, whatever, that takes magic away from whoever she wants, do you think she'll just give it back to me because I ask her? She's too manipulative for that, and I don't even know if she *can*. Besides, I'm not going to help her do whatever she's doing. That's not the way it's supposed to work. Everybody makes their own decisions about whether to keep their magic or not. That goes for you and us."

"But not the humans whose souls you take?"

"Are you so sure about that?"

Scout growled, and I could see we were getting nowhere fast. It was time to talk about concrete options or they were going to start slap fighting right here on the bridge.

"Fine," I said. "You two can agree to disagree." I looked at Sebastian. "Does Jeremiah know about Fayden?"

"Not yet. She's my cousin," he said, pity in his voice. "He'll go postal. I don't want her to get hurt."

"Where can we find her?" Scout asked.

"I don't know. Her apartment is in Hyde Park near U of C. She wasn't there. I've called her a few times, but no answer. I haven't talked to her mom yet. I didn't want to scare her if I wasn't sure what was going on."

"She hasn't been in Chicago very long," I said. "How many hiding places could she even know about? Wait." I pointed at Sebastian. "You played tour guide. Where did you take her? I mean, did she seem really interested in anywhere in particular? Was there anything unusual she really wanted to see?"

He frowned and looked down at the ground as he considered. "Not that I can think of. I showed her all the tourist spots. Field Museum. Navy Pier. Wrigley Field. The planetarium. She hadn't been to Chicago in years. She wanted to see pretty much everything."

I nibbled on the edge of my thumb as I racked my brain, trying to figure out our next move. This was when the crew from *Scooby Doo* or *Buffy* or *Star Trek* or one of those other shows where people solved a mystery at the end would have been really handy.

"If I tell Jeremiah," he finally said, "he'll rush in and try to take whatever is there for his own use."

"He's your boss."

"But that doesn't mean I do everything he tells me. And that definitely doesn't mean I want him using Fayden. If this is really her doing, I'm not a fan of it. But I wouldn't be a fan of Jeremiah doing it, either, and I don't think he could stop himself. Not when there's that much power up for grabs."

Scout and Sebastian looked at each other for a minute, like they were taking each other's measure.

"Perhaps an agreement could be worked out," he carefully said.

"I'm listening," Scout said.

"You need Jeremiah off your back. I need you to take care of Fayden because you'll be nicer to her than he would."

"How do we know we can trust you?" Scout asked.

"You can't. That's the nature of trust—it's always a risk. And I'm not crazy about trusting someone I know hates me. But what better options do we have?"

Hands on her hips, Scout looked at him for a minute. Finally, she held out a hand. "Deal under those terms. The détente is extended between your crew and mine until Fayden is neutralized."

He held out his hand, and they shook on it. "Deal." He gave me a nod, then turned and headed back down the bridge again. He met Alex and the tall girl and must have given them a little bit of a summary because they both gave us dirty looks. Maybe they weren't thrilled about the plan . . . or maybe he'd told them what Scout had said about Reapers.

When I turned around again, Scout was leaning over the railing, her fingers linked together over the water. I joined her.

"Do you think he's telling the truth?"

She laughed, but it wasn't a happy laugh.

"What about the confidentiality stuff? Do you think they're really helping people?"

She sighed, and it sounded tired. "A few years ago, there was a big Dark Elite PR campaign about Reapers being secret government weapons—helping solve crimes and fix problems and stuff. But no one believed it. It was made up."

That was the part that bothered me—how could she know it was made up any more than she could know it was true?

"So what do we do now?"

"We tell Daniel," she said. "And we hope he likes the deal we just worked out."

My fingers were crossed.

16

After the excitement of our morning meeting, classes passed by in a blur. The teachers still technically did the teaching, but everybody was focused on parents' night. Dinner was actually awesome—the girls attending parents' night got a full-on catered meal, so the kitchen staff didn't have time to cook a separate round of slurry for us. Instead, they ordered pizzas. A lot of pizzas. The bites I choked down were delicious, but I was nervous enough about our lingering problems that I didn't have much of an appetite.

Study hall was also canceled, which made our evening plans a lot simpler. As soon as we made it back to the room after dinner, Scout dialed up Gaslight Goods, switched it to speakerphone, and put the phone down on the table.

"Gaslight Goods. Let us be your light in the midst of life's darkness, the sunlight in your foggy day, the candle in your wind. This is Kite. How can I help you today?"

I grimaced. That was their opener?

"Kite, it's Scout."

"Hi, Scout. What can I do you for?"

"Information," she said. "We need to know what Fayden Campbell bought from your store. Do you by chance remember what that was?"

"I'm sorry, Scout, I don't. I didn't process her order."

"Kite," Scout said, her tone serious. "We have a really strong suspicion that she's behind the blackout. If you tell me what she bought, that might help us stop her. But if we can't stop her, and no one has magic, pretty soon she will be your *only real customer*. I will not be dropping my parents' hard-earned dough on the newest-fangled salt because I will have no magic. And nobody else will, either. Is that what you want?"

There was silence on the line. Then Kite said, "I don't know . . . but I could probably look it up on the computer for you."

Hands in the air, Scout did a weird little dance that was fifty percent running, fifty percent jumping, and one hundred percent awkward.

"Yes, please," she said.

" 'Kay," he said. "And sorry; you know I have to do this."

I didn't know what he was about to do, but it sounded suspicious to me. But not to Scout, apparently.

"Go ahead," she said.

Kite cleared his throat. "Gaslight Goods is a nonparty to any disputes among members of the Dark Elite. Gaslight Goods has an official position of neutrality with respect to any such disputes, and the provision of information to one party or other is not an indication in a change in that position, nor a statement of support. All rights of Gaslight Goods are reserved. Phew," he added. "Sorry about that."

"No worries."

"So, now that that's out of the way, here's what she bought."

Scout snatched up the same notebook she'd been using for our list and a purple pen, tilted and ready to write.

"Quartz. Pink salt. Some heavy-duty magnets. Dried feverfew. Oh, and a rod of copper. That just came in yesterday, actually."

"That's it?" she asked.

"That's it."

"Okay. Thanks, Kite. If it turns out we're right, you'll be the first person we call."

"I'd appreciate it. I've got to run. Later, Scout." Kite hung up the phone, and Scout stuffed hers away again.

"What was with the legalese?" I asked.

"That's the official disclaimer that they're still neutral even if they give you information. It's so they don't get blamed for stuff the Reapers or Adepts do."

"Why didn't they have to do it before—when we were in the store, I mean?"

Scout shrugged. "That was just chatting. You get official, with people looking up records, and they want to keep their names out of the discussion. That's the disclaimer."

Magical rules were just bizarro. But that wasn't important. "So we know what she bought. Does that help you?"

Scout looked down at her paper. "This isn't stuff you just buy for the heck of it. So whatever she's doing with the blackout, it's magical. She has created a spell, a hex, a machine, something that has taken away all of our power—"

"Except hers," I finished.

"Exactly. I don't know exactly what she's brewing up. I'm going to have to think about it, let it float around in my head a little. But I'll figure it out." She waved the notebook. "This is the key, Lily. We still have work to do, but this is the key."

Thank goodness I'd finally done something right.

An hour later Scout had scribbled through a bunch of pages in the notebook and she'd chomped through half a pack of gum.

"I chew gum when I'm working magical equations," she said.

I still wasn't entirely sure what was meant by "equations." I flipped through the pages of her notebook, which were filled with what looked like those puzzles where a picture is supposed to symbolize a word—an image of an eye is supposed to mean "I" and so forth.

In Scout's case, the drawings looked a lot like Egyptian hieroglyphics. "Are you, like, trying to add salt to quartz and then subtract the magnets or—"

She flopped back on the bed. "I have no idea what I'm trying to do. None of these things go together. It's like trying to add blue and twelve and a dandelion. That kind of math doesn't work."

"So you don't have any ideas?"

"Not unless"—she picked up her notebook and turned it so that she was reading it upside down—"Fayden Campbell is attempting to work bacon-typewriter-earmuff magic."

"That seems unlikely."

"Yep." She tossed the notebook back on the bed and rubbed her hands over her face. "What am I missing? What am I missing?"

"Is there, like, a secret ingredient? Like a catalyst or something? Like, you have to heat everything up, or maybe you have to use the things in a particular order?"

"That's magic 101, Parker. All accounted for."

It might be introductory magic for an Adept who'd been doing it for years, but it was pretty advanced stuff for me.

"So we know what she bought, but we don't know why she bought it?"

"Yep."

"And we can't try to fix the magical blackout if we don't know how she made it happen in the first place."

"Since we have no magic because of said magical blackout, that is correct."

I put a hand on her arm. "It may be time to accept temporary defeat. Or at least to call Daniel."

She sighed. "I'll call him," she promised. "But I'm not calling it defeat. How about 'temporary not-knowingness'?"

"Whatever gets you through the night, Scout."

She updated Daniel, and he invited us into the Enclave to work on the magical problem.

When we emerged from her room to head out into the tunnels, the suite was empty; Amie and Lesley were probably both at parents' night.

The school was equally empty. We could hear the sounds of chatting and music as we walked through the buildings, but we never actually saw the party. We walked silently to the basement door and through the giant metal one, then pulled it shut behind us.

We made it only twenty yards before we stopped short, hearts suddenly pounding.

The tall girl who'd been at the bridge with Sebastian stood in the middle of the tunnel. She wore jeans, knee-high boots, and a long-sleeved top, and she bobbed to the sound of music we could hear faintly from her white earbuds. She had no flashlight, and had apparently been skulking in the dark waiting for us to arrive.

I swallowed down fear, and both Scout and I held up our flashlights like baseball bats. They were the only weapons we had. "Don't come one step closer."

She pulled out her earbuds, stuck them in a jeans pocket, and held up her hands. "I'm not going to."

"Then why are you in our tunnels?"

"It's nice to meet you, too. I'm Kiara. Sebastian sent me."

Scout's eyes narrowed. "To do what?"

"To keep an eye on the door and make sure none of Jeremiah's Reapers get into the school tonight."

You could have pushed me over with a feather.

"Could you say that again?" I asked, and Kiara smiled a little.

"You made a deal on the bridge," she said. "You agreed to help Sebastian's cousin without turning her over to Jeremiah. In return, we agreed to keep him out of your hair." She shrugged. "At least as much as we can without giving ourselves up."

"You aren't fans of his, either?" I wondered.

"Let's just say we have different opinions about how the Dark Elite should operate."

She seemed sincere to me, but Scout wasn't so easily persuaded. "How do we know you aren't just making this up? That you won't sneak into the school as soon as we walk away?"

Kiara shrugged. "You don't. But I could have waited for you to leave and snuck in without your knowing it. Sebastian trusts you, or at least he trusts her." She gestured toward me. "And I trust Sebastian."

"What will you do if Jeremiah's Reapers show up?" I wondered. "Won't they be suspicious if you don't let them into the school?"

Her eyes sparkled a little. She looked even prettier when she did it, but a little scarier, too. "You let me worry about that."

Scout and I looked at each other for a moment, silently debating what to do.

"Could you excuse us for a minute?" Scout asked. Without waiting for Kiara to answer, she grabbed my hand and pulled me down the tunnel and around the corner.

"Crap on toast. Could these people just give us a break for, like, a couple of days?"

"Apparently not," I said. "What do you want to do?"

Scout scratched her head and looked really confused. "I don't know. I mean, can we just leave her here? In the tunnels right by the school?"

"She didn't have to tell us she was here. She made a good point."

"Yeah, but maybe that's just some kind of ploy so she can walk right in."

Maybe, but I doubted it. It wouldn't have surprised me if Sebastian had multiple motives in helping us out—like getting his own magic back—but this didn't seem like the kind of thing he'd waste effort on.

"How about this," I suggested. "Let's trust her for now, and as soon as we get to the Enclave, we tell Daniel. Maybe he knows more about this movement of underground Reapers or something, and if it's really stinky he can send us back out or call Foley and give her a heads-up."

Scout pointed at the tunnel. "Technically, wouldn't they be underground-underground Reapers?"

"Not the point. Is that okay with you? And I don't think we have a better option," I added when she didn't respond.

"Fine, fine. But let's add this to the list of things you get to explain to Daniel."

"Why do I have to explain it?"

"Because you got us mixed up in this Reaper mess."

I rolled my eyes and walked back to where we'd left Kiara. Scout eventually followed me.

"You know," I told her, "technically the brat pack got me wrapped up in this Reaper mess, since they're the ones who locked me in the City Room. Can't we just blame it on them?"

She nodded. "You're right. We should blame it on them. That just feels good."

Or at least as good as it was going to get tonight.

We made Kiara swear on her iPod that she meant no harm to the school. I'm sure that probably didn't have much impact on whether she'd wreak havoc or not, but it seemed to make Scout feel better.

Meeting Kiara in the tunnel gave the night a weird vibe, and that vibe continued when we got to the Enclave. Katie and Smith were absent, and they weren't the only ones. Jason hadn't shown up.

Apparently noticing the same thing, Scout squeezed my hand when we walked inside.

While we might have been missing an Adept, we had a ton more *stuff.* The room was full of goodies pulled directly from the shelves at Gaslight Goods. Candles. Icons. Salts in every color. Squares of velvet and silk. Herbs in tiny glass jars. The empty Gaslight Goods bags were scattered on the floor where they'd been emptied.

"Kite must really want his customers back," Scout said, grinning wildly.

"He's spending money to make money," I suggested.

"I guess so." She started darting around the room from pile to pile, checking out all the stuff Kite had left. "Oh, my God, it's like those books where you fall asleep in a museum and you get to use all the cool stuff while you're asleep *except I'm actually awake.*"

She bubbled on for ten more minutes. And when she was done with her inspection, she threw her messenger bag on the table, pointed at Jill, Jamie, and Paul, and put them to work mixing ingredients and writing out that weird hieroglyphic math on a dry-erase board Kite had also donated.

As far as I could tell, cat plus monkey equaled water bottle.

"And so we begin," she said, and sat down at a table. Full of energy and ready to work, she immediately pulled out a notebook and started writing.

Two hours later things had gone completely downhill.

Scout wasn't any closer to a solution than she had been when we arrived, even with all the goodies, and the Enclave looked like a *wreck.* There were balled up pieces of paper everywhere, open books, and the dry-erase board was covered on both sides. She seemed completely flustered by the set of materials Fayden had bought, and couldn't figure out how to reverse-engineer whatever magic Fayden had worked.

I tried to help when I could, but since I was the least experienced Adept, there wasn't a lot I could do.

We took a break when Daniel brought in turkey sandwiches, veggie sandwiches with extra hummus, and drinks for a late-night supper. Since I hadn't eaten much at dinner, I pretty much scarfed it down. Scout ate more slowly, picking at her own sammie as she stared hopelessly at the clutter around her. I knew she was frustrated, and I hated that I couldn't do anything. But I didn't get the magical math, so I had no idea how to help. It was also getting late. We were all tired, and irritable, and missing our magic. That was a pretty bad combination.

Scout, finished with her sandwich, suddenly threw a dry-erase marker across the room.

The Enclave went silent.

"Scout?" Daniel asked.

"I'm just . . . I am so *mad*. Who does she think she is, that she has the right to do this? To control who has and doesn't have magic, and when they get to use it? How is that possibly fair?"

"Hey, we're all in the same boat," Paul said. "It's not like you're the only one with troubles."

"Oh, I am well aware of that, Paul. Well aware." Her voice was snippy and tired, and from the way they glared at each other across the room, this conversation wasn't going to end well. It seemed most likely to end at the First Immanuel recovery room—as had the last Adepts who'd gotten snippy with one another.

"Hey, hey," Daniel said. "Everybody bring it down a notch."

"How am I supposed to bring it down when I am the only one here working on this? I'm trying to reverse engineer magic I haven't even seen. I don't even know where she is, much less what she's managed to make!"

"We're all trying," Daniel said. "All of us. You know what? Let's call it a night. We're all tired and we're all stressed out. We can reconvene tomorrow night after classes. We'll leave all the experiments right where they are, and you can come right back to them."

"Tomorrow is the dance," Michael said. "We can't miss Sneak."

"I forgot about Sneak," Daniel said. "I know you all have lives and things to do. This situation isn't great, but until Fayden makes another move, it's not crucial. Let's just all get some sleep, and maybe we'll have some sort of brainstorm tomorrow. I'll talk to the Council and see if they have any leads on Fayden, maybe where she is. We'll figure this out," he promised.

If only the rest of us could be so sure.

We'd closed the door on the Enclave only when Jason emerged from the tunnels in jeans and a long-sleeved T-shirt. He looked uncomfortable, and he wasn't the only one. Seeing him was like a punch in the gut. What was I supposed to say? Supposed to feel? Glad to see him? Angry that I was only just seeing him now?

"Hey," Michael said.

Jason nodded.

"Michael," Scout said, "why don't we go talk about . . . the . . . color of your tuxedo for the dance."

"I have to wear a tuxedo?" he whined, but followed along when Scout dragged him down the hall.

"How are you?" Jason asked.

"I'm fine." It was a lie, but what was I supposed to say?

"I wanted to talk to you about all this."

"I'm sorry I hurt you," I said. "It wasn't my intention."

He nodded. "I know. It's just—we've come into this world differently. You see things differently than I do, and differently than my family does. I don't know. I'm just really confused right now, and my family is putting all this pressure on me. I just needed you to be on my side."

"I am on your side," I said. "But sometimes right and wrong aren't as clear as we want them to be. If you can't trust me right now, I understand. I don't agree with it, but I understand it. It's just that sometimes I have to trust myself. And this is one of those times."

He nodded. "I know."

We stood there in silence for another few minutes, and it felt like we hadn't known each other at all. And I guessed we definitely weren't going to the dance together.

"Well," he finally said, "it's late. I should get going."

I couldn't do anything but nod and watch as he walked away.

I met Scout a couple of tunnels up, and at her questioning eyes, shook my head. She strode toward me and gave me a hug.

"He'll come around," she whispered. "He'll come around, or he won't. And if he doesn't, it's his loss."

"Thanks," I said.

We walked quietly back to St. Sophia's, and approached the

door to the school expecting to see Kiara. But she was gone. She'd been replaced . . . by Sebastian.

He was sitting on the floor, his back to the door. He stood up as we approached.

"What are you doing here?" I asked.

"Guarding the school. Kiara has a paper due, so it was my turn. How are . . . plans?" he carefully asked.

"They're fine," Scout said, "which is all you need to know."

At her snippy tone, Sebastian looked at me. I shrugged. "We're working on it."

"You won't hurt her?"

"We don't plan on it," Scout said. "And the odds go up a lot if we can get our work done without Reaper intervention."

"That's why I'm here."

"And we appreciate it," I added, earning me an elbow jab from Scout.

"I'm standing right here," he dryly said.

"He doesn't have to be standing here," I pointed out. "And I'm not taking anyone's side, but right now both sides need all the friends we can get and all the sleep we can get, too, 'cause I'm really tired. So can we all be happy and just go to bed, please?"

Scout's lip was still curled, but she nodded. "Fine. But if he destroys the school while we sleep, I'm blaming you."

"I accept that blame," I said, and waited until Sebastian moved over a little to unlock and open the vault door. Scout scooted inside, but I glanced back at Sebastian.

"If this is all a ploy—" I began, but he reached out and touched my chin.

"I told you we'd make a good team, and we do. Someday, maybe you can do a favor for me."

Our eyes met for a brief but weirdly electric second. Then I turned away.

"And so it begins," I muttered, and walked through the door, my skin still tingling where he'd touched me.

I spun the door's flywheel and slid home the metal bar that locked it in place. I nearly jumped when I turned around and found Scout leaning against the wall and staring at me, arms crossed.

"What?"

"Flirting much?"

"I wasn't flirting."

"He was."

Yeah, probably so. But I didn't have any more energy to deal with Sebastian Born today. I'd worry about him tomorrow. . . .

17

The St. Sophia's alumnae who paid the rental fee for the Field Museum may have been wealthy, but they weren't so wealthy that they could close down the museum for the entire day. That meant we had a full day of classes before we could head out to hang decorations. Although only a few of us were on the planning committee, everybody got dragged into the decorating. We had only a few hours between the closing of the museum and the start of the party, so we needed as many "St. Sophia's Girls" as we could find to get things ready.

When classes were over, everyone hustled around, grabbing their dresses, makeup kits, and final party decorations. The school was in a mad rush.

Since I hadn't had time to arrange anything else, I took Scout up on her offer to let me borrow her green dress. It may have cost a fortune—and I was still nervous about the putrescence issue—but it was better than wearing my St. Sophia's uniform to Sneak, even if I didn't have a date. I had no idea what she came up with, but she had a dress bag, too, when she met me in the common room for our trip downstairs.

The limos were all gone tonight, replaced by orange school buses that would ferry us over to the Field Museum. Scout and I got in line with everyone else, the two least excited girls in the pack.

At least she had a date.

St. Sophia's was a boarding school, so it had been months since I'd been on a bus. There was no need to travel to school when you slept next door to it. Turned out, I hadn't really missed much. The cool but dangerous girls still sat in the very back. The uncool girls sat in the front, and the middle was like a no-man's-land of left-overs. It was a minefield.

The bus dropped everyone off in front of the Field Museum. We trudged inside. Honestly, I just wasn't that excited. Not even considering the boy and magic troubles, I wasn't much of a museum person. I loved to draw, but museums were usually quiet and stuffy, and I wasn't one for walking around in silence staring at paintings. Don't get me wrong—I liked the paintings—it was the atmosphere that sucked. Galleries should be loud, happy places, full of people talking about art and thinking about art and enjoying the experience. Instead, they felt more like libraries, where you were only supposed to whisper. That was not my cup of tea.

But when we arrived, I thought maybe I hadn't given the Field Museum enough credit.

From the outside, the museum looked like a giant palace. It was a white stone rectangle building with huge columns in front. And the inside wasn't bad, either. Scout and I took a minitour before getting down to the decorating. There was a giant open room in the middle of the first floor. It was two stories high and held the skeleton of an entire Tyrannosaurus rex. The rooms to the side held glass cases full of historical bits. Clothes, tools, jewelry, baskets, weapons, and everything else you could think of. There were rooms of Native American artifacts, Aztec pottery, and Egyptian sculptures.

The party was being held in the main room on the first floor. Half the space had been filled by round tables arranged by the rental company our wealthy alumnae had hired. One of the Montclare boys was playing DJ at the other end in front of a dance area.

When the decorations went up, this place was going to look unbelievable. At least, if you were at the dance with a date and were into that kind of romantic stuff. Me? I'd been dumped by someone who didn't even have the guts to tell me I'd been dumped.

I wasn't sure whether to be sad or angry. I opted for angry. It felt a lot better.

We spent an hour hanging up garland and black glittery decorations, although the rental company had done most of the hard work. They put huge black candelabra on the tables and hung a banner that read ST. SOPHIA'S SNEAK from one of the balconies. The stuff we'd made definitely added a cool "graveyard" vibe, but the alumnae had already gone all out.

When the decorations were done, we headed off to a couple of conference rooms to get ready. I wasn't thrilled about changing clothes in front of everyone else, but everyone was so worried about their own hair and makeup that they hardly noticed anyone else was in the room.

Scout's parents may be self-centered, but they knew how to pick out a dress. Luckily, we were about the same size so it fit like a glove. I paired it with some black heels, and Scout helped me pin my hair into a messy updo with lots of twisty tendrils falling around. Add some eyeliner, and I was done.

Scout surprised me, too. When she unzipped her own dress bag, I just about fell over. Inside it was a really simple, but totally beautiful, black dress. It was a sleeveless sheath that fell just below her knees, and had a heart-shaped neckline that was totally flattering. She wore bright yellow heels and some chunky jewelry, and put enough product in her hair that it did the porcupine/pincushion thing.

"You look like a Goth princess," I told her.

"Oh, my God, I was going to say the same thing to you. You know, cheesy as this party is, we should totally get a picture of ourselves. Who knows when we'll have time to dress up again?"

"So true," I said, and pulled out my cell phone for a picture. I was playing with the dials to figure out how to get the flash to work, when genius struck me.

I froze, then looked at Scout.

"What?" Scout said, eyes wild. "Is there a Reaper in here?"

"I know how we can find out where Fayden is."

She smiled a little, and nodded. "I knew that dress was going to work for you, Parker, I just knew it."

Dressed in our party finest, we popped back into the hallway, and I dialed up Sebastian. My nerves were already taut, and the fact that he didn't answer until the fifth ring didn't exactly help.

"Lily?"

"Camera!" I exclaimed. "Fayden had that big camera around her neck. When you gave her the tour of the city, did she take pictures of anything in particular?"

"As a matter of fact, I kept making fun of her because she had that huge camera but didn't take pictures of anything until . . ."

"Until what?" I asked, my heart beginning to race as we got closer to our answer.

"The old pumping station on Michigan Avenue—it's not far from the Hancock building. It used to have all these pipes inside, but I'm not sure what's in there now. It's all boarded up for remodeling or something."

"And she took pictures of it?" I asked.

"Yeah, and we had to be careful because there were No Trespassing signs all over the place. I guess they want to turn it into some kind of museum, but the money hasn't come through."

"So she took a bunch of pictures of an empty industrial building," I summed up. "That doesn't sound at all suspicious. Thanks, Sebastian."

"Sure. If you find anything out, will you let me know?"

"Of course," I said, not entirely sure whether I meant it or not. I hung up the phone and looked at Scout. "I think there's a pretty good chance we know where Fayden Campbell is." I explained what Sebastian had said.

"I need to look at the pumping station," she agreed. "That's the only way I'm going to make any progress on the spell."

I checked the time. "The dance starts in, like, an hour. Maybe we should wait for Michael."

"So Fayden can run away from us again? No, thanks." She pulled out her own phone. "I'm just going to have him meet us at the Enclave—and everyone else. God willing, I'll figure something out and we can get the spell working tonight."

"Fine," I said, putting my phone away again. "Let's go see the evil Reaper headquarters."

Scout jumped around and clapped her hands like I'd given her a unicorn for her birthday.

We headed for the museum's front door, but didn't make it very far.

"Where do you think you're going?"

We glanced back at Mary Katherine, who stood behind us in a slinky gold dress that left very little to the imagination. Veronica and Amie stood behind her, also dressed for the dance. Their gowns were longer and more princessy than M.K.'s.

"We were just going to get some fresh air. Stuffy in here in all this makeup," Scout said, fanning her face.

"We haven't seen you around lately," M.K. said to me.

"We've been working in our rooms. You know, 'cause we're uncool and we never leave them." The words sounded corny, but what else was I supposed to say? We have a magical prodigy to go spy on?

Not surprisingly, M.K. didn't look convinced. But this time, it was Veronica who spoke.

"Just leave them alone," she said. "We need to put the confetti on the tables."

M.K. slowly looked behind her, apparently shocked that she'd intervened. I understood the emotion. "Are you serious?"

"I'm serious about the party," Veronica said, grabbing her hand. "I don't want these little twerps getting in the way. Let's go."

M.K. rolled her eyes, clearly not convinced she shouldn't make fun of us for a while, but let Veronica pull her back toward the party room. They bounced back into the main hall, but not before

Veronica glanced back and looked right at me. She didn't say anything before turning around again.

"What do you think that was about?" Scout whispered.

"Maybe Nicu told her about us? I don't know, and I'm deciding not to worry about it. There are just not enough hours in the day."

"I hear ya."

We were pretty far down Michigan Avenue, so we snuck out to a cab for the ride to the pumping station. When we arrived a few minutes later, we stopped near a group of trees and scoped it out.

The building was located in a little park tucked between skyscrapers—the type people tended to ignore as they rushed around to high-end shops. It was short and made of big chunks of rough stone. There were rectangular windows all the way around it, two on each side, all placed the same distance apart. If you sliced it down the middle like a cake, both sides would look exactly the same.

And all the windows were covered on the inside with blue paper. It was thick enough that I couldn't tell whether the lights inside were on or off, but there was no movement in or around the building, so we moved closer.

A sign had been posted a few yards away from the door. It was from some development company and talked about how the building was going to be rehabbed. But that rehab was months away, which explained the NO TRESPASSING warning below it.

"It doesn't look like we can see much from out here," I whispered.

"Let's walk around," Scout said, and we tiptoed around three of the building's four sides. Every window was covered, so we couldn't get even a small peek inside.

Finally, on the fourth and final side, we struck gold. Someone hadn't been entirely careful putting the blue paper over one of the windows, and the bottom corners had started to roll up, giving us two little views of the interior of the building.

Scout and I nodded at each other . . . and leaned in.

She squeaked almost immediately.

Sebastian had been right—there were huge pipes in the room, each one probably three or four feet wide. They lay across the floor in a complicated grid pattern, and at the end of each pipe was a huge piece of machinery. Maybe a generator or something. The size of the things was just amazing. But that wasn't the most interesting thing about the pumping station.

The entire room was filled with bright blue light—emanating from a huge circle that floated in the air above the pipes. It had to be twenty feet wide, and it was empty in the middle—like a giant's bracelet. It rotated slowly, humming as it moved.

"Oh, my God, Lils, are you seeing this?"

"I'm seeing . . . I'm seeing something. I'm not sure what."

Scout pressed a hand to the glass, and she didn't look nearly as horrified as I'd expected.

"This is a bad thing, remember?"

"Oh, I know," Scout said. "But it's like the kid in the science fair who creates face-eating bacteria. The idea is awful, but you have to be impressed by the initiative."

"I guess. What is it, exactly?"

"Some kind of magic spool, I think. Like a spindle." Her voice got even quieter, and I think she forgot I was there. It sounded like she was just talking it over. "Pulling all the magic into it, maybe, with some kind of controls so she can take it away in parts. First the Adepts, then the Reapers. That's probably the big plan for later—use it to divvy up the magic so she can hand it over to whomever she wants whenever she wants."

While Scout thought it through, I scanned the rest of the room. Fayden Campbell stood in one corner dressed in a black bodysuit like a comic book bad girl, her hair pulled into a high ponytail, her signature glasses perched on her nose.

And she wasn't alone. There were a few other people in the room. I guess they wanted to be part of her new world order, at least if our theory was right. And one of them looked familiar. . . .

"That's Charlie Andrews," I told Scout, pointing him out. "The Reaper who was attacking Lisbeth. The guy I hit with a suitcase."

"We wondered why he was Reaping out in the open," she said. "I guess we know."

"She isn't working alone," I whispered. "That explains how she managed this with firespell. Maybe it's also why you haven't been able to figure out how she made the magic—why the equations didn't make sense. It's because she's not the only one doing it. It's the combination of *their* magic, too."

"Holy toast, Parker, that is a good idea. Grab your phone," she added, as she pulled hers out. "Get pictures of their faces. Maybe we can figure out who the rest of them are and what their powers are."

"And if we do that, you have a little more information to add to the equation."

She nodded and began snapping photos. I did the same, and hoped we'd find the answers she needed.

We didn't press our luck, and got out of there was soon as we had enough pictures. And as soon as we were a safe distance away from the building, we called Daniel and filled him in. All the Adepts—except Jason—agreed to meet back at the Enclave to work on the magic solution. I wasn't sure if seeing the spindle was going to actually help out Scout, but she definitely seemed energized. It certainly couldn't have hurt.

The problem was, we were blocks from St. Sophia's, and we were even farther from the Enclave. And, we were aboveground. There were ways to get into the tunnel from street level without having to sneak back into St. Sophia's and out again. But they involved walking through the Pedway.

The Pedway was a system of tunnels and passageways that ran through buildings in downtown Chicago and gave people a way to move through the city in the wintertime. There were access points from the Pedway to the tunnels, but there was a catch. The Pedway was the territory of vampires, and vampires didn't like Adepts. They also didn't really like competing vampire covens. That was precisely the fight Veronica had walked into.

"We need the Pedway," Scout said, looking at a map on her phone. "There's an entrance in a building a block from here, and we can hop right into the tunnels. It will be so much faster than going the long way."

"And it risks getting caught in a vampire fight that will take us a lot longer to deal with," I pointed out.

"There is one thing we could do."

"What's that?"

"You could call your favorite vampire and ask him for an escort."

I just blinked at her. "You cannot be serious. I already had to run one errand for him this week."

"Speed," Scout stressed. "We need it. He can give it to us."

I sighed, but knew I'd been beaten. So I dialed up Nicu and when he answered, gave him our address. "We need to get into the tunnels, and we have to go into the Pedway to do that. Can you meet us and, like, escort us through?"

His voice was grumbly and cold. "What will you do for me in return?"

I rolled my eyes. "Haven't I done enough for you this week? Like, given you a happily-ever-after with one of St. Sophia's finest?"

"I do not understand your sarcasm."

Scout tapped her watch impatiently.

"Fine," I said. "What do you want in return?"

He was quiet for a moment. "I wish to attend this dance I have heard about."

You could have bowled me over. "Are you asking my permission to take Veronica Lively to Sneak?"

Scout made a gagging sound.

"It is your territory," Nicu said. "It is only appropriate that I ask for your permission before I enter it."

"Fine," I said, glad *someone* wanted to go to the dance. "Go to the dance. Live happily ever after. Can you just meet us?"

"I will meet you. Two minutes."

I figured he was exaggerating, but it took three minutes for

Scout and me to take the elevator down into the building's basement Pedway access, and Nicu was already waiting for us.

In a *tuxedo*.

I'll be honest—he cleaned up pretty well.

"You look . . . lovely," he said, glancing between Scout and me.

"Thanks," she said. "But let's get this show on the road. We have spells to cast."

"You can teach me to slow dance?" he asked, as we walked down the Pedway.

Could this night possibly get any weirder?

18

Why did I even ask questions like that? Because no sooner did I ask it than I ended up in a room beneath the city, trying to explain to a bunch of teenagers how we'd just seen a magical floating spool in a deserted building on Michigan Avenue.

Unfortunately, even having seen the pumping station and the magic Fayden had made, Scout didn't have any better ideas about how to stop it. For nearly an hour—while the rest of the St. Sophia's girls were starting to get their dance on—Scout frantically scribbled numbers and figures and symbols that didn't mean anything to me on the dry-erase board . . . and unfortunately didn't seem to mean much to her, either.

Right now it looked like a bad abstract drawn by a bunch of kindergartners. I could do better than that. I may not be able to understand their equations . . . but I could draw.

Ooooh, I thought. That was something. "Maybe we're going about this the wrong way."

"How so?" Daniel asked.

"We need a new perspective." I walked over to the dry-erase board. "Can I erase this?"

"Not that it's doing any good," Scout said, so I took that as permission, swabbed it down with an eraser, and grabbed a marker.

"Let's think about the magic like a story."

"Like a story?" Paul asked. "How?"

"Um," I said for a second, pausing as I tried to actually figure out what I might have meant. Thank goodness, an idea popped into my head. "Well, instead of thinking about how the parts go together, like a recipe, we'll storyboard it, like we're deciding which scenes to put in a movie."

I drew a grid on the board, three squares across and two squares down, six squares in all. "Now we need to fill in the pictures." In the last square, I drew a little caricature of Scout casting a spell.

"The happily-ever-after is that we get our magic back," Paul said.

"Exactly. So, what has to happen in the square before that one for you to get your magic back?"

Scout leaned forward at the table, and that's when I knew I had her attention. "Fayden's magic has to be interrupted."

"Like, um, a cog in the wheel?" I asked.

"Yes!"

In the next to last frame, I drew Fayden's circle, then smudged away a little part at the top to show that it had been broken; then I looked back at the room.

"So maybe we don't have to dissect the spell exactly, or know the exact combination of stuff they used to make it. Maybe all we need is to figure out a way to break the circle. And there has to be more than one way to do that, right? Like, um, could we throw something through the circle and break it?"

As an example, in the square before the circle was broken, I drew another, smaller circle with an arrow flying toward it. "Like that? The circle looked like it was just made of light. That should break pretty easily."

"But it's magic," Scout said. "A physical object won't interrupt that kind of magic. Otherwise every time a bit of dust hit the circle the thing would explode."

"Okay," I said, "then we need something magic to throw." I drew little squiggly lines along my arrow.

"Is that supposed to be magic?" Daniel asked, but there was a smile on his face. I blushed a little, forgetting that my studio art teacher—at least when we actually had time for class—was standing in the room.

"Those are magical indication lines. It's a very, you know, technical phenomenon," I totally made up. But he chuckled, and I felt better that the mood was a little lighter. "If only we had some, you know, magic."

Scout jumped off her chair and ran around one table to another, where she flipped through a book on the table. "Parker, Parker, Parker, I love you almost as much as I love strawberry soda. You might actually have something there." She scanned the page, then ran over to the board and snatched up another marker. She popped off the lid and started scribbling.

"So we don't actually have any magic, right? But we need magic to blow a hole in the circle and destroy the spell."

She moved back one more square and drew another arrow.

Then she drew a plus sign and something that looked like a beaker.

"What's in the jar?" I asked.

She put the marker down, then looked back at everyone else in the room, who had gone completely silent. "A pre-spell," she said, fanning out her hands for effect. "An almost-spell. A spell-to-be." She looked back at me. "A spell that isn't actually a spell until it hits the magical catalyst."

"The circle," I guessed.

"Exactly. We rig some kind of projectile, and since we can't actually activate any magic right now, we equip it with a pre-spell. The circle is magic, so as soon as our projectile hits the circle, *ka-pow*. The spell activates and breaks apart the circle, and we all get our magic back."

Dang. I guess drawing on the board had been a pretty good idea. I leaned toward Scout. "I get credit for this, right?"

"Totes," she said, and wrapped me in a big hug. "You helped me get my mojo back."

"Just get me a projectile with pre-spell," I told her. "Then we'll worry about mojo."

And just like that, we went back to work. Which as far as I could tell, meant Jamie, Paul, and Jill mixed ingredients in a big glass bowl while Scout worked out the incantation to go along with the spell. See, there were three parts to every magic spell—intent, incantation, incarnation. She definitely had the intent, and the stuff being mixed together would form the incarnation. The incantation was the part you said aloud that made the spell take root—assuming Scout's theory was right, and putting the spell into the circle would give it enough magic to make the spell work.

Unfortunately, it didn't seem like Scout was feeling the rhymes today.

She stood at the dry-erase board with giant black earphones over her ears, bobbing along to the beat of some hip-hop song she'd downloaded. Every few seconds, she'd lift up her marker and start scribbling something out, and then she'd immediately erase it again.

She had magical writer's block. So far, she'd rejected "Break this circle, so our magic we can encircle!" and "Break this circle, or you're a big fat jerk-el."

Those were truly awful, but to be fair, not much rhymed with "circle."

Hip-hop didn't help. Switching to country didn't help. Musical soundtracks didn't help. Nothing helped until we found a station for Scout that played ragey alternative stuff. Those people were *angry*. But it worked. Scout draped the earphones from a corner of the dry-erase board, and we bounced around to the music until Scout got in the mood. And when the rhyme finally came, I wrote it down while she called it out.

"It's a circle of fear," she sang. "A circle of control. You wanna wreak havoc? Then you have to pay the toll. You take our power. You try to take our souls. But in this case, honey, it's you who's gotta go. We're breaking your circle; we're tearing up your goal, and most of all we're taking back the magic that you stole!"

The room went silent.

For five full minutes, Scout walked back and forth in front of the board, fingers on her chin, mulling it over, deciding whether it passed some unspoken incantation test.

And then, finally, she spoke.

"Okay," she said. "That's our rhyme."

Every Adept in the room let out a *whoop*.

We carefully wrote down the incantation on three different pieces of paper. I had a copy, Scout had a copy, and we gave the third to Daniel for safekeeping. But when it came time to pick the projectile—the thing we'd actually use to break the spell—we were at a loss again.

"If only we really had an arrow," Michael said.

"Then we'd also have to have a bow and someone with really good aim," Scout pointed out. "Too complicated."

"What's our plan to get into the pumping station?" I asked, and everyone looked at me. "The object we pick should be easy to get into the building, right? And easy to actually get into the circle?"

"Right," Scout said with a nod. "We'll want something inconspicuous. They aren't going to want to let us into the building just because we ask nicely."

"Pizza delivery?" Michael suggested.

"Or Chinese," Paul said. "Lots of little containers to hide things."

"I doubt a building of Reaper rejects are going to have takeout delivered to their secret headquarters."

I looked down, and caught sight of the room key around my neck. I'd forgotten to take it off when I'd changed for the dance.

"They probably wouldn't order takeout," I agreed. I pulled the key off and held it out by its ribbon. "But they might talk to a girl with firespell who's all confused about Adepts and Reapers and why they exist."

The room was quiet for a moment.

"You can't," Scout finally said. "You've already risked enough this week."

I shook my head. "Like it or not, I'm the only one they'll believe. Fayden saw me talk to Sebastian, so she knows I'm willing to talk to Reapers. And I'm sure someone has filled her in about how I became an Adept and that I'm new to the scene. It makes more sense that I have doubts about Adepts than anyone else."

"She has a point," Daniel said.

"I don't like it," Scout said. "But it is a good plan."

She held out her hand, and I handed over my key. Silently, she placed it on the top of the table, then sprinkled the concoction the twins had made—which looked like the gray stuff in the bottom of a vacuum cleaner—over it.

But nothing happened. The key just lay under its pile of gray fluff.

"Don't you at least want to say some magic words?" I asked.

She gave me a dry look while wiggling her fingers over the tile. "Hocus pocus alamagokus."

"Really." My voice was flat.

"Abracadabra," she said, this time with more flourish.

"Is something supposed to, I don't know, spark up or something?" I asked.

"It's pre-spell," Scout said, tilting her head at the key. "I'd hoped it might at least light up a little, but until I've actually got magic again, none of my spells have juice. So it won't trigger—it won't spark—until it hits the circle." She looked at me. "Repeat the incantation when you get in there, and then immediately throw the key into the circle."

"What if she misses?" Michael asked.

"She won't miss."

"I won't miss."

Scout and I answered simultaneously. She carefully dusted off the key, then handed it back to me. I put it on again and tucked it into my dress. I probably wasn't going to get zombie putrescence on it, but magical ash and Reaper putrescence? Much more likely.

"As soon as we get our magic back, we'll come rescue you."

I nodded and blew out a breath, and hoped it worked just like that. But I wasn't going to bet on it.

With Nicu having been excused to get to the dance, the Adepts of Enclave Three—except for their werewolf—popped back to street level through a secret shortcut Daniel knew about, and walked toward the pumping station. We stopped at the corner one building over. The pumping station looked the same as it had when we'd snuck out to look at it, the blue paper still covering the windows.

The key around my neck felt like a heavy weight—I was too aware of the magic it held and its importance to Adepts. I was going to have one chance to make this work. If I threw the key and missed, Fayden would undoubtedly figure out that I was up to something and put a stop to it. And if I missed—I'd have no magic.

I had to get this right, and that was a lot of pressure for a not-quite-sixteen-year-old girl. I couldn't legally drive, but I had the fates of hundreds of people with magic in my hands. Awesome.

Luckily, the street was pretty empty, so if we had trouble dealing with Fayden, there were fewer bystanders to injure. But I tried not to think about that. I tried to focus on how relieved I'd feel if the circle was broken and everything was back to (relative) normal again.

"*When*," I reminded myself quietly. "*When* the circle is broken."

But I was really nervous. Even my palms were sweaty. These kinds of things never went as well as they were supposed to.

I touched the key around my neck, then looked at Scout.

"You remember the incantation?"

I nodded. I'd repeated it over and over and over until it was second nature. "I remember. I'll get it done."

"Good girl," she said, and wrapped her arms around me. "Be careful."

"I will."

I blew out a breath, and stepped into the darkness between the buildings. It wasn't but thirty or forty yards to the pumping station, but the walk felt like forever.

Heart racing, I walked up the few steps and knocked on the door. It took two more loud knocks, but finally it squeaked open.

A girl with suspicious eyes and jet-black hair stared back at me. She looked down at my green and lace dress and clearly wasn't impressed. "What?"

My heart was pounding, but I forced myself to smile. "I'm here for the tour."

"Wrong time, wrong place." She gave me an evil smile and tried to close the door again, but I stuck a foot in it.

"I'm pretty sure there's a tour."

The girl growled and opened the door just enough to step outside and glare down at me. "You have the wrong address, kid. Go make trouble somewhere else."

"I have the right address. I need to talk to Fayden."

She blinked at me, then stepped back inside and closed the door in my face. But before I could knock again, she opened it, and this time she was grinning.

It was a predatory grin, and it didn't make me feel any better.

"Come in," she said.

I walked inside and onto a metal balcony that overlooked the giant pipes. I jumped when she slammed the door shut behind me, and blinked from the glare of the circle, which made a low *thrush* sound every time it completed a rotation.

"You're Sebastian's friend."

I turned around. The dark-haired girl was gone, replaced by Fayden Campbell. She wore the same black bodysuit Scout and I had seen her in earlier.

"And you're his cousin. The Reaper."

"I really don't care for that name. It's inaccurate. We borrow energy that replenishes itself. There's no Reaping. But that's not the point. Why are you here?"

I almost started to argue with her, and it took me a second to remember the part I was supposed to play.

"I'm not . . ." My voice sounded nervous, so I cleared my throat and started again. "I'm not sure about this Adept thing."

Fayden arched a very carefully plucked black eyebrow. "Not sure about it?"

Play the role, I told myself, and turned to lean against the railing that overlooked the well of pipes and pumps.

"They just give up," I said. "I'm not saying I agree with what you're doing, but that can't be right, either, can it?" I looked back at her. "Can it?"

Her eyes narrowed, clearly not sure whether to take me seriously. "You tell me," she said.

"I've talked to Sebastian about it. He thinks everything is gray—not just black or white—that I'm being brainwashed by the Adepts. But I don't know what to believe. When I lost my magic, I figured out that you were responsible, and that you can turn magic on and off again. I like that idea."

"Mmm-hmm," she said.

She wasn't buying it. My mom had once told me that the best way to make friends wasn't to tell them about yourself, but to ask them about themselves. So I changed tactics.

"So this circle thing. It turns off magic?"

She looked over at it, admiration in her eyes. She was proud of what she'd made. "It provides control over the distribution of magic."

"So you can be in charge of everyone?"

"So that we can be in charge of ourselves. We are superheroes. We have powers. We can do important things in the world. But not the way we currently exist. Right now we hide from the world. The majority of the Dark Elite eke out an existence while Adepts take the moral high ground. We waste our energies on internal battles fought by teenagers in tunnels. But with this, we become unified again."

"So instead of people making their own decisions about magic, you get to make them on their behalf?"

"That's vastly oversimplified."

It seemed accurate to me.

"The Scions are old-school leaders," she said. "They don't direct. They don't lead. They don't do anything new or interesting. They follow old rules and use old tactics. Jeremiah is the reason I left for California. 'Join us or leave,' he'd said. What kind of option is that? Who does he think he is?"

Her words were coming faster now, and her tone was more intense. There was no doubt she believed what she was saying.

"I did some research. Studied, with my friends, the way of magic." She looked back at me. "There are so many things we can do that he doesn't even know about. But was he swayed? No." Her eyes narrowed. "It's time for him to know what it's like not to have control. To have someone else be in charge for a little while."

"So are you doing this to teach him a lesson, or to make life better for members of the Dark Elite?"

She scowled. However mixed her motives may have been, she didn't like my pointing that out. "My plan, little girl, is magical socialism. We all have a role to play. We will all contribute equally, and we will all have a little magic to use as we will."

While she talked, I nudged a little closer to the railing, judging the distance I had to throw the key. It was at least forty feet. Could I get it that far? I wasn't sure.

I looked back at Fayden. "That's all well and good, but you haven't exactly figured out how to do that, have you? I mean, you clearly know how to take magic away—but you haven't yet figured out how to give it back."

Her expression darkened. "What do you want?"

I'd hit a nerve. Her patience with me wasn't going to last much longer. I was getting close to crunch time, when I was going to have to throw the key. But before I did, since I had only one shot, I thought I might as well ask her to be rational.

"I want you to turn this thing off and give our magic back."

"Fat chance of that." Our conversation apparently over, she took a step forward. I took my chance, reared back my arm, and prepared to throw the key as hard as I could—but something grabbed my hand.

I looked back. It was the dark-haired girl, and her fist was wrapped around mine.

Frick.

"What's this?" she asked.

"My room key," I said, snatching my hand back. "I was going to, you know, throw it at her as a distraction."

The dark-haired girl growled. Fayden had better instincts.

"Let me see that," she said, taking another step closer.

"I would really rather not," I said, peeking over the rail at the pipes below. The drop was a good ten feet. Just far enough that I might make it . . . or I might not. But if I did, I'd have better access to the circle.

What a horrible night to wear a borrowed dress and three-inch heels.

Fayden took another step closer and held out a hand. "I'm going to need you to give me that key right now."

I wrapped the ribbon around my hand, entwining it in my fingers so I wouldn't drop it when I fell.

"I don't think so," I said. I put a hand on the railing, and I jumped.

19

'm not going to lie—it hurt. The pipe was made of metal and the top was round, so I hit it on my knees and then rolled halfway off. The pain startled me enough that the key skittered from my fingers.

"Get her," Fayden yelled from the balcony. Two of her minions made a run for it.

Grimacing, I pulled myself back onto the pipe, then crawled forward to find the key. It had fallen between my pipe and another, and I had to dig my fingers between them to find it. I'd just barely managed to get a finger around the ribbon when a shot of firespell exploded above my head.

"Uncool!" I yelled out. "You shouldn't use magic against people who don't have it." A little more grappling, and I managed to get my pinkie in a loop of ribbon. I pulled up the key and slipped it around my neck again

I glanced back. Two of Fayden's minions—already on the ground floor—were heading toward me.

The pipe was just wide enough to run along, so I hauled butt across it—a pretty impressive feat in heels. As I ran, I began the chant. "It's a circle of fear, a circle of control."

I stopped right in the middle of the pipes, equal distance between the balcony walls and right in the middle of the circle. It was louder down here, the circle *whooshing* as it spun nearly drowning out Fayden's yelling.

But not quite.

"She's chanting a spell!" Fayden yelled out. "Stop her!"

I jumped from one pipe to another, barely avoiding the hands of a minion who reached for me. "You wanna wreak havoc? Then you have to pay the toll."

"You little brat," she said. "You have no idea how hard I've worked for this."

And I don't really care, I silently thought.

Aloud, I kept repeating the incantation. "You take our power. You try to take our souls. But in this case, honey, it's you who's gotta go."

Someone grabbed my ankle, but I kicked myself free. I pulled the key from around my neck and chanted the last bit of the spell.

"We're breaking your circle, we're tearing up your goal, and most of all we're taking back the magic that you stole!"

I lobbed the key—and it landed right in the middle of the spinning wheel. Sparks suddenly flew across the room. I ducked and put my hands over my head as the wheel expanded into a spinning sphere, then exploded in a burst of light and sound and energy that made my hair stand on end. The windows exploded outward, and the pipes creaked and groaned around us as energy shot the length of the pumping station.

After a moment, the room went silent.

I looked up. The wheel of light was gone, leaving a dull blue haze in the room. Neither Fayden nor her minions were anywhere in sight.

Time to make a run for it.

I left the key behind, hopped over the pipe, and hit the ground. I pulled off my shoes and ran toward the stairs, my party heels dangling from my fingers. I took the stairs two at a time, the metal treads biting into my bare feet as I ran. But I didn't care. I just wanted to get out of the building and away from Fayden. I made it to the balcony, ten feet from the door, when she stood up in front of me.

There was a cut on her cheek from where she'd fallen to the floor. She looked mad, and I could feel her energy swell as she gathered it up for a strike.

It took me a minute to remember that I had magic of my own—or I was supposed to, anyway.

I opened myself up to the power in the room, and there was plenty of it. And for a glorious second, I could feel the firespell gathering in my bones.

But only for a second. The more firespell Fayden tried to make, the less I could gather up. It was like there was only a certain amount of power in the room, and she was pulling it all toward her.

"Oh, this is going to be bad," I muttered.

"Yes," she said, an evil grin on her face. "It is. And you deserve it. You ruined what I made. You did this—destroyed something I built. And for what? Because you didn't believe in me? Because you didn't agree with me?"

I wasn't sure if she was talking to me, or just thinking about the things she really wanted to say to Jeremiah.

Either way, this was going to be bad. I tried to pull in a little more firespell of my own, just to reduce the amount she had to work with. It wasn't going to do much good, I knew, but what else could I do?

"When all this falls apart," she said, "it will be your fault."

She wound up her arm to throw the firespell at me, and I closed my eyes, bracing for impact . . . when I heard the roar of a wolf.

My eyes shot open. Fayden was on the ground, a giant silver wolf atop her, little bits of glass in his fur.

It was Jason. He'd come through the window . . . to save me.

He fought with Fayden, but she couldn't get enough traction to throw the firespell. They rolled around and tumbled a bit, and as they did, the power in the room filled up again.

I closed my eyes for a second, blocking out the burst of joy from seeing Jason again, and concentrated on gathering up power.

She slapped at his hide, and he whined a little.

"Jason," I yelled out, when I was as primed as I was going to be. "On three. One, two, three!"

Jason leapt away, and Fayden sat halfway up to stare at me.

"Your turn," I said, and I let the firespell go, sending the entire burst of it directly toward her. Her image wavered as the air warped, and then she fell back and hit the ground with a thud.

Just in time, the other Adepts rushed in through the door, but I had eyes only for the wolf at the other end of the balcony, chartreuse eyes shining. He looked at me, but he didn't come any closer.

"Thank you," I said, but he disappeared out the door.

My heart broke again. Did he hate me so much that he couldn't even stand to be in the same room with me, even after saving me from Fayden?

It was heartbreaking that he'd left, but I tried not to think about it. I did not want to cry in front of a room of Adepts and minions.

Scout jogged over to check me out. "You're okay?"

"I'm fine. The spell worked. The spool exploded. There are still minions down there, I think." To confirm, I looked over the rail. They were definitely still down there, waking up groggily after being hit full-on with the impact of the exploding magic.

"Is she wearing spandex?" Paul asked, tilting his head as he stared down at Fayden.

"Yep. She most definitely is." I looked at Daniel. "She wanted to start some kind of magical socialism, where the amount of everyone's magic was controlled. But mostly I think she was just angry at Jeremiah."

"What a weirdo," Paul said.

"And an unconscious weirdo," Scout said, putting an arm around my shoulders. "And that's what really counts."

One victory at a time, I thought.

We had our magic back. Of course, so did all the Reapers in the city. But it was hardly worth the trouble of going back to fight if we didn't at least stop to celebrate. Scout helped me clean up, and she, Michael, and I headed back to the Field Museum. Daniel promised to get the pumping station cleaned up—and to explain to the cops exactly how Fayden had managed to blow the windows out.

The lights were down and the music was up when we walked back into the party. The place looked phenomenal. Fancy and spooky at the same time, and impressive either way.

Michael didn't waste any time pulling Scout onto the dance floor. She looked back at me, worry in her eyes, but I waved her off. Just because I wasn't going to have a fantastic time didn't mean they shouldn't. Besides—my ex-boyfriend had just saved my life. That was something, right?

Nicu, having gotten us safely to the tunnels, didn't squander his favor. He and Veronica were dancing together in the middle of the room. And although the room was filled with people who looked very happy and very smitten—at least for tonight—there was no mistaking the emotion in their eyes. They looked kind of perfect together, and he even looked kind of normal. Just like a guy at a dance, except for the fact that with one good look in his eyes you could see he wasn't a normal teenager. There was too much knowledge there. He looked like he had an old soul, if that made sense.

I, on the other hand, had a young soul. And a thirsty one. I decided I could use some punch.

I walked around the dance floor to the table with drinks and snacks. There were a few girls nearby, mostly the ones who hadn't come with dates.

I poured a cup of the punch—but sniffed before drinking it. There was no telling what kind of illegal stuff a bunch of rich sixteen-year-olds would sneak into the Sneak punch bowl. But it smelled like fruit punch and ginger ale. Classic punch ingredients. Not great, but not awful.

"Is there any more of that?"

I glanced back.

Jason Shepherd, the disappearing werewolf, stood behind me in a black tuxedo—black bow tie and everything.

He looked so handsome—and I was so surprised to see him there—I couldn't think of a single thing to say. I also nearly dropped my cup.

"I'll maybe just have a drink of yours," he said, gently taking the cup from my hands and finishing it off in a single gulp.

Words returned. "Thanks for the rescue."

"You're welcome," he said, putting the cup down on the table. "I'm sorry I ran off. I had to get dressed."

"You look . . . very nice," I carefully said.

"And you look gorgeous, Lily Parker. But we have unfinished business." While the rest of the dateless girls looked on, Jason took my hand and led me out the door and into the hallway. He pulled me into a quiet alcove, then looked down at me, his blue eyes intent.

"You scared me," he said. "I wasn't sure who to trust. You're new to this and you have this bravery that the rest of us don't have. You have different ideas about what's right and what's wrong. And that's a difficult thing to get used to. Do you think you can forgive me for running away?"

His lips were so close to mine—just hovering there, like a butterfly just out of reach.

"I think you should kiss me," I whispered, and he did.

I felt that kiss all the way from my lips to my toes and back again. His arms were around me, his hands hot against my back, a sharp contrast to the chill in the air. That heat seemed like proof that he was something *else*. Something not like me or Scout or the rest of the Adepts. No better, no worse. Just very, very different.

"I want to try again," he said.

The statement scared me out of my wits, my heart beating like a bass drum in my chest.

"What if you change your mind?" I asked. "What if you disagree with something I do, and you run away because of it? How am I supposed to trust that?"

He put his forehead on mine. "I will always come back, Lily Parker. Because that's who you are to me."

My heart burst with something unimaginably good, and I took his hand, ready to begin.

Read on for an excerpt from
the first title in the Dark Elite series
by Chloe Neill,

FIRESPELL

Available now!

1

They were gathered around a conference table in a high-rise, eight men and women, no one under the age of sixty-five, all of them wealthy beyond measure. And they were here, in the middle of Manhattan, to decide my fate.

I was not quite sixteen and only one month out of my sophomore year of high school. My parents, philosophy professors, had been offered a two-year-long academic sabbatical at a university in Munich, Germany. That's right—two years out of the country, which only really mattered because they decided I'd be better off staying in the United States.

They'd passed along that little nugget one Saturday in June. I'd been preparing to head to my best friend Ashley's house when my parents came into my room and sat down on my bed.

"Lily," Mom said, "we need to talk."

I don't think I'm ruining the surprise by pointing out that nothing good happens when someone starts a speech like that.

My first thought was that something horrible had happened to

Ashley. Turned out she was fine; the trauma hit a little closer to home. My parents told me they'd been accepted into the sabbatical program, and that the chance to work in Germany for two years was an amazing opportunity for them.

Then they got quiet and exchanged one of those long, meaningful looks that really didn't bode well for me. They said they didn't want to drag me to Germany with them, that they'd be busy while they were there, and that they wanted me to stay in an American school to have the best chance of going to a great college here. So they'd decided that while they were away, I'd be staying in the States.

I was equal parts bummed and thrilled. Bummed, of course, because they'd be an ocean away while I passed all the big milestones—SAT prep, college visits, prom, completing my vinyl collection of every Smashing Pumpkins track ever released.

Thrilled, because I figured I'd get to stay with Ashley and her parents.

Unfortunately, I was only right about the first part.

My parents had decided it would be best for me to finish high school in Chicago, in a boarding school stuck in the middle of high-rise buildings and concrete—not in Sagamore, my hometown in Upstate New York; not in our tree-lined neighborhood, with my friends and the people and places I knew.

I protested with every argument I could think of.

Flash forward two weeks and 240 miles to the conference table where I sat in a button-up cardigan and pencil skirt I'd never have worn under normal circumstances, the members of the Board of Trustees of St. Sophia's School for Girls staring back at me. They interviewed every girl who wanted to walk their hallowed halls—

after all, heaven forbid they let in a girl who didn't meet their standards. But that they traveled to New York to see me seemed a little out of the ordinary.

"I hope you're aware," said one of them, a silver-haired man with tiny round glasses, "that St. Sophia's is a famed academic institution. The school itself has a long and storied history in Chicago, and the Ivy Leagues recruit from its halls."

A woman with a pile of hair atop her head looked at me and said slowly, as if talking to a child, "You'll have any secondary institution in this country or beyond at your feet, Lily, if you're accepted at St. Sophia's. If you become a St. Sophia's girl."

Okay, but what if I didn't want to be a St. Sophia's girl? What if I wanted to stay home in Sagamore with my friends, not a thousand miles away in some freezing Midwestern city, surrounded by private-school girls who dressed the same, talked the same, bragged about their money?

I didn't want to be a St. Sophia's girl. I wanted to be me, Lily Parker, of the dark hair and eyeliner and fabulous fashion sense.

The powers that be of St. Sophia's were apparently less hesitant. Two weeks after the interview, I got the letter in the mail.

"Congratulations," it said. "We are pleased to inform you that the members of the board of trustees have voted favorably regarding your admission to St. Sophia's School for Girls."

I was less than pleased, but short of running away, which wasn't my style, I was out of options. So two months later, my parents and I trekked to Albany International.

Mom had booked us on the same airline, so we sat in the concourse together, with me between the two of them. Mom wore a shirt and trim trousers, her long dark hair in a low ponytail. My father wore a button-up shirt and khakis, his auburn hair waving over the glasses on his nose. They were heading to JFK to connect to their international flight; I was heading to O'Hare.

We sat silently until they called my plane. Too nervous for tears, I stood and put on my messenger bag. My parents stood, as well, and my mom reached out to put a hand on my cheek. "We love you, Lil. You know that? And that this is what's best?"

I most certainly didn't know this was best. And the weird thing was, I wasn't sure even she believed it, considering how nervous she sounded when she said it. Looking back, I think they both had doubts about the whole thing. They didn't actually say that, of course, but their body language told a different story. When they first told me about their plan, my dad kept touching my mom's knee—not romantically or anything, but like he needed reassurance, like he needed to remind himself that she was there and that things were going to be okay. It made me wonder. I mean, they were headed to Germany for a two-year research sabbatical they'd spent months applying for, but despite what they'd said about the great "opportunity," they didn't seem thrilled about going.

The whole thing was very, very strange.

Anyway, my mom's throwing out, "It's for the best," at the airport wasn't a new thing. She and Dad had both been repeating that phrase over the last few weeks like a mantra. I didn't know that it was for the best, but I didn't want a bratty comment to be the last thing I said to them, so I nodded at my mom and faked a smile, and let my dad pull me into a rib-breaking hug.

"You can call us anytime," he said. "Anytime, day or night. Or e-mail. Or text us." He pressed a kiss to the top of my head. "You're our light, Lils," he whispered. "Our light."

I wasn't sure whether I loved him more, or hated him a little, for caring so much and still sending me away.

We said our good-byes, and I traversed the concourse and took my seat on the plane, with a credit card for emergencies in my wallet, a duffel bag bearing my name in the belly of the jet, and my palm pressed to the window as New York fell behind me.

Good-bye, "New York State of Mind."

Pete Wentz said it best in his song title: "Chicago Is So Two Years Ago."

Two hours and a tiny bag of peanuts later, I was in the 312, greeted by a wind that was fierce and much too cold for an afternoon in early September, Windy City or not. My knee-length skirt, part of my new St. Sophia's uniform, didn't help much against the chill.

I glanced back at the black-and-white cab that had dropped me off in front of the school's enclave on East Erie. The driver pulled away from the curb and merged into traffic, leaving me there on the sidewalk, giant duffel bag in my hands, messenger bag across my shoulder, and downtown Chicago around me.

What stood before me, I thought as I gazed up at St. Sophia's School for Girls, wasn't exactly welcoming.

The board members had told me that St. Sophia's had been a convent in its former life, but it could have just as easily been the setting for a Gothic horror movie. Dismal gray stone. Lots of tall, skinny windows, and one giant round one in the middle. Fanged, grinning gargoyles perched at each corner of the steep roof.

I tilted my head as I surveyed the statues. Was it weird that nuns had been guarded by tiny stone monsters? And were they supposed to keep people out . . . or in?

Rising over the main building were the symbols of St. Sophia's—two prickly towers of that same gray stone. Supposedly, some of Chicago's leading ladies wore silver rings inscribed with an outline of the towers, proof that they'd been St. Sophia's girls.

Three months after my parents' revelation, I still had no desire to be a St. Sophia's girl. Besides, if you squinted, the building looked like a pointy-eared monster.

I gnawed the inside of my lip and scanned the other few equally Gothic buildings that made up the small campus, all but hidden from the rest of Chicago by a stone wall. A royal blue flag that bore the St. Sophia's crest (complete with tower) rippled in the wind above the arched front door. A Rolls-Royce was parked on the curved driveway below.

This wasn't my kind of place. This wasn't Sagamore. It was far from my school and my neighborhood, far from my favorite vintage clothing store and favorite coffeehouse.

Worse, given the Rolls, I guessed these weren't my kind of people. Well, they *used* to not be my kind of people. If my parents could afford to send me here, we apparently had money I hadn't known about.

"This sucks," I muttered, just in time for the heavy double doors in the middle of the tower to open. A woman—tall, thin, dressed in a no-nonsense suit and sensible heels—stepped into the doorway.

We looked at each other for a moment. Then she moved to the side, holding one of the doors open with her hand.

I guessed that was my cue. Adjusting my messenger bag and duffel, I made my way up the sidewalk.

"Lily Parker?" she asked, one eyebrow arched questioningly, when I got to the stone stairs that lay before the door.

I nodded.

She lifted her gaze and surveyed the school grounds, like an eagle scanning for prey. "Come inside."

I walked up the steps and into the building, the wind ruffling my hair as the giant doors were closed behind me.

The woman moved through the main building quickly, efficiently, and, most noticeably, silently. I didn't get so much as a hello, much less a warm welcome to Chicago. She hadn't spoken a word since she'd beckoned me to follow her.

And follow her I did, through lots of slick limestone corridors lit by tiny flickering bulbs in old-fashioned wall sconces. The floor and walls were made of the same pale limestone, the ceiling overhead a grid of thick wooden beams, gold symbols painted in the spaces between them. A bee. The flowerlike shape of a fleur-de-lis.

We turned one corner, then another, until we entered a corridor lined with columns. The ceiling changed, rising above us in a series of pointed arches outlined in curved wooden beams, the spaces between them painted the same blue as St. Sophia's flag. Gold stars dotted the blue.

It was impressive—or at least expensive.

I followed her to the end of the hallway, which terminated in a wooden door. A name, MARCELINE D. FOLEY, was written in gold letters in the middle of it.

When she opened the door and stepped inside the office, I assumed she was Marceline D. Foley. I stepped inside behind her.

The room was darkish, a heavy fragrance drifting up from a small oil burner on a side table. A gigantic, circular stained glass window was on the wall opposite the door, and a massive oak desk sat in front of the window.

"Close the door," she said. I dropped my duffel bag to the floor, then did as she'd directed. When I turned around again, she was seated behind the desk, manicured hands clasped before her, her gaze on me.

"I am Marceline Foley, the headmistress of this school," she said. "You've been sent to us for your education, your personal growth, and your development into a young lady. You will become a St. Sophia's girl. As a junior, you will spend two years at this institution. I expect you to use that time wisely—to study, to learn, to network, and to prepare yourself for academically challenging studies at a well-respected university.

"You will have classes from eight twenty a.m. until three twenty p.m., Monday through Friday. You will have dinner at precisely five o'clock and study hall from seven p.m. until nine p.m., Sunday through Thursday. Lights-out at ten o'clock. You will remain on the school grounds during the week, although you may take your exercise off the grounds during your lunch breaks, assuming you do not leave the grounds alone and that you stay near campus. Curfew is promptly at nine p.m. on Friday and Saturday nights. Do you have any questions?"

I shook my head, which was a fib. I had tons of questions, actually, but not the sort I thought she'd appreciate, especially since her PR skills left a lot to be desired. She made St. Sophia's sound less like boarding school and more like prison. Then again, the PR was lost on me, anyway. It's not like I was there by choice.

"Good." Foley pulled open a tiny drawer on the right-hand side of her desk. Out of it she lifted an antique gold skeleton key— the skinny kind with prongs at the end—that was strung from a royal blue ribbon.

"Your room key," she said, and extended her hand. I lifted the ribbon from her palm, wrapping my fingers around the slender bar of metal. "Your books are already in your room. You've been assigned a laptop, which is in your room, as well."

She frowned, then glanced up at me. "This is likely not how you imagined your junior and senior years of high school would be, Ms. Parker. But you will find that you have been bestowed an incredible gift. This is one of the finest high schools in the nation. Being an alumna of St. Sophia's will open doors for you educationally and socially. Your membership in this institution will connect you to a network of women whose influence is international in scope."

I nodded, mostly about that first part. Of course I'd imagined my junior and senior years differently. I'd imagined being at home, with my friends, with my parents. But she hadn't actually asked me how I felt about being shipped off to Chicago, so I didn't elaborate.

"I'll show you to your room," she said, rising from her chair and moving toward the door.

I picked up my bag again and followed her.

St. Sophia's looked pretty much the same on the walk to my room as it had on the way to Foley's office—one stone corridor after another. The building was immaculately clean, but kind of empty. Sterile. It was also quieter than I would have expected a high school to be, certainly quieter than the high school I'd left behind. But for the click of Foley's heels on the shining stone floors, the place was graveyard silent. And there was no sign of the usual high school stuff. No trophy cases, no class photos, no lockers, no pep rally posters. Most important, still no sign of students. There were supposed to be two hundred of us. So far, it looked like I was the only St. Sophia's girl in residence.

The corridor suddenly opened into a giant circular space with a domed ceiling, a labyrinth set into the tile on the floor beneath it. This was a serious place. A place for contemplation. A place where nuns once walked quietly, gravely, through the hallways.

And then she pushed open another set of double doors.

The hallway opened into a long room lit by enormous metal chandeliers and the blazing color of dozens of stained glass windows. The walls that weren't covered by windows were lined with books, and the floor was filled by rows and rows of tables.

At the tables sat teenagers. Lots and lots of teenagers, all in stuff that made up the St. Sophia's uniform: navy plaid skirt and some kind of top in the same navy; sweater; hooded sweatshirt; sweater-vest.

They looked like an all-girl army of plaid.

Books and notebooks were spread on the tables before them, laptop computers open and buzzing. Classes didn't start until tomorrow, and these girls were already studying. The trustees were right—these people were serious about their studies.

"Your classmates," Foley quietly said.

She walked through the aisle that split the room into two halves, and I followed behind her, my shoulder beginning to ache under the weight of the duffel bag. Girls watched as I walked past them, heads lifting from books (and notebooks and laptops) to check me out as I passed. I caught the eyes of two of them.

The first was a blonde with wavy hair that cascaded around her shoulders, a black patent leather headband tucked behind her ears. She arched an eyebrow at me as I passed, and two other brunettes at the table leaned toward her to whisper. To gossip. I made a prediction pretty quickly that she was the leader of that pack.

The second girl, who sat with three other plaid cadets a few tables down, was definitely not a member of the blonde's pack. Her hair was also blond, but for the darker ends of her short bob. She wore black nail polish and a small silver ring on one side of her nose.

Given what I'd seen so far, I was surprised Foley let her get away with that, but I liked it.

She lifted her head as I walked by, her green eyes on my browns as I passed.

She smiled. I smiled back.

"This way," Foley ordered. I hustled to follow.

We walked down the aisle to the other end of the room, then into another corridor. A few more turns and a narrow flight of limestone stairs later, Foley stopped beside a wooden door. She bobbed her head at the key around my neck. "Your suite," she said. "Your bedroom is the first on the right. You have three suitemates, and you'll share the common room. Classes begin promptly at eight twenty tomorrow morning. Your schedule is with your books. I understand you have some interest in the arts?"

"I like to draw," I said. "Sometimes paint."

"Yes, the board forwarded some of the slides of your work. It lends itself to the fantastic—imaginary worlds and unrealistic creatures—but you seem to have some skill. We've placed you in our arts track. You'll start studio classes within the next few weeks, once our instructor has settled in. It is expected that you will devote as much time to your craft as you do to your studies." Apparently having concluded her instructions, she gave me an up-and-down appraisal. "Any questions?"

She'd done it again. She said, "Any questions?" but it sounded a lot more like "I don't have time for nonsense right now."

"No, thank you," I said, and Foley bobbed her head.

"Very good." With that, she turned on her heel and walked away, her footsteps echoing through the hallway.

I waited until she was gone, then slipped the key into the lock and turned the knob. The door opened into a small circular space—the common room. There were a couch and coffee table in front of a small fireplace, a cello propped against the opposite wall, and four doors leading, I assumed, to the bedrooms.

I walked to the door on the far right and slipped the skeleton key from my neck, then into the lock. When the tumblers clicked, I pushed open the door and flipped on the light.

It was small—a tiny but tidy space with one small window and a twin-sized bed. The bed was covered by a royal blue bedspread embroidered with an imprint of the St. Sophia's tower. Across from the bed was a wooden bureau, atop which sat a two-foot-high stack of books, a pile of papers, a silver laptop, and an alarm clock. A narrow wooden door led to a closet.

I closed the door to the suite behind me, then dropped my bag onto the bed. The room had a few pieces of furniture in it and the school supplies, but otherwise, it was empty. But for the few things I'd been able to fit into the duffel, nothing here would remind me of home.

My heart sank at the thought. My parents had actually sent me away to boarding school. They chose Munich and researching some musty philosopher over art competitions and honors society dinners, the kind of stuff they usually loved to brag about.

I sat down next to my duffel, pulled the cell phone from the front pocket of my gray and yellow messenger bag, flipped it open, and checked the time. It was nearly five o'clock in Chicago and would have been midnight in Munich, although they were probably halfway over the Atlantic right now. I wanted to call them, to hear their voices, but since that wasn't an option, I pulled up my mom's cell number and clicked out a text message: "@ SCHOOL IN ROOM." It wasn't much, but they'd know I'd arrived safely and, I assumed, would call when they could.

When I flipped the phone closed again, I stared at it for a minute, tears pricking at my eyes. I tried to keep them from spilling over, to keep from crying in the middle of my first hour at St. Sophia's, the first hour into my new life.

They spilled over anyway. I didn't want to be here. Not at this school, not in Chicago. If I didn't think they'd just ship me right back again, I'd have used the credit card my mom gave me for emergencies, charged a ticket, and hopped a plane back to New York.

"This sucks," I said, swiping carefully at my overflowing tears, trying to avoid smearing the black eyeliner around my eyes.

A knock sounded at the door, which opened. I glanced up.

"Are you planning your escape?" asked the girl with the nose ring and black nail polish who stood in my doorway.

2

"Seriously, you look pretty depressed there." She pushed off the door, her thin frame nearly swamped by a plaid skirt and oversized St. Sophia's sweatshirt, her legs clad in tights and sheepskin boots. She was about my height, five foot six or so.

"Thanks for knocking," I said, swiping at what I'm sure was a mess beneath my eyes.

"I do what I can. And you've made a mess," she confirmed. She walked toward me and, without warning, tipped up my chin. She tilted her head and frowned at me, then rubbed her thumbs beneath my eyes. I just looked back at her, amusement in my expression. When she was done, she put her hands on her hips and surveyed her work.

"It's not bad. I like the eyeliner. A little punk. A little Goth, but not over-the-top, and it definitely works with your eyes. You might want to think about waterproof, though." She stuck out her hand. "I'm your suitemate, Scout Green. And you're Lily Parker."

"I am," I said, shaking her hand.

Scout sat down on the bed next to me, then crossed her legs and began to swing a leg. "And what personal tragedy has brought you to our fine institution on this lovely fall day?"

I arched a brow at her. She waved a hand. "It's nothing personal. We tend to get a lot of tragedy cases. Relatives die. Fortunes are made and the parentals get too busy for teen angst. That's my basic story. On the rare but exciting occasion, expulsion from the publics and enough money for the trustees to see 'untapped potential.'" She tilted her head as she looked at me. "You've got a great look, but you don't look quite punk enough to be the expulsion kind."

"My parents are on a research trip," I said. "Twenty-four months in Germany—not that I'm bitter about that—so I was sentenced to lockdown at St. Sophia's."

Scout smiled knowingly. "Unfortunately, Lil, your parents' ditching you for Europe makes you average around here. It's like a home for latchkey kids. Where are you from? Prior to being dropped off in the Windy City, I mean."

"Upstate New York. Sagamore."

"You're a junior?"

I nodded.

"Ditto," Scout said, then uncrossed her legs and patted her hands against her knees. "And that means that if all goes well, we'll have two years together at St. Sophia's School for Girls. We might as well get you acquainted." She rose, and with one hand tucked behind her back and one hand at her waist, did a little bow. "I'm Millicent Carlisle Green."

I bit back a grin. "And that's why you go by 'Scout.'"

"And that's why I go by 'Scout,'" she agreed, grinning back.

"First off, on behalf of the denizens of Chicago"—she put a hand against her heart—"welcome to the Windy City. Allow me to introduce you to the wondrous world of snooty American private schooldom." She frowned. " 'Schooldom.' Is that a word?"

"Close enough," I said. "Please continue."

She nodded, then swept a hand through the air. "You can see the luxury accommodations that the gazillion dollars in tuition and room and board will buy you." She walked to the bed and, like a hostess on *The Price Is Right*, caressed the iron frame. "Sleeping quarters of only the highest quality."

"Of course," I solemnly said.

Scout turned on her heel, the skirt swinging at her knees, and pointed at the simple wooden bureau. "The finest of European antiques to hold your baubles and treasures." Then she swept to the window and, with a tug of the blinds, revealed the view. There were a few yards of grass, then the stone wall. Beyond both sat the facing side of a glass and steel building.

"And, of course," Scout continued, "the finest view that new money can buy."

"Only the best for a Parker," I said.

"Now you're getting it," Scout said approvingly. She walked back to the door, then beckoned me to follow. "The common room," she said, turning around to survey it. "Where we'll gossip, read intellectually stimulating classics of literature—"

"Like that?" I asked with a chuckle, pointing at the dog-eared copy of *Vogue* lying on the coffee table.

"*Absolument*," Scout said. "*Vogue* is our guide to current events and international culture."

"And sweet shoes."

"And sweet shoes," she said, then gestured at the cello in the corner. "That's Barnaby's baby. Lesley Barnaby," she added at my lifted brows. "She's number three in our suite, but you won't see much of her. Lesley has four things, and four things only, in her day planner: class, sleeping, studying, and practicing."

"Who's girl number four?" I asked, as Scout led me to the closed door directly across from mine.

Her hand on the doorknob, Scout glanced back at me. "Amie Cherry. She's one of the brat pack."

"The brat pack?"

"Yep. Did you see the blonde with the headband in the study hall?"

I nodded.

"That's Veronica Lively, the junior class's resident alpha girl. Cherry is one of her minions. She was the brunette with short hair. You didn't hear me say this, but Veronica's actually got brains. She might not use them for much beyond kissing Foley's ass, but she's got them. The minions are another story. Mary Katherine, that's minion number two—the brunette with long hair—is former old money. She still has the connections, but that's pretty much all she has.

"Now, Cherry—Cherry has coin. Stacks and stacks of cash. As minions go, Cherry's not nearly as bad as Mary Katherine, and she has the potential to be cool, but she takes Veronica's advice much too seriously." Scout frowned, then glanced up at me. "Do you know what folks in Chicago call St. Sophia's?"

I shook my head.

"St. Spoiled."

"Not much of a stretch, is it?"

"Exactly." With a twist of her wrist, Scout turned the knob and pushed open her bedroom door.

"My God," I said, staring into the space. "There's so much . . . *stuff.*"

Every inch of space in Scout's tiny room, but for the rectangle of bed, was filled with shelves. And those shelves were filled to overflowing. They were double-stacked with books and knick-knacks, all organized into tidy collections. There was a shelf of owls—some ceramic, some wood, some made of bits of sticks and twigs. A group of sculpted apples—the same mix of materials. Inkwells. Antique tin boxes. Tiny houses made of paper. Old cameras.

"If your parents donate a wing, you get extra shelves," she said, her voice flat as week-old soda.

"Where did you get all this?" I walked to a shelf and picked up a delicate paper house crafted from a restaurant menu. A door and tiny windows were carefully cut into the facade, and a chimney was pasted to the roof, which was dusted in white glitter. "And when?"

"I've been at St. Sophia's since I was twelve. I've had the time. And I got it anywhere and everywhere," she said, flopping down onto her bed. She sat back on her elbows and crossed one leg over the other. "There's a lot of sweet stuff floating around Chicago. Antiques stores, flea markets, handmade goods, what have you. Sometimes my parents bring me stuff, and I pick up things along the way when I see them over the summer."

I gingerly placed the building back on the shelf, then glanced back at her. "Where are they now? Your parents, I mean."

"Monaco—Monte Carlo. The Yacht Show is in a couple of

weeks. There's teak to be polished." She chuckled, but the sound wasn't especially happy. "Not by them, of course—they've moved past doing physical labor—but still."

I made some vague sound of agreement—my nautical excursions were limited to paddleboats at summer camp—and moved past the museum and toward the books. There were lots of books on lots of subjects, all organized by color. It was a rainbow of paper—recipes, encyclopedias, dictionaries, thesauruses, books on typology and design. There were even a few ancient leather books with gold lettering along the spines.

I pulled a design book from the shelf and flipped through it. Letters, in every shape and form, were spread across the pages, from a sturdy capital *A* to a tiny, curlicued *Z*.

"I'm sensing a theme here," I said, smiling up at Scout. "You like words. Lists. Letters."

She nodded. "You string some letters together, and you make a word. You string some words together, and you make a sentence, then a paragraph, then a chapter. Words have power."

I snorted, replacing the book on the shelf. "Words have power? That sounds like you're into some Harry Potter juju."

"Now you're just being ridiculous," she said. "So, what does a young Lily Parker do in Sagamore, New York?"

I shrugged. "The usual. I hung out. Went to the mall. Concerts. TiVo *ANTM* and *Man vs. Wild.*"

"Oh, my God, I *love* that show," Scout said. "That guy eats everything."

"And he's hot," I pointed out.

"Seriously hot," she agreed. "Hot guy eats bloody stuff. Who knew that would be a hit?"

"The producer of every vampire movie ever?" I offered.

Scout snorted a laugh. "Well put, Parker. I'm digging the sarcasm."

"I try," I admitted with a grin. It was nice to smile—nice to have something to smile about. Heck, it was nice to feel like this boarding school business might be doable—like I'd be able to make friends and study and go about my high school business in pretty much the same way as I could have in Sagamore.

A shrill sound suddenly filled the air, like the beating of tiny wings.

"Oops, that's me," Scout said, untangling her legs, hopping off the bed, and grabbing a brick-shaped cell phone that was threatening to vibrate its way off one of the shelves and onto the floor. She picked up the phone just before it hit the edge, then unpopped the screen and read its contents.

"Jeez Louise," she said. "You'd think I'd get a break when school starts, but no." Maybe realizing she was muttering in front of an audience, she looked up at me. "Sorry, but I have to go. I have to . . . exercise. Yes," she said matter-of-factly, as if she'd decided on exercise as an excuse, "I have to exercise."

Apparently intent on proving her point, Scout arched her arms over her head and leaned to the right and left, as if stretching for a big run, then stood up and began swiveling her torso, hands at her waist. "Limbering up," she explained.

I arched a dubious brow. "To go exercise."

"Exercise," she repeated, grabbing a black messenger bag from a hook next to her door and maneuvering it over her head. A white skull and crossbones grinned back at me.

"So," I said, "you're exercising in your uniform?"

"Apparently so. Look, you're new, but I like you. And if I guess right, you're a heck of a lot cooler than the rest of the brat pack."

"Thanks, I guess?"

"So I need you to be cool. You didn't see me leave, okay?"

The room was silent as I looked at her, trying to gauge exactly how much trouble she was about to get herself into.

"Is this one of those, 'I'm in over my head' kind of deals, and I'll hear a horrible story tomorrow about your being found strangled in an alley?"

That she took a few seconds to think about her answer made me that much more nervous.

"Probably not *tonight*," she finally said. "But either way, that's not on you. And since we're probably going to be BFFs, you're going to have to trust me on this one."

"BFFs?"

"Of course," she said, and just like that, I had a friend. "But for now, I have to run. We'll talk," she promised. And then she was gone, her bedroom door open, the closing of the hallway door signaling her exit. I looked around her room, noticing the pair of sneakers that sat together beside her bed.

"Exercise, my big toe," I mumbled, and left Scout's museum, closing the door behind me.

It was nearly six o'clock when I walked the few feet back to my room. I glanced at the stack of books and papers on the bureau, admitting to myself that prepping for class tomorrow was probably a solid course of action.

On the other hand, there were bags to be unpacked.

It wasn't a tough choice. I liked to read, but I wasn't going to spend the last few waking hours of my summer vacation with my nose in a book.

I unzipped and unstuffed my duffel bag, cramming undergarments and pajamas and toiletries into the bureau, then hanging the components of my new St. Sophia's wardrobe in the closet. Skirts in the blue and gold of the St. Sophia's plaid. Navy polo shirt. Navy cardigan. Blue button-up shirt, et cetera, et cetera. I also stowed away the few articles of regular clothing I'd brought along: some jeans and skirts, a few favorite T-shirts, a hoodie.

Shoes went into the closet, and knickknacks went to the top of the bureau: a photo of my parents and me together; a ceramic ashtray made by Ashley that read BEST COWGIRL EVER. We didn't smoke, of course, and it was unrecognizable as an ashtray, as it looked more like something you'd discover in the business end of a dirty diaper. But Ashley made it for me at camp when we were eight. Sure, I tortured her about how truly heinous it was, but that's what friends were for, right?

At the moment, Ash was home in Sagamore, probably studying for a bio test, since public school had started two weeks ago. Remembering I hadn't texted her to let her know I'd arrived, I flipped open my phone and snapped shots of my room—the empty walls, the stack of books, the logoed bedspread—then sent them her way.

"UNIMPRESSED RR," she texted back. She'd taken to calling me "Richie Rich" when we found out that I'd be heading to St. Sophia's—and after we'd done plenty of Web research. She figured that life in a froufrou private school would taint me, turn me into some kind of raving Blair Waldorf.

I couldn't let that stand, of course. I sent back, "U MUST RE-SPECT ME."

She was still apparently unimpressed, since "GO STUDY" was her answer. I figured she was probably onto something, so I moved back to the stack of books and gave them a look-see.

Civics.

Trig.

British lit.

Art history.

Chemistry.

European history.

"Good thing they're starting me off easy," I muttered, nibbling on my bottom lip as I scanned the textbooks. Add the fact that I was apparently taking a studio class, and it was no wonder Foley scheduled a two-hour study hall every night. I'd be lucky if two hours were enough.

Next to the stack of books was a pile of papers, including a class schedule and the rules of residency at St. Sophia's. There wasn't a building map, which was a little flabbergasting since this place was a maze to get through.

I heard the hallway door open and shut, laughter filling the common room. Thinking I might as well be social, I blew out a breath to calm the butterflies in my stomach, then opened my bedroom door. There were three girls in the room—the blonde I'd seen in the library and her two brunette friends. Given Scout's descriptions, I assumed the blonde was Veronica, the shorter-haired girl was Amie, the third of my new suitemates, and the girl with longer hair was Mary Katherine, she of the limited intelligence.

The blonde had settled herself on the couch, her long, wavy hair spread around her shoulders, her feet in Amie's lap. Mary Katherine sat on the floor in front of them, her arms stretched behind her, her feet crossed at the ankles. They were all in uniform, all in pressed, pleated skirts, tights, and button-down shirts with navy sweater-vests.

A regiment of officers in the army of plaid.

"We have a visitor," said the blonde, one blond brow arched over blue eyes.

Amie, whose pale skin was unmarred by makeup or jewelry except for a pair of pearl earrings, slapped at Veronica's feet. Veronica rolled her eyes, but lifted them, and the brunette stood and walked toward me. "I'm Amie." She bobbed her head toward one of the bedrooms behind us. "I'm over there."

"It's nice to meet you," I said. "I'm Lily."

"Veronica," Amie said, pointing to the blonde, "and Mary Katherine," she added, pointing to the brunette. The girls both offered finger waves.

"You missed the mixer earlier today," Veronica said, stretching out her legs again. "Tea and petits fours in the ballroom. Your chance to meet the rest of your new St. Sophia's chums before classes start tomorrow." Veronica's voice carried the tone of the wealthy, jaded girl who'd seen it all and hadn't been impressed.

"I've only been here a couple of hours," I said, unimpressed by the attitude.

"Yeah, we heard you weren't from Chicago," said Mary Katherine, head tilted up as she scanned my clothes. Given her own navy tights and patent leather flats, and the gleam of her perfectly straight hair, I guessed she wouldn't dig my Chuck Taylors (the board of trustees let us pick our own footware) and choppy haircut.

"Upstate New York," I told her. "Near Syracuse."

"Public school?" Mary Katherine asked, disdain in her voice.

Oh, how fun. Private school really *was* like *Gossip Girl.* "Public school," I confirmed, lips curved into a smile.

Veronica made a sound of irritation. "Jesus, Mary Katherine, be a bitch, why don't you?"

Mary Katherine rolled her eyes, then turned her attention to her cuticles, inspecting her short, perfectly painted red nails. "I just asked a question. You're the one who assumed I was being negative."

"Please excuse the peanut gallery," Amie said with a smile. "Have you met everybody else?"

"I haven't met Lesley," I said. "I met Scout, though."

Mary Katherine made a sarcastic sound. "Good luck there. That girl has *issues.*" She stretched out the word dramatically. I got the sense Mary Katherine enjoyed drama.

"M.K.'s just jealous," Veronica said, twirling a lock of hair around one of her fingers, and sliding a glance at the brunette on the floor. "Not every St. Sophia's girl has parents who have the cash to donate an entire building to the school."

I guess Scout hadn't been kidding about the extra shelves.

"Whatever," Mary Katherine said, then crossed her legs and pushed herself up from the floor. "You two can play Welcome Wagon with the new girl. I need to make a phone call."

Veronica rolled her eyes, but swiveled her legs onto the floor and stood up, as well. "M.K.'s dating a U of C boy," she said. "She thinks he hung the moon."

"He's pre-law," Mary Katherine said, heading for the door.

"He's twenty," Amie muttered after Mary Katherine had stepped into the hallway and closed the door behind her. "And she's sixteen."

"Quit being a mother, Amie," Veronica said, straightening her headband. "I'm going back to my room. I suppose I'll see you in the morning." She glanced at me. "I don't want to be bitchy, but a little advice?"

She said it like she was asking for permission, so I nodded, solely out of politeness.

"Mind the company you keep," she said. With that gem, which I assumed was a shot at Scout, she walked to Amie. They exchanged air kisses.

"Nighty night, all," Veronica said, and then she was gone.

When I turned around again, Amie was gone, her bedroom door closing behind her.

"Charming," I muttered, and headed back to my room.

It was earlier than I would have normally gone to sleep, but given the travel, the time change, and the change in circumstances, I was exhausted. Finding the stone-walled and stone-floored room chilly even in the early fall, I exchanged the uniform for flannel pajamas, turned off the light, and climbed into bed.

The room was dark, but far from quiet. The city bustled around me, the thrum of traffic from downtown Chicago creating a backdrop of sound, even on a Sunday night. Although the stone muffled it, I wasn't used to even the low drone of noise. I had been born and bred amongst acres of lawns and overhanging trees—and when the sun went down, the town went silent.

I stared at the ceiling. Tiny yellow-green dots emerged from the darkness. The plaster above me was dotted with glow-in-the-dark stars, I assumed pasted there by a former St. Sophia's girl. As my mind raced, wondering about tomorrow and repeating my to-do list—find my locker, find my classes, manage not to get humiliated in said classes, figure out where Scout had gone—I counted the stars, tried to pick out constellations, and glanced at the clock a dozen times.

I tossed and turned in the bed, trying to find a comfortable position, my brain refusing to still even as I lay exhausted, trying to sleep.

I must have drifted off, as I woke suddenly to a pitch-black room. I must have been awakened by the closing of the hallway door. That sound was immediately followed by the scuffle of trip-ping in the common room—stuff being knocked around and mumbled curses. I threw off the covers and tiptoed to the door, then pressed my ear to the wood.

"Damn coffee table," Scout muttered, footsteps receding until her bedroom door opened and closed. I glanced at the clock. It was one fifteen in the morning. When the common room was quiet, I put a hand to the doorknob, twisted it, and carefully pulled open the door. The room was dark, but a line of light glowed beneath Scout's door.

I frowned. Where had she been until one fifteen in the morn-ing? Exercise seemed seriously unlikely at this point.

That mystery in hand, I closed the door again and went back to bed, staring at the star-spangled ceiling until sleep finally claimed me.

Photo by Jeremy Dixon

Chloe Neill was born and raised in the South, but now makes her home in the Midwest—just close enough to Cadogan House and St. Sophia's to keep an eye on things. When not transcribing Merit's and Lily's adventures, she bakes, works, and scours the Internet for good recipes and great graphic design. Chloe also maintains her sanity by spending time with her husband (also her favorite landscape photographer) and their dogs, Baxter and Scout. Visit her on the Web at www.chloeneill.com.